Basilisk

Basilisk

N M BROWNE

BLOOMSBURY

Acknowledgements

Thanks to Stuart (Marsden) and Jerry (Procter) for an inspirational dinner with 'Parfait Amour.'

Thanks to Jessica Liebmann, Deborah Lane and 3H (2002/3) of Hampton School, Hampton, for their perceptive comments on the draft version of *Basilisk* and to Louise Rawstorne for her kind help.

Thanks are also due to my agent, Mic Cheetham, and to my editors at Bloomsbury: Ele, Victoria and Georgia.

Thanks to Paul for his support, and to my children for putting up with very haphazard domestic arrangements and a lot of oven chips, pizza and bad temper during the writing of this book.

Published by Bloomsbury, New York and London
Distributed to the trade by Holtzbrinck Publishers, LLC
Library of Congress Cataloging-in-Publication Data
available upon request

ISBN 1-58234-876-6

1 3 5 7 9 10 8 6 4 2

Bloomsbury USA Children's Books
175 Fifth Avenue
New York, New York 10010

All papers used by Bloomsbury Publishing are natural, recyclable products made from wood grown in well-managed forests. The manufacturing processes conform to the environmental regulations of the country of origin.

For William, Morgan, Owen and Christa –
may you always see bright suns in blue skies

Chapter One

Rej started awake in the total darkness of Below. He'd had that dream again. It was a moment before he realised where he was; the dream had a brightness and a clarity that made it seem more real than the damp darkness.

There were no dragons. He knew that, and yet again he had seen them soar above Lunnzia – wingspan wider than that of an eagle, scales tawny-gold like the heraldic symbol of the city, glinting in the sun. He had never seen the sun and yet he knew the quality of its light. He was shaking and his eyes watered as if from the brightness. Could it be tears that choked him, salt tears that streamed down his face? He did not think so. It was so long since he had cried it did not seem that it was something he could still do.

The sense of loss he felt was real. There had been a sky of a pure, pellucid blue, like no colour he had ever seen. It was everywhere and nowhere. He had been there, soaring through it – in it but not of it – with the city below; and all around him, everywhere, that colour – luminous, perfect. Then there had been the clean wind, smelling of strangeness and the pleasure of flight. Rej felt a new heaviness in his burial niche, a new sense of the gravity of his situation. The air smelled suddenly stale and fetid to senses that had never smelled anything else. The dream had been a kind of ecstasy, a gift maybe of the Creator, Arché – a sign? He did not know, and the grief of loss was overwhelming.

There would be hours yet until the dim glow from the treaty lights would signal day. Rej wrapped himself more completely in his fur and retreated deeper into the narrow cave he had made his own with proper ceremony. It was too much to hope that the dream might return, and yet he sought sleep as eagerly as some of his combe-mates sought unawareness. There were no dragons. He knew it and yet …

Donna woke along with everyone else and with the pale dawn light seeping through the shuttered window. The call to morning prayer sounded, a hand bell rung too loudly. She had no choice but to get up immediately. The sleeping arrangements at the university campus barracks for the preliminary scribes were cramped and everyone lay pretty well wherever they could. Gayla of the long limbs and flirtatious smile stretched and kicked her sharply in the ribs.

Donna did not complain. It could have been worse. This season the women were all together, since most of the men had joined the Lunnzia militia and gone off on the spring campaign fighting the army of High Verda. They were still gone, though the campaign season was long over. Food was still in short supply after the heavy autumn rains had destroyed much of the limited harvest that had got through the Verdan blockade, so that celibacy was this year's community duty; there would be no blessed birthings this winter. Celibacy was not a hardship for Donna; she did not relish the prospect of motherhood or even the prospect of getting with child. Donna had unpleasant memories of the last time an extra ration of beer had turned the barracks bedding-down time into a free-for-all in a old-time Liberty brothel.

She still bore the scars of her humbling after Darlish had reported her to the priest for pride and possessionism when she had refused to accommodate his demands. It was easier to keep her personal privacy intact in a women-only dorm. She knew most of the girls from previous work details and they left her alone. She wanted that – had encouraged it – and then again, sometimes she didn't want to be quite so alone. This morning she would have liked to tell someone of her extraordinary dream. It was a dream of rare lucidity, a dream in which she had known herself to be flying free, high above the city of Lunnzia like the golden dragon–basilisk of Arché in her dragon phase. Of course, she did not tell anyone.

She stretched less extravagantly than Gayla and got up like the rest, participating as minimally as possible in the grumbling early morning conversation. She tried not to wrinkle her nose at the pungent female odours surrounding her that never seemed to bother anyone else. She had stayed with her mother too long; even after four years of communal living she still found it difficult. She rolled up her bedroll with neat, economical movements and stowed it in one of the wooden 'bird boxes' that lined the walls. Because they were scribes they were privileged to have their own personal bird boxes labelled with their name. It was not quite a sin of ownership, more the privilege of permanent borrowing. It was one of the reasons Donna had striven for this work tour. Should she be selected as a secondary scribe there would be other privileges, and she – strange, sinful, corrupted creature that she was – yearned for private space, for quietness. It was a desire she rarely dared confess. For her, as for all oppidans, service of the state was the rule of life, for only in self-surrender could there be perfection. Donna knew herself to be resolutely imperfect, resolutely different – a bird trying to swim. Some days she felt like a festival freak.

Today she had room for no such thoughts, for nothing but her memory, her memory of the dragon and those that had flown with her. Distractedly, she followed her work detail to the refectory and the morning rations. The cold stone of the flag floor brought her back to reality. The soles of her slippers were wearing thin – there was a shortage of leather this season.

The refectory was a beautiful room with a high vaulted ceiling and complex stonework. Each of the main craft masters had worked on the halls so that the walls were bright with frescos by the chief imagers of the city and lit by windows of magnificent glass depicting the myth of Arché, the creator dragon whom God had sent to seed the world and who, as the dark basilisk, would one day destroy it. It was hard to escape images of the dragon in this hall and, as she chewed on the weevily dark bread, Donna allowed herself briefly to recall the glorious liberation of flight. The red-garbed priest, the Most Humble Servant Hortim, was intoning the general confession of humility. Donna scarcely listened, busy with her own thoughts.

'Oppidan Donna.'

The slave had to address her twice before she heard him. His green-stained face looked sickly in the filtered light – by his tattoo he had been a native of the conquered city of Lambrugio.

'How will you serve me?' Donna answered softly in response.

'The Doctor Esteemed Melagiar would have you scribe for him, Oppidan.'

Donna had never heard of Melagiar, but the university was stuffed full of Doctor Esteemeds so that was unsurprising. It was unusual to be asked for by name, but then she, when her humility failed her, had to admit she was an excellent scribe. She tried harder than most of her fellow acolytes, who were not interested in making this more than the usual three-month work tour.

She stuffed the remaining bread up her sleeve and, bowing vaguely in the direction of her peers and genuflecting towards the Most Humble Servant, followed the slave through the cloisters to the library and study rooms. It was even colder in the cloisters, where frost had petrified the spiders' webs that decorated the tracery of the arched portals into the finest silver filigree. The slave's bare feet were blue with cold and Donna was rapidly losing all feeling in her own. There would be no fires lit until midwinter, by order of the Arkel – the High Priest of Arché and the unacknowledged ruler of the Council of Ten. The Council blamed the war for the shortage of fuel, if not for the cold – even the most loyal of oppidans might find that hard to swallow.

The slave indicated a narrow arched stairway and said flatly, 'Oppidan Donna will find the Doctor Esteemed Melagiar at the top of the South Tower.'

His voice sounded so weak and unsteady that Donna found herself looking at the man, not the messenger. He was tall and cadaverous, with the characteristically high-cheekboned face of his country-men. Older than Donna by some years, he looked ill even in the daylight, and the green stain with which he had been marked looked lurid and ugly on his finely chiselled face. His breath was tainted with the sweetness of berenslip. His eyes had a hectic gleam. The war with High Verda must have been going even more badly than they'd heard – berenslip, as Donna knew from her mother's training, not to mention her own work tour with the apothecaries, was an elixir which gave the sensation of fullness in an empty belly; it simulated health in the weak. It was given to those on the point of starvation. It occurred to her that when oppidans – free citizens of Lunnzia – were given coarse black bread, there could be no reserves left for the slaves. With uncharacteristic generosity she found herself giving the man the remaining hunk of food from her sleeve. He looked at her dazedly.

'Eat it! It is health-giving,' she commanded, before climbing the dim stairwell.

'Oppidan Donna.' She turned to see the slave looking at her intently. 'In my city that is now no city, I would have said to you – be wary.'

Donna met his eyes and saw something there she did not expect to see in the eyes of a slave. She bowed an acknowledgement and continued on her way. He should not have spoken to her except to pass on a message, but he'd given her something as payment for the bread. That was how things worked in Lambrugio – or so it was said. In that brief exchange which had turned her generosity into a transaction she had seen a flicker of pride in the man's feverish eyes. In accepting that payment, she had allowed him to embroil her in the corruption of his kind. She shook her head to rid herself of such unwelcome thoughts and to focus her mind on the important part – what did the warning mean?

Chapter Two

'You owe me!' Strong hands dragged Rej from a heavy sleep. He was startled into full wakefulness.

'For frakking Light's sake, Moon – deve off and let me sleep.'

Rej kept his voice irritated and sleepy while he groped under his fur for his weapon. He didn't want to use his knife; it was a proscribed weapon in the combes. Rej found what he was looking for – one of the items he kept in his hide at all times: a stone-mason's mallet, filched from Above, precious as Light. Moon was not a serious threat. There were others he was afraid of – he owed them more.

Moon let go when Rej spoke. Not sure how much Moon could see, Rej affected a stretch and an exaggerated yawn. It was after what passed for dawn down in the combes. Rej could see nothing but he knew exactly where Moon was. There was only one place he could be that would allow him to lean inside the cave – the hearth ledge.

'What the frakk are you bothering me for this early?'

As Moon started to grumble an answer Rej suddenly kicked his legs out with enough force to unbalance Moon from the hearth ledge, the precarious foothold just outside Rej's hide-cave. The roof of the cave was low – too low to do much besides sleep – but Rej twisted himself clear of the hide with the sudden swiftness of a snake and, holding on to the grip-hold above the cave, raised the mallet high in the other hand. He could have knocked Moon over and down into the Styx below. He could see now, he could see Moon's eyes in the dirty yellow, filtered light of morning. Below them the sheer cliff of the burial wall, holed with niches, ended in the stinking waters of the effluent river, and there was much that could not be seen, much that disappeared in the deep shadows where the murky sunshine of treaty lights never reached. Moon was clearly scared: hardly anyone chose to live in this section of the catacombs. Today the stench of sulphur was choking, making eyes stream. The dampness of Moon's eyes reflected light like shiny, silvered mirrors. Rej could see how they darted furtively to the left, as if looking for back-up.

'You'll get what you're owed when I've got it – unless you want this first.' Rej shook the mallet to make his point. His voice was low – he was so close to Moon that he could feel Moon's breath on his face, see the tiny beads of perspiration form on his upper lip, though the air was cold and damp. Moon had always been a coward, a minor player in the fluid hierarchy of the catacombs. He would not take on Rej – would not even have tried if he had not been expecting support. Rej wondered who had let Moon down this time – his reinforcements had obviously not yet arrived. Rej relaxed. Moon would back down.

Moon grinned nervously, showing the rotten stumps

of teeth that were the result of too much stenk-chewing. He had a wad of the foul stuff as he spoke and Rej could see the juices dribble a little from the corner of his mouth. Its strange bitterness tainted the air between them. The stench made Rej's gorge rise – he had not eaten since the night before. Stenk affected your judgement – Moon certainly had none.

'Hey, Rej – don't go up with it, comber. Getting bad dreams again, eh, Rej? I know where you can get some good stuff for that.'

Moon repeated Rej's name with a kind of bravado, a reminder that they had grown up together. They had never been friends, yet it worked. Rej allowed Moon to place a trembling hand on the rough rock wall of the combes. Moon's balance was as wrecked as his judgement. Touching the cold rock seemed to give him confidence. He spoke in his usual wheedling voice, as if he had never breached Rej's threshold, as if Rej was not within his rights to treat him as badly he liked.

'And just what do you know of dreams?'

You never knew with Moon. Most of what he said was ordure of the most useless kind, but he'd grabbed Rej's interest. It was probably nothing, but Moon had only survived long enough to have stenk-rotted teeth by finding things out, putting things together and telling only what he wanted told. Every now and again he was worth listening to. Moon also had the survivor's instinct for another man's weaknesses – he knew he had found Rej's.

'What's it worth to you to know?'

Rej waved the mallet. 'You've forgotten who's got the chips here, comber.'

Moon shrugged. 'A man can't think when he's threatened.'

Rej sighed and cautiously lowered his arm. After his disturbed night's sleep he didn't have the stomach for a fight, even an easy win. His head ached and the acrid smells from the Styx and from Moon made him nauseous.

'You've got five heartbeats – your last five heartbeats if you've nothing to say.'

Moon nodded, licking his lips, his face earnest in the dimness. 'I know an oppidan Above – deals with me sometimes – kinsman, sort of. He's a master of alchemy, a dream-maker!'

'And?'

Moon, watching Rej's face with fierce concentration, seemed disappointed by Rej's reaction.

'He knows I take stenk.'

'So, you twazzock, you don't need the arts of an Inquisitor to know that.' Rej was getting impatient.

Moon started to speak more quickly. 'He gave me something – purple stuff. He told me to try it and see if it had any effect on my dreams.'

'Did you?'

Moon hesitated fractionally, but too long.

'You didn't try it, did you?'

Moon shook his head grudgingly. 'What kind of a linny d'you think I am? The man's an oppidan – they hate us, don't they? Light, I've worked as a bread-taster down here before now – you probably don't remember – but comber before me died of it. No, I don't trust a city man, an Abover, but –'

'But what? Why do I want to know this, Moon?

You've three heartbeats left.'

'People have heard you, Rej – raving at night. Maybe someone slipped you some of that stuff. Can't say you've got no enemies, can you? Looks to me like a good number will be turning up any time around –'

Rej reacted swiftly. He'd seen the movement an instant before – a couple of figures, crawling via the roof ropes in the dark shadows of the vaulted roof of the vast cavern. He guessed their identities – the others he owed. They would be on him in moments. Rej shoved Moon forward with a sharp kick of his right foot and launched himself at the leather grip-hold of the nearest combe – deserted since old man Harly had died. It was a huge leap but Rej made it and hung there, weighing his options. The catacombs predated the sewers which flowed under the city of Lunnzia – predated the city which was built upon them. The huge stone cliffs riddled with burial chambers like wormholes in wood were the city's foundations and the combers' whole world. No one knew all their secrets but Rej knew more than most.

He glanced back to see four men, not two, closing in on him. The hapless Moon had fallen up to his chest in the Styx. The splash and his howls of anguish as the poisons ate through his clothing echoed chillingly in the cavernous space. Here, under the university towers where the alchemists poured their mistakes down the privy, the Styx was deadly but the stench kept combers away and Rej liked his peace from time to time. All Moon had to do was pull himself out of the water before the poisons putrefied his flesh – even he should have been able to manage that. Above Rej the network of ropes and guide lines that the combers used to move over the river hung like the web of some drunken or stenk-addicted spider. He could see them twitching under the weight of men. He could not escape from them that way – spider ropes could be cut; it was easy to be trapped. Climbing, insect-like, across the uneven surface of the combes themselves, he stayed just ahead of his pursuers. Luck his Lady, who failed him regularly, had at least granted him the right physique for his life underground. Tall and lankily-limbed, he was light and strong with a long reach and near-perfect balance. His pursuers were heavier men and had to shout to one another to be sure they didn't overburden the rope lines. Rej had made sure that only poor quality rope made its way into this section of the catacombs.

He heard another echoing yell and sensed rather than saw a man fall, scrabbling for purchase on the rough walls of the cliff face with a panicky tirade of expletives. Dove Grey – he recognised the voice. Dove Grey was bad news – Rej accelerated towards the total darkness of the shadows. Dove Grey, having recovered his balance, was not far behind – the trick now was silence. Rej slowed down, moving as noiselessly as possible, feeling his way for unseen hand-holds, recognising the route by small changes in the feel of the stone, by the sounds of the river and by the distinctive smells of the many refuse streams from the university Above cascading down the once sacred rock of the catacombs. Here, in this damp darkness, strange moulds and slimy textured things flourished, making rock slick as ice and flesh recoil. Rej concentrated hard – straining to hear his pursuers, struggling to find a refuge. It was treacherous climbing and once he nearly slipped and fell. He had to stop for a moment to calm himself.

It was then he found it – the narrow entrance he had discovered years before. It was little more than a fissure in the rock, an uncomfortable squeeze even for a man as thin and angular as Rej. He cursed silently; he scraped the flesh of his shoulder as he forced himself through. He fought the panic that never entirely left him in tight, dark spaces. There was room for him – he had hidden there before. He imagined the unseen walls closing in on him, crushing him, their weight on his chest making it impossible to breathe, the air so stale it must surely be without wholesomeness. Stop it! He thrust all such thoughts from him. He had spent every day of his life in caves. There was no light for his eyes to adjust to so he shut them and stilled his breathing, which was rasping, rapid and about to give away his position to anyone listening as hard as his pursuers would surely be. In a moment he would move on.

It was all the fault of his dream. After his vision of open space and perfect light the darkness was more oppressive than ever. He wondered briefly if there had been any truth in Moon's story. He didn't believe that anyone might try to poison him deliberately – why go to the trouble? There were too many other ways to kill someone underground. But who knew what substances found their way to the catacombs? Above, from his mother's tales, was a place of elaborate intrigue, of contentious guilds and extravagant arts of which the art of poison was but one. He did not have time to think the idea through, to worry about such abstract threats. His mind fluttered between thoughts; he tried to force himself to calmness. He was Rej: comber, survivor, debtor, occasional beloved of the Lady Luck, and he was not afraid.

'I know you're frakking in there, Rej, and I'm telling you I'll get you if I've got to dig you out. Dove Grey's pickaxe will have you. I want you, Rej, Hara's son – your mother would have skinned you herself if she were still alive. A comber pays his debts – boy! You hear me! Come out and I'll still leave you your hide.'

The voice – Barna's voice – was close, no more than an arm's reach away. The darkness lessened fractionally. By the thousand scents of shit, they'd got a light! Rej forced himself to breathe evenly and quietly. The threat echoed around the combe. No one would help him if Barna was against him. He tried to work out how he could have crossed Barna – he'd had no debt with him. Barna must have bought it off one of the others.

Rej's mouth was dry. There was a further, narrower channel that led deep into the rock of the combe. It went back a long way, then joined other wider channels. His mother Hara had called them ghost tunnels because, according to the common sense wisdoms, the men of the far long ago who had dug the catacombs had been sealed in with the dead. In despair and madness they had dug the narrow channels with their dying strength in a desperate effort to escape. Most of the tunnels went nowhere and petered out, some went upwards to the surface – all were no wider than the shoulders of a small man. Rej was not a small man – although he was thin, emaciated even, his frame was large. He was also for the first time in years genuinely afraid – not just of the narrow space, but of Barna. Barna had murdered men before – no one could prove it, but everybody knew. He was an old man by some combers' standards, but tough with the hardness of bedrock, and in long ago pre-revolutionary days had fought as a mercenary in distant wars.

Rej had a straight choice: he could risk Barna or the tunnels. His hand found the fissure in the rock that was the ghost tunnel's entrance. He wrapped his clothes tightly around him, removing the thick coil of rope that every comber carried from around his waist. He could not afford its extra bulk. He carried his illegal knife, of course, and, working in the cold darkness, cut the rope into lengths and loosely wrapped his knees, hands and elbows with the hemp. He would have to crawl and he did not wish to invite the green death. He took a hunk of tested bread from his food pouch and stuffed it into his mouth. He did not want the distraction of hunger, but his mouth did not have enough spit and he struggled to swallow the hard bread. He'd made his decision: he'd take his chance in the tunnel. There were worse ways to die than in the tunnels and rumour had it that Barna knew them all.

The thought did not help much. Rej'd not been through this tunnel for a long time, not since he was a boy, with a boy's foolhardiness and a boy's flexibility. He was a man now; could he still make it through? He began to manoeuvre himself by touch alone into the narrowest of apertures. He would find out.

Chapter Three

Donna mounted the shadowed staircase to the rooms of the Doctor Esteemed Melagiar. It was hard to see, and she gripped the smooth wood banister with anxious hands. Why had she been asked for by name? Perhaps she was due advancement, as she was good at her current job, having longed for a chance to do something connected to her earlier life. Before the military Council of Ten had imposed their 'Humble Road' she could already read and write in a quick clear hand the three main languages required of a scholar and had had the requisite grounding in practical theology and metaphysics.

Donna hesitated at the dark door of the Doctor's study. Her nature sought preferment, though her common sense preferred obscurity. There was much to lose. She could hear a scuffling behind the door and she bowed her head, steeling herself to accept the humiliation that seemed so much a part of the life of an oppidan. After four years as an oppidan she still found it difficult.

A woman opened the door – a woman in the heavy silk and brocade of that other time, before the Sumptuary Laws, before the Humble Road, before the

Revolution. Donna lowered her eyes hastily in good oppidan fashion, before they could register her surprise. The woman indicated that she should enter with a wave of a pale, elegant hand which, even in the dimness, flashed with decadent diamonds.

Donna fought the urge to curtsey an old world response: oppidans bowed to each other but all who worked together under the rule of the Council of Ten were equal – so she stood uncomfortably at the threshold. The room was not cold. That was the first thing that she noticed. The unmistakeable sweetness of wood smoke scented the warm air and in the narrow fireplace a fire blazed with the intensity of the basilisk's breath – for, thought Donna, one who so flagrantly flaunted the rules of the Council of Ten could surely be heading for the basilisk's last, fatal kiss.

'Come into the light that I might see you, child.' The Doctor appeared from behind a carved screen that separated the large room in two. He spoke the now obsolete court language and Donna did not know if she were supposed to understand him or not. He was younger than she had expected, with a refined, ascetic face.

'Forgive me – I slip too easily into the old ways. Please come forward, Oppidan. I desire to inspect your suitability for the task I have in mind.'

This time he spoke in the vulgar tongue and Donna stepped forward, grateful that she could at least admit to understanding that. The heat from the fire thawed the vellum stiffness of her face; she had forgotten how good such warmth felt. She maintained her careful impassivity; it was no longer essential to cultivate such a look as a sign of good manners, but her mother had schooled her too well and it was impossible for her to do otherwise.

There was an awkward silence while the Doctor viewed her as he might a cow. Donna knew that she was beautiful. Her mother had been a celebrated courtesan, the First Low Lady of the kingdom before the Revolution. Even lacking the advantages of good cosmetics and jewels Donna was quite as lovely as her mother. She acknowledged the fact without particular pride. Her beauty was an incidental: deep blue eyes, dark brows and lashes, luxuriant black hair and good teeth were all gifts of the whim of Arché. It was through luck that she had avoided the pockmarking of disease and addiction and still maintained – that rarity in Lunnzia – flawless skin. She knew that others did not always regard her beauty so lightly. She remained expressionless under the Doctor Esteemed's careful scrutiny.

'What rank were you before this ridiculous "Humble Road", Oppidan?'

Donna raised her eyes to catch the gleam of malice in her questioner's eyes. She kept her voice firm and even. 'Doctor Esteemed Melagiar – I am an oppidan only. I know of no other rank.'

'And men don't fart and the river flows upstream, I suppose. Very well, as you will have it. I understand from my … sources … that you write with a fair hand and with some speed. I have need of a scribe and you, my dear Oppidan, are she. Do your task well and you will be accredited secondary rank – do it badly and ...' He waved a long and seemingly boneless hand with foppish elegance. Donna found it a sinister gesture, for no reason that she could name. He continued, 'Your first task is to make fair copies of some rough notes I have left – use the desk by the window. My sister will watch over you. She does not speak due to some congenital disease, though she may from time to time make noises. Do not trouble yourself with them. She is not of sound mind, but she will do you no harm.'

The woman certainly seemed to have little awareness of her surroundings. Her eyes had a chilling blankness about them that reminded Donna of the stenk addicts who had lived by the docks in her childhood. The woman stood so close to the fire that the long velvet train of her gown threatened to catch light.

'Immina! 'Ware the fire!' The Doctor Esteemed Melagiar spoke to the poor woman in much the same tone in which the street clearers spoke to the feral dogs that had scavenged for food in better days. Immina seemed briefly aware and moved away from the fire. Melagiar, seeing Donna gazing at it, spoke again in a more conversational tone.

'My work here is vital to our security and to the timely conclusion of the war against High Verda. I have not been blessed with a strong constitution and, as warmth is essential to my continued health, the Council of Ten have granted Immina, who assists me, and myself many privileges. Do not abuse them while you attend me. There are many oppidans who would do much for a warm room and congenial work.'

Was she oversensitive, or had the Doctor placed just a little too much emphasis on 'much' for her comfort? Donna felt his eyes on her again and forced herself to retain the outward modesty appropriate to an oppidan on work detail. Not for the first time she wished that the war had not deprived her of her chosen profession. No Low Lady would be spoken to in such a way, at least not since the guilds of courtesan and assassin had combined forty years previously; Donna's mother, like many courtesans, also excelled in the latter role.

'It will be a pleasure to serve you.' Donna bowed and answered carefully.

Melagiar omitted the polite response: 'We serve each other.' Instead he had moved briskly on. 'I will see you again tomorrow, if today's work proves satisfactory. Do not be late.'

He disappeared behind a velvet curtain and did not reappear. Perhaps there were further chambers beyond this large warm room, or the curtain disguised another exit? It was a matter of hidden pride to Donna that, in spite of her enforced career change, she worked still on the lessons necessary to a 'Poison Lady' of the assassins' guild. One of the first she had been taught was 'Know all exits and all entrances'. She lacked the small poisoned pin that made the next injunction possible: 'Never forget that the death door is also an exit'. That she had regretted more than once.

Immina had moved from the fire and drifted towards the window. Donna followed her and was pleased to find a fine writing stand with good quality inks and quills ready for her use. She was to copy something called *A Treatise on Dreams*. Something had been written beneath it and scored out so heavily that the paper had torn. The name now written beneath the title in extravagant script was 'Nikris Melagiar, Doctor Esteemed of the University of Lunnzia'.

Immina stared for a moment out of the glazed mullioned window at the herb garden beneath and Donna followed her gaze. A work detail were busily covering the ground with fresh straw and dung to protect the more delicate plants from the winter frost. A few of the workers were wearing old cloaks to protect them from the cold – this was illegal, of course, but perhaps they would be permitted their unlawful warmth as an alternative to frostbite. Donna was suddenly grateful for the warm room and the easy work – whatever it entailed.

Immina did not seem to register what she saw; her eyes stared unseeingly past Donna so that Donna was able to look at her more carefully. The rich maroon of her dress only accentuated the unhealthy pallor of her thin face. Her flax-coloured hair was piled on her head in a fashion not seen in Lunnzia since Donna's own mother had been a child, and a string of pearls marked the division between forehead and shaved hairline. Her eyes were a faded blue, watery and vague. She could not have been very much older than Donna herself and yet she exuded a kind of frailty and a whiff of something else. Donna's sense of smell was particularly acute: her early training had seen to that. She could not recognise the scent as one of the main poisons, but then it was disguised by attar of damask rose. Immina's dress had been coffered in lavender and that too confused Donna's nose still further, yet there was something familiar about it, something that pulled at the very edges of her memory. Her mother would recognise it, she knew.

Donna shut her eyes and tried to describe the scent to herself, but was jerked from her speculation by an unexpectedly hard slap. Immina was not as vague as she appeared. Donna started and was startled to see Immina's smile, an apparently random expression as strange and unexpected as the slap. Donna's face stung. Immina had turned away without acknowledging what she had done and begun another apparently aimless perambulation of the room. She was clearly not in her right mind, and Donna was even more uncomfortable in her presence than before. But in these post-revolutionary times madness was not remarkable; it was merely that everyone not conforming to the prevailing spirit of sharing self-sacrifice, including those lost in their own private worlds, had a tendency to disappear. Sometimes the usefully moon-witted were tolerated so long as they did not upset anybody. Immina's eccentricity would have to be borne. Donna did not wish to upset Melagiar, and said nothing to Immina herself – there seemed little point. She tried to settle to her work; she wanted to be promoted to secondary scribe.

The writing on the manuscript was cramped and almost illegible in places so that Donna had to concentrate hard to transcribe it. She focused entirely on her task, a gift for attentive study that she had perfected under the stern eye of a succession of tutors. When she next looked up from the pages it was to discover that the daylight had almost gone and the fire had all but died in the grate. Most disturbingly, Immina lay prostrate in front of the fire, shaking silently. Donna had no way of knowing how long she had lain like that, and rushed to her side.

'My Lady – I mean, fellow Oppidan.'

The woman made no reply but thrashed from side to side as if experiencing a fit. Long ago Donna had watched her mother deal with stenk-eaters fitting and foaming at the mouth. Stenk addiction was common enough in the dockside and the illegal Liberty – but rare among the once high-born and the oppidans. She remembered her mother's calm competence and copied it now, forcing Immina's mouth open to prevent her from swallowing her tongue. Donna almost shouted out in shock; the woman's tongue was no more than a stump; it had been cut out. So much for her congenital condition. She loosened the stays of the woman's dress so that the bodice opened to reveal a second shock: a gilt tattoo of a dragon which coiled around her left breast so that its reptilian head was all but buried in her cleavage. Tattoos were commonly used to brand slaves but Donna had never seen anything like this one, a work of art so incongruously placed on this woman's breast.

Donna did not know what more she could do to calm Immina, but fortunately she seemed to revive without further intervention. Her vague eyes opened and focused briefly on Donna's own. The look she gave Donna was not that of a mad woman; it was cool and appraising, as with an imperious gesture she demanded Donna's assistance in getting to her feet.

Immina self-consciously rearranged the neckline of her gown to hide the strange tattoo. Donna, acting the part of co-operative sister oppidan, carefully re-laced Immina's bodice in silence. She watched as Immina poured herself a drink from the beautifully decorative pitcher by the fire with tremulous fingers. Donna's fingers were clumsy – she had never laced a bodice before, and this one was particularly awkward as the eyelets were small and the original thread had been replaced by some coarser, thicker stuff which did not quite fit.

When she had finished she looked again at Immina, expecting some gesture of thanks, and was bemused again: the woman who had briefly seemed to regard her so coolly was gone and some other vague and hapless creature had returned. Immina sank into a kind of stupefied trance then, and slumped on the chair. Donna was guiltily relieved and was careful to do nothing else to draw attention to herself. Immina was not her concern. Even so, it was a relief when the light failed and the single candle provided proved inadequate.

Donna slipped gladly away. Free from Immina's strangely intimidating presence, she could think about her more rationally. She carried a clear picture of the dragon tattoo in her mind because it was already so familiar. It was not the usual religious, iconic representation of Arché. Most disturbingly, it was the exact form and colour of the dragon of her dreams.

Chapter Four

It was the dream that kept Rej going; remembering it, fixing it in his head. He held on to it like he'd grip one of the spider ropes that criss-crossed over the Styx. Frakk, he was scared. He kept his eyes closed. It hurt them less if he did not strain to see where nothing could be seen. It was cold in the tunnel and his limbs trembled with both the cold and his fear. He struggled to breathe, certain that the air was bad. He tried to make himself breathe normally in and out; he tried to link his breathing with this painful movement forward.

The pressure of the rock was almost too much for him. It felt as if the whole weight of the earth was bearing down on him and that at any moment he would be crushed. The rough rock scraped his skin raw as he crawled on all fours, keeping his head so low he feared his neck would snap with the effort of it. The base of the channel was littered with small stones that stabbed at him, so that each laborious movement made his knees and elbows bleed, in spite of his attempt to pad them with his hemp rope. He feared that the channel would become too narrow with every twist of the tunnel. He had to hunch his shoulders and twist his back in order to fit himself within the space and keep going. That was all that it was about: keeping going, keeping on trusting that Luck, his fickle Lady, chose today to favour him. He did not want to think of what would happen if she did not; the possibility was too much in his thoughts already. He had to fight not to think of it, he would freeze, petrified into rock, if he allowed those thoughts to grow. The voices of his pursuers dropped away and the only sounds were his own ragged breath, his too rapidly beating heart, and the rattle of the dislodged stones as he laboured over them.

At length it seemed to him that he could see the dragons in his mind's eye swooping and soaring in the brilliant sunlight. He tried to make himself believe that it was the dragons that were real and that this tortuous progress through his own worst nightmare was no more than a dream. His shaking became a little less convulsive. He tried to make himself believe that if only he could carry on dragging his unwilling limbs through the constricting tomb that enclosed him, he would in the end emerge into the sunlight. He had heard that there was a poor feeble crawling creature like himself that buried itself in a close, encasing tomb of fibres which on bursting from its burial sack, spread jewelled wings and flew. He could almost believe that might be possible for him. The dream had made his life underground seem like the grim, pupal stage before something better, something free.

He knew such thoughts were a kind of madness, but he persisted with them because they kept the fear away and helped to take the edge off the pain in his cramped limbs and the sharp discomfort. Protruding rock grazed his cheek and he dropped his head so that his chin almost scraped the ground and his neck muscles complained. The ground rock became smoother, less covered by shale, and he became a slithering creature moving more easily as the slickness of his blood, from the many lacerations and abrasions that he suffered from the rock shards, lubricated his passage.

It was impossible to gauge time. He did not know if he had crawled through the total darkness for a quarter day or for very much less. His stomach grumbled but he was too disturbed to eat, even if that had been possible. He was tired, but weariness was only a small portion of the pain he had to fight to move on. Despair was not too far away when Rej at last detected a slight widening in the channel, a slight lessening of the intolerable burden of weight upon his shoulders. He emerged, bloodied and battered, into the blessed, broader space of a burial niche on the other side of the combes. He was still Rej; no metamorphosis had occurred; his Lady had not deserted him; and he was still alive.

The burial niche was big – more of a cave. The space made him giddy and he stretched to unknot his limbs. Now that he was safely through the ghost tunnel, he immediately turned his attention to the next problem: the green death. It was not one shade less black in the cave than it had been in the tunnel, so that Rej had no way of establishing the extent of his injuries. Worse than that, within a heartbeat he became aware of breathing that was not his own.

The breath was laboured, rasping, and a voice said in the ringing tones of an oppidan, 'Who is that? Who disturbs me? I will not tell you more – no more.' The voice sounded desperate, exhausted, but the unwritten codes of the combers demanded an answer.

'I'm not an enemy,' said Rej from the dust dryness of his throat and his sudden overwhelming exhaustion. He sank to the floor of the cave and hoped that the statement was a true one. Certainly the man did not sound like anyone he owed credits to, though of course it was impossible to say whether the voice belonged to someone who may have bought his debt.

The stranger continued, as if he had not heard. 'No! No! No! Come no closer, there is nothing I will tell you.'

'Have you the means of light?' Rej's need to see again after the long hours of crushing darkness was overwhelming. He stepped towards the direction of the voice, keeping his own tone as reassuring as possible. 'It's all right, I mean no harm – I need to find a light.'

Most combers kept the means to make light very close at hand – the combes were too treacherous by night (the greater part of them were still treacherous even when daylight shone through the treaty lights to dimly illuminate what lay below with borrowed sunlight). Rej must have dropped his own tinder box in his flight from Barna's men; he had not even heard it fall. He groped gently around the recumbent form of the man. The man screamed and sobbed wildly. Rej gained an impression of movement too, as if the frenzied creature flailed his limbs. Rej's hand sought the reassurance of his knife blade – just in case the stranger attacked him. The man made no attempt to hinder Rej's careful fingertip exploration of the combe floor and Rej found what he was looking for. With trembling, eager fingers he coaxed a spark from the flint and, by touch alone, undid the simple catch of the stranger's storm lantern to light the candle within.

The warm light brought the world back into being. He had never seriously doubted that he could still see, but it was good to know that the terrible darkness was due only to a lack of light. Rej held the light aloft and was shocked when it revealed the emaciated form of the combe's owner. The man's eyes were swollen shut and his face was so badly battered that it was hard to guess at the nature of his features; his nose was broken, and blood caked his face. His body was scarcely any better. It was painfully thin and inadequately covered by a coarse blanket; all the exposed flesh was bruised and bloody. Without the cleansing power of bitter herbs, this man would die the green death as surely as would Rej himself. The man's sobbing ceased abruptly, as if he did not have the strength to sustain it. Rej quickly checked his own body for open cuts – there were too many to count, though few were particularly deep. He was most concerned about the slice to his cheek which stung badly and which he could not see.

'I'm just going to touch you to see if you have a fever,' Rej said to the figure. The man seemed to have retreated back into himself. He made no attempt to open his eyes – maybe he could not open them – but the thin body was still wracked by a silent shuddering spasm that might have been a result of his injuries or the effect of a particularly malignant poison. There were too many things about the man's situation that Rej could not understand. Rej wiped his own hand on his dirty tunic as best he could and tried not to touch the man's bloodied skin with any of his own open wounds. There were poisons that passed blood to blood and the comber's life bred caution. The man had a fever, which might account for his frenzied screaming earlier – but Rej thought differently. On the man's seal finger he wore a ring of some value that marked him, as clearly as his accent, as a high-ranking oppidan. It was strange that it had not been removed; it was valuable and would identify him to another oppidan. The fingers of his hand appeared to have been broken in the manner favoured by the Inquisitors of Lunnzia; he had been tortured. Rej passed the lantern over the lower part of the man's body; his feet were badly cracked and blistered in a way that to Rej suggested hard and unfamiliar use rather than torture. There was a satchel of soft leather by the stone slab that formed the sleeping platform of the burial niche. Once, this platform, like all others in the combes, had been the resting place for a corpse. It seemed likely that it would fulfil that function again very soon.

'It's all right – combe-mate,' said Rej softly. 'I'm not here to hurt you.'

Rej had always had this weakness, this tendency towards sympathy. It was often less than helpful – a weakness he had inherited from his mother. Rej set about searching the man's possessions, for information, for valuables, for anything that might be useful. The satchel contained little more than papers torn into tiny fragments. It contained no gaming pieces or bone-disc credits, so the stranger really was no comber – if proof of that assumption were needed. Every comber carried gaming pieces, for without them, how could they win credits to eat? What kind of a man escaped torture and brought only a rough blanket and an expensive satchel of leather into the combes? At least he had had the wit to bring a lantern and a tinder box. What worried Rej most was not the man's condition – he had seen worse. The man was at least still alive. Most of the recipients of the Inquisitors' arts were dead before their corpses washed up on the combers' underground shores. No, what worried Rej was the fact that this man had either walked or crawled to the combes of his own volition. That made him crazier than a stenk-head – or it meant that someone, someone from Above, had dumped him there. Both possibilities made Rej very suspicious indeed.

Rej made a decision. He shook the man gently by the shoulder. 'Hey, combe-mate – you're from Above?'

The man was startled into vigorous, distressed arm-flailing, and would have begun screaming again except that Rej lightly covered his mouth with his hand.

'Hush – I want to help you. Your wounds need dressing, but I need to know who you are and why you're here.'

The man licked bloodied lips. 'Water?'

'I'll get safe water when I go to the Light – the Light

Hall of Distribution.' Rej was vaguely aware that the man may not know the comber customs so he added the briefest of explanations. 'It's the place where there are the most treaty lights – it's where we trade in the combes. I will help you – do you understand? But I need to know how you got here.'

'The Basilisk Contrivance!' The man shrieked and tried to sit up, but was too weak. His eyelids fluttered. Rej spat on a corner of his cloak and carefully wiped the man's eyes, as he suspected it was congealed blood that glued them shut – he could not let a man suffer in unnecessary darkness when there was light. The man blinked and tried to focus on Rej's face. Rej realised belatedly that he was probably not a reassuring sight.

The man's face contorted into something that could have been a smile, though it was grim and strained. 'They won't make it work – it's dangerous, too dangerous – how can they not know that? You know that, don't you?'

Rej nodded encouragingly. 'Of course, my friend, my dear friend …'

Rej let the sentence hang there, in the hope that he would furnish his name – the man obligingly introduced himself. Even battered and bloodied his politeness was reflexive; he was of the same generation as Rej's dead mother.

'The Doctor Esteemed Harfoot, of the University of Lunnzia.'

'I am pleased to renew our acquaintance,' Rej continued. His mother had told him stories of Lunnzia in the old days, and the characters in her stories had spoken in this strange stilted way. It amused Rej to realise that she had not made that up; that somewhere people really spoke like that. He wondered if she'd ever believed what she'd so often said – that he'd find that out for himself one day.

'Doctor Esteemed Harfoot, could you tell me how you came to be here, underground, in the catacombs?'

The Doctor's eyes clouded and became unfocused as though he no longer saw Rej at all. His voice was chillingly calm, though his words made no sense. 'They will come for you too – the basilisk! Quite hopeless!' And then he started to scream.

Rej patted the madman softly on his poor abused arm. He would have to go to the Light. In addition to herbs to repel poison from his wounds, the man needed food, water and some kind of philtre to calm his nerves. There were combers who regularly made illegal forays Above, trading in stenk, to bring treasures Below to supplement the basic goods they were granted by treaty. Rej was out of credits but it may be possible to trade information on the whereabouts of one Doctor Esteemed. He slid the ring from Harfoot's misshapen finger and put it carefully inside his chest pouch. Maybe the shredded paper in the satchel was worth something too, or why else would a man drag such useless excess into the combes? The bag was large enough to have brought useful trade goods. On the other hand, the man was intermittently mad and perhaps had not thought rationally at all. Rej took the satchel and slung it over his left shoulder and over his chest. If there was any value in its contents he would have to work that out for himself.

'I am going to have to leave you now, sir. I will be back soon with water and supplies. I'll leave the light on so you know that there is no harm here.' Rej tried to make his voice as reassuring as was possible. Harfoot only groaned a response.

There was nothing more that Rej could do. He felt fear tighten its vice-like grip on his innards. Instinct suggested that by arriving here he had not moved to the safe haven he'd required. There was too much risk in going to the Light alone. He was likely to be recognised and there was no disguising his gangling height. There was only one person he trusted to trade on his behalf. He would have to find Scrubber and face her derision. He had run out of options.

Rej left by the front entrance – over the hearth ledge – and immediately recognised his location. He could not rid himself of the suspicion that he was being watched.

Chapter Five

The manicured lawn of the quadrangle in front of the Doctor Esteemed's staircase was stiff with frost as Donna slunk gratefully from the building. She began to shiver uncontrollably as the icy curtain of cold engulfed her. She hardly noticed the discomfort as she struggled to make sense of the strange coincidence of Immina's incongruous tattoo and the dragon of her dream. There was something wrong, very wrong. She mistrusted the warmth of Melagiar's rooms, the predatory glint in his eye when he had looked at her. Melagiar's world was the world her mother had trained her for and yet, faced with all that richness, she felt only fear and uncertainty – a fish trying to fly. She did not want to return to the campus barracks; she could not face the jibes and the thousand small acts of malice which made life there so uncomfortable.

There was a little time before she would be missed. She found herself walking towards the old docks. She did not skulk, although what she was doing was strictly forbidden. It was not quite the time of curfew but the cold kept most people indoors; even the slaves who swept the streets and washed the treaty lights' thick Lunnzian glass had found some excuse to be under shelter. A few flakes of snow landed on her eyelashes. Donna silently cursed the Arkel and the Council of Ten for demanding the destruction of all fur and fur-lined garments the previous winter; the current clothing allowance was better suited to a warm spring day than to approaching midwinter. She casually checked to ensure that there was no one around to observe her slip between two disused brick warehouses, abandoned since the beginning of the Verdan blockade that was the source of much of their misery. Lunnzia no longer stored luxury goods for import and export, and had lost almost all of its merchants under the regime of the Council of Ten. She breathed deeply; the buildings seemed to retain the faintest aroma of spice, the memory of riches.

There was no light in the dark spaces of the alleyways, the jumble of buildings and narrow corridors that led through the old wall to the dockside – the Liberty, the traditional haunt of the lawless. Hidden eyes watched her progress. If she had carried anything of value she might have been in danger, but the poverty of her oppidan's dress and the status it denoted offered a kind of protection. Moreover, she was the Low Lady's daughter, and all in the Liberty must know it. She walked calmly and fearlessly, trying not to hunch against the cold. Her neck prickled and her knees trembled with the fear of ambush. She turned into the darkest alleyway and found the rough wood of her mother's door, groping around for the knocker. She rapped on it in the staccato rhythm that denoted the presence of a friend. She waited to be observed in one of the numerous disguised spy cracks that riddled the walls like holes in cheese, then Grimper let her in.

'Donna, sweet child, come in!'

It was not the warmth of home that made her suddenly unclench muscles she had not known were tensed, but the familiar smell of childhood – it almost made her sob and she fell into the arms of the woman who waited, grim-faced, behind Grimper's shoulder. The woman carefully relinquished the halberd she'd been holding and wrapped both arms around her daughter.

'Donna, what in the name of all holiness are you doing here? You bring danger on us. Were you seen?' The former Low Lady spoke harshly but her embrace was tender.

Donna shook her head and released her mother. 'No, Lady, I'm sorry – no one saw me – well, only Liberty men, but I had no reason to come here. I'm sorry, but …' She felt hot with sudden embarrassment: she'd made a mistake again. However hard she tried she was always wrong in her mother's eyes, she always misjudged things: the strength of a potion, the timing of a curtsey, this spontaneous visit. The thought brought pain. Grimper seemed to understand. Grimper seemed able to read her carefully expressionless face as her mother never did.

'Leave her be, Estelle,' he said crossly. 'I'm glad to see her, even if you're not. Come and share the fire.' As Donna widened her eyes she saw his gnarled face crease further into a grin. 'Not here – down below. The chimney is hidden from the Watch and we've got a nice bit of something in the pot.'

Donna might have known that her mother would find a way to survive even when all of Lunnzia was on minimum rations. She smiled back at her mother's bodyguard, her mother's sometime lover. He was always good to her and she wondered, as she always did, if he were her blood father. She could think of no one she would prefer to have sired her, but her mother, in accordance with the tight-lipped rules of her guild, would never say.

Donna followed Grimper's enormous bulk as he led her down the narrow stairs, through a series of rotting doors and the echoing emptiness of abandoned storerooms into her mother's basement hide. The smell of beef hotpot made her feel suddenly faint with hunger; her hands trembled when Grimper handed her a chipped bowl of aromatic liquid and a hunk of white bread. It was years since she had tasted white bread, months since she had tasted black bread without weevils. She did not ask where such wealth came from; it was probably better that she did not know. Her mother had contacts throughout the city and in all probability outside it; more than that, she was adept at making every contact count. Even in the pleasure of the moment Donna felt ashamed that she had so little of her mother's skill; she had found no way to gain power and influence even though she lived nearer the centre of authority. Her mother always made her feel like an ignorant child, a novice at the game of living.

The Low Lady Estelle moved house regularly and compulsively for safety's sake; everything she had could be stowed in a couple of large trunks.

Nonetheless she had a gift for making everywhere she lived seem opulent as a palace. The walls and floor of the small windowless room were covered in hangings the Low Lady had fashioned from scraps of her most exotic gowns, for scraps were all that remained. Her wealth and business had been all but destroyed in the uprising following the Arkel's imposition of the Sumptuary Laws four years previously – it had been a bad year, the year in which the twelve-year-old Donna had been registered as an oppidan orphan and taken her reluctant place in the official world of Lunnzia. Donna could not forget that thanks to the Arkel and the Council of Ten, her mother had been obliged to send her away to live the communal life she so despised.

There was nothing left of the fine furniture that she had once taken for granted, the extravagantly liveried servants and the beautiful vessels of imported porcelain, gold and silver, yet her mother sat with aristocratic élan on a velvet cushion on an old wine crate as if it were a carved court chair in the grand style of Regana the Third. Donna noted with some relief the familiar form of her mother's poison chest acting as the table on which was placed a flask of wine. There was real wealth in that 'table' and the Low Lady Estelle guarded it closely. The small glass vials neatly stowed within its elegant craftsmanship contained death enough to destroy half the city and the means to concoct perfumes of the most sublime beauty. That was the smell of home for Donna: food, wine, her mother's subtly distinctive scent, and poison.

Donna smiled at the figure watching her silently in

the candlelight. 'It's good to be home, Mother.'

'Donna, this is dangerous. We are still outlawed, you know, and you have been too gently raised to deal with this life.'

'I am not a child.'

Her mother cast a professional eye over Donna's well-proportioned figure. 'No, you are not a child, and if things were different we might have talked about your entry into the guild, but things are different. I did not foresee this change in our fortunes or I would have guided you differently. You are not equipped to be a fugitive – the mere fact that you came here without arrangement proves it.'

As Donna opened her mouth to argue, her mother gave her one quelling glance and Donna closed her mouth again. She knew that her mother was right. She had been prepared for a life she could never have and then abandoned to a life for which she was utterly unprepared. She was sure of herself only in her dreams and now she did not want to talk of those. What were dreams to her mother who had come from the streets and made herself the most renowned Low Lady in Lunnzia and, perhaps, beyond? They were exactly the kind of unrealistic juvenile fantasies for which her mother had always chastised her. Donna pulled herself together, aware that her mother was still talking, using the soft, persuasive voice that was as much her stock in trade as her carefully preserved beauty.

'You are too precious to me for me to risk you in our life. You know that. I kept you with me until you were twelve – until I could risk you no longer.' The Low Lady smiled her rare, genuine smile that made the room seem brighter. 'You must go back and do the best you can as an oppidan and stay safe. This regime will not last for ever, the Arkel has made too many mistakes – this ridiculous war among them. His army is gone to fight a cause it cannot win – undermanned, badly led and overstretched.' She paused as if to gain possession of herself and when she spoke again it was in a voice with a harsher passion than Donna had ever heard. 'Trust me, Donna, one day even the Arkel and the Council of Ten will topple, you can count on that. Until then you are safer, as one oppidan among many, than I could keep you here.'

Donna looked down. Her mother had known hardship that Donna had not, and had survived. When Donna had been very small she had sometimes been allowed to watch her mother dress for an important client. She had watched the care with which her mother had applied cosmetics with her own hand to the many scars that marred her body. Once she had asked her mother what had scarred her and got for her enquiry a hard slap and a single answer, 'Pain'. She had never asked again.

'The hotpot is good,' Donna said at length. 'Food is running low at the refectory – black bread.'

'Ah,' said her mother. 'You'll have more, then?'

Donna luxuriated in the warmth and safety of her mother's home. It did not matter that her mother and Grimper were outcasts on the run, that they lived in constant danger as two of the very few survivors of the assassin's guild: when she was with them in the privileged ambit of their company she always felt safe. She warmed her cold limbs in the heat of her mother's fire and finally felt her sense of isolation and loneliness melt away like the snow on her clothes.

It was at least two hours later that Grimper escorted Donna, loaded with hidden gifts, back to the campus barracks, using the alleyways of the waterfront and the darkest shadows made by moonlight to avoid the Watch. Grimper moved with silent economy in spite of his size and, with his hooded cloak pulled well over his head, it was almost impossible to see him in the night. He hung back when she reached her destination but she sensed him, still waiting, watching her in the darkness, to see her safely inside. She could not go through the front door or the night porter would have reported her to Martrin, the Redman who was overseer in charge of her work detail. The building was a tall and imposing one that had once housed the wealthy Fiorini family; her room was on the second floor. Donna tried to measure distances with her eye. There was a window open on the first floor, but it was in an exposed position which would leave her vulnerable to the eye of the Watch, and she had never learned to climb. She was studying her possible route so intently that she did not notice the soft sound of footsteps in the snow or sense the subtle sweetness of berenslip until she felt a cold hand over her mouth. She signalled frantically to Grimper to stay hidden, though she could see him rise from the shadows out of the corner of her eye.

'It is me, Capla, the slave of Lambrugio. Don't scream!'

He removed his hand and she turned to face him.

She could not make out his face in the darkness but she could see the scarecrow outline of his body.

'What do you want? How dare you –' Donna stopped before she could continue with her proud tirade. She was at risk here in the night when she should be indoors. She snapped her mouth shut and simply waited for a reply.

'I wanted to tell you, Oppidan, that should you have need of me you will find me in the household of the Arkel. There is much that I know that could be of use to you. I know for example that there is a servants' entrance at the back of this building that is unguarded for the moment because the Watchman is sick.'

Donna reached in her sleeve for the half loaf of soft white bread her mother had given her. It pained her to give it away. She hoped that he would not question the source of such luxury.

'Show me, Capla of Lambrugio.'

In giving him such a name she gave him respect. He nodded his acknowledgment. She let him lead her round the back of the building and, when Capla's back was turned, risked a quick wave in the direction of Grimper's hiding place. If Capla noticed he gave no sign.

Chapter Six

Scrubber was less amused by Rej's narrow escape than he had expected her to be.

'Frakk, Rej, I don't like the sound of this. You don't mess with Barna.'

'Will you go to the Light for me or not?'

Scrubber wrinkled her nose in a way that made her wizened, monkey-like face look odder than ever.

'I'll do it. But I'm not touching them bits of paper. You can take an extra candle – then you frakking deve off, combe-mate. I don't want Barna on my tail.'

Rej hugged Scrubber warmly. She had been his mother's friend years back – the two of them had fallen foul of the ruling party even before the Revolution of the Ten sixteen years previously, and together had taken refuge Below. Scrubber was the nearest thing to family Rej had left.

'Deve off, you're as mad as a stenk-head. Hey, did you see Moon get out of the Styx, or are we finally free of the runt?'

Rej shrugged. His confrontation with Moon already seemed days away. He had bigger things to worry about.

Scrubber's sharp eyes missed nothing. 'I can get you

out, you know,' she said softly. 'I know every leak in the frakking system. I could get you Above. Not that it's any better than down here right now, but you'd be away from Barna.'

Rej shook his head. 'Thanks, Scrub. It's not that bad yet.'

He smiled at her. He did not know why he had said 'no'. He surprised himself; he wanted to go Above, had always wanted to go Above. Was it fear that had made him refuse her, his desire not to run away from a mess of his own making, or was it that he didn't want to get involved with her business? They never talked about her smuggling. Rej wasn't completely happy with her dealings in stenk so they never spoke of it. Scrubber was of his mother's generation, the group who thought all those above ground were 'degenerates'. His mother's main criticism of Scrubber had been that she didn't wash enough. That memory always made him smile – these days nobody washed. Untreated combe water made your skin peel off, and it was better to be dirty than thirsty.

Scrubber passed him a candle and an oil lamp. The extra brightness revealed the dark lines on her face where dirt had filled the creases of her skin and made it a tracery of wrinkles. Her teeth were chipped and rotten but still clear of the tell-tale damage of stenk. She'd been an addict once, long ago, when Rej was a child. His mother had helped her free herself of it; it made her continued trade in the stuff the more incomprehensible to him.

'Read your bits of paper – I won't be long. You frakking owe me after this, Rej. You'll harvest for me yet.'

He'd never agreed to harvest stenk for her, but he had nothing left to trade, only debt and the torn secrets of a broken oppidan – and Harfoot's ring, of course. Rej nodded.

'Thanks, Scrub.'

She'd given him ointment and insisted on treating his every wound with her own filthy hands. The unguent she'd used was traded from Above and smelled pungently of unknown herbs and stung like broken glass. Somehow he felt that was a good sign.

'I'll be back soon – don't leave the hide. If you don't hear my signal – use the ghost tunnel!'

She wasn't joking. He'd learned about the ghost tunnels from Scrubber. Wherever she lived – and she moved around often – she always found a niche with a back door. She was, however, a tiny woman, half Rej's size, who weighed no more than one of the larger combe rats. She tended to pick places with very narrow back doors.

When she had gone Rej gnawed on the bread she had left him and tried to assemble the pieces of paper from Harfoot's satchel into some kind of order. It was absorbing work. There were several scientific drawings much annotated in a spidery and almost illegible hand, and many abbreviations. He could make sense of only two fragments – a section of a diagram, and the words 'Basilisk Contrivance', the words the oppidan had shouted in his confusion. The diagram, as far as it was possible to tell, had no link with any pictures of the basilisk Rej had come across, nor with anything in the city which might owe its name to the city's emblem. He knew more than most young combers about the city Above from his mother's stories, but this had him truly puzzled.

He gave up in disgust and lay down on Scrubber's corpse stone. He did not dream, and it seemed like it was only a moment later that he heard a low whistle that indicated Scrubber's return.

'Its frakking mayhem down there,' she announced, tossing him another candle to replace the stub that had all but burned out. 'Moon, the frakking prallock, is in a bad way – major blisters from the water, and there are rumours that Barna trapped you in a dead-end ghost tunnel! Bad news travels fast. I got you what you asked for and you owe me sixty credits' worth of stenk gathering – double or quits?' She rattled her gaming dice wickedly and Rej hesitated. His Lady may well be with him again – luck had after all seen him through the ghost tunnel; on the other hand the Doctor Esteemed Harfoot lay dying.

'Later Scrub, I'll wipe you out, but I'd better go.' He caught the packages she threw at him and stowed them in Harfoot's satchel. 'Thanks!'

'Don't you worry. I'll make you frakking pay!' Scrubber returned cheerfully, and Rej eased his way into the half-darkness of this part of the combes. He climbed carefully, avoiding the parts he knew to be inhabited. Most combers lived in those niches closest to the treaty lights and the Light Hall of Distribution. Only the solitary, awkward ones like himself or combers up to no good like Scrubber preferred the outer sections where there was little light and more danger.

He made it to Harfoot's burial niche, fairly

confident that he had not been seen. Harfoot's lantern had burned out, but he knew the moment he stepped on the threshold stone that something was wrong. There was no breathing. He found that his hand was on his knife and that his own breathing had stopped. He moved hesitantly into the deep darkness. He sniffed the air; there were trace scents of things he did not recognise: spice and the sour sweat of strangers. He fumbled his first attempt at striking a flame and when he finally lit the pitch-soaked torch that Scrub had got him he almost dropped it in his shock.

There was blood everywhere. Someone had bled Harfoot as he'd once seen combers bleed a pig. The main vessel at his neck had been severed and then he'd been stabbed with a sword through the heart. Rej felt his legs melt under him and he sank to the floor. There was no doubt about it – no comber would have done that. No comber he knew had ever had a sword, not even Scrubber, and she broke most of the rules of the combes. There was something very wrong here. Rej had seen death before, many times. The combes had many ways of killing the unwary and murder was not unknown among them. No, what shocked him was the clear involvement of Abovers, banned by the fifteen-year treaty from setting foot underground. Were things so bad Above that they had to bring their problems Below? Was the long feared war against Above about to start? He steeled himself to check the niche for any further clues as to the murderer's identity. There was no blood on the entrance to the ghost tunnel so it seemed unlikely that the attacker, who must have been splattered in blood, could have left in that direction.

Rej sighed. As the finder of the body it fell to him to perform the funerary rites which were the duty of every comber, and one of the few that even Scrubber wouldn't have denied. Ironically, there was no form of burial in the catacombs; bodies were always burned. Rej took the small vial of oil that he'd got from Scrubber for his lamp and poured it over the dead man's body. He emptied the paper from the satchel and scattered that too over the dead man – the fragments made no sense and were no use to trade. He covered the man's face with his coarse, blood-stained blanket. Then Rej began to sing words from a rite so ancient it predated the catacombs, remembering an earlier time when corpses were always burnt.

'When the world was but nothingness
God sent Arché to breathe fire and bring the world
to life
At the beginning there was fire and at the end there
is fire
May the breath of Arché take you back through the
breath of death
To life in the place from which all breath comes.'

It was not necessary that he remain to watch the corpse burn, but he waited anyway at the threshold stone after he'd thrown the torch on to the body. The oil burnt with a sudden flare of flame and the intense heat made his own skin burn. The rough walls of the combe glowed orange, the smell made him gag and the smoke made his eyes water. He made himself stay at the threshold, turning away only to breathe the cool, damp air outside. His responsibility was not over. His mother had taught him about honour and debt. She had died helping a comber avenge himself for his sister's murder. There was a blood debt here and only Rej to pay it. It did not matter that he was no relation to the man or that they were strangers to one another. There were no laws in the combes, only customs, and some people thought it discouraged a prospective murderer to know that any death would be avenged. He took the man's ring from his pocket and muttered ritual words. It was not important that there was no one to witness the deed; he would be true to it.

> *'From the light of your death flame*
> *Light the flame of my vengeance,*
> *Burn in my blood's fire*
> *Until the death flame is lit again.'*

Rej put the ring back in its safe place and contemplated what he'd just done. He thought of Scrubber's offer. He had a duty to leave the combes now; whatever compulsion had made him refuse Scrub's offer was lifted. If this death was the work of an Abover he had to find out what was going on. Something within him quickened at the very thought. With this blood debt hanging over him he could justifiably leave Barna and his other problems below ground in the combes: there could be no shame in that. Perhaps Luck, his Lady, was smiling on him, giving him the kick he needed to see the wide sky for himself. For an instant he remembered the soaring sensation of his dragon flight. He was sad that Harfoot had died. He was worried that Abovers were involved, but for once duty, luck and his own inclination were pushing him in the same direction – up and out. Scrubber had told him she could fix it for him. He would not refuse her again. With as much joy as fear in his heart, he set out to find her again.

Chapter Seven

Donna woke to the squalor of the shared dormitory and a queasy sense of fear. She did not want to return to the Doctor Esteemed Melagiar's chamber, in spite of its warmth and the pleasure she took in her work there. She had not dreamed of the dragon but her dreams had been full instead of unknown dark horrors and a pervading atmosphere of gloom. She felt stale and disgruntled. The fact that she had eaten well the night before served only to make her hungrier. Her stomach growled for more than black bread and souring ale.

She battled for space at the meagre basin, ignoring the jostling and catcalls of the other oppidans. Her mind was too full of other places for her even to respond with her favourite vindictive fantasy of poisoning the lot of them. There was a fine gilded mirror in the hall and she tidied up her ramshackle appearance as best she could, without drawing attention to herself. She quickly braided her long hair into a severe style, tying it back with a scrap of cloth she had found in the street. She intended to emphasise her worthiness and seriousness; she wanted to become a secondary scribe. It was not a great advancement up the hierarchy that was supposed to be no hierarchy, but it would be a start. In fact the severe hairstyle served to accentuate the fine, rather too prominent bones of her face and the startling beauty of her eyes.

The door to the Doctor Esteemed's study was opened by his sister Immina. It was scarcely possible, but she seemed if anything more wan and bloodless than she had the day before. She was elaborately dressed in an old-fashioned, high-necked gown of heavy blue damask silk. The dress was as lovely as any in Donna's mother's collection and Donna had to contain her desire to touch it; it was decorated with tiny cream-seed pearls arranged in a pattern of trailing briar roses. Immina smiled, but the smile was a smile of chilling vacancy. Her eyes had an absent, unfocused look as if she gazed not at Donna but at some creature of her own imagining. Donna felt ice creep down her already rigid spine. She did not want to be alone with this woman.

A fire still blazed in the hearth and the room was hot and heavily scented with some perfume that made her head swim. Something burned on the fire, which gave out a sickly sweetness – averaine? Becomon? Neither was a powerful poison but they brought their own gifts of stupefaction and quietude. Donna was not sure that she could work in such an environment; it was hard to breathe and harder still to think. Immina directed Donna to her seat at the window with a vague gesture of her elegant hand. A square-cut ruby, the size of her thumbnail, flashed on her middle finger. Donna felt a rising nausea. The haze of fumes within the room distorted her vision so that everything seemed oppressive and sinister. She reached for the latch of the casement and, with what seemed like enormous effort, flung the window open, not wide, but far enough to allow a breath of cold, fresh air into the room; it cut like a knife through the fug of fumes.

Donna breathed deeply and her head cleared; the room was no more than a room again. She was surprised to find Immina at her side, breathing deeply of the untainted air. A measure of awareness returned to Immina's faded blue eyes. She gave Donna a cool look, raised a long finger to her lips as if to silence her and then, to Donna's complete surprise, bit her own finger savagely so that blood oozed. Donna was too shocked to act. How mad did you have to be to bite your own flesh to draw blood? It was not a small wound either, yet Immina had made no sound. Donna looked around for something with which to staunch the blood, but Immina gripped her by the shoulder with vice-like strength. Her long fingers pinched into Donna's flesh like the talons of a predatory bird, or the claws of the basilisk. Immina held her so that Donna had no choice but to look into her pale, haunted face. Immina made a sound in her throat, a frightening inhuman noise, and then very deliberately opened her mouth to reveal the stub of tongue. Donna recoiled. The sight was no less shocking than it had been the day before. Donna was afraid. Immina's strength was terrifying, her madness beyond doubt. Then, unaccountably, she released her grip on Donna's shoulder. Donna's stared at her, transfixed by fear, revulsion and sudden unexpected sympathy: Immina had her full attention. Immina's eyes looked almost normal now, as if the pain had brought her back to herself – was that why she had bitten her own finger?

Silently Immina picked up the quill pen that lay on the desk, dipped it in the ink well and wrote on the palm of her own now bloody hand.

Help me!

The writing was unsteady and there was too much ink on the quill so that the ink ran and mingled with the blood, frustrating her purpose, but the words were clear enough. When Immina showed her open palm to Donna there was no doubt about the meaning she intended, nor any doubt about the desperation in her now clear, pale eyes.

There was a sound as if someone had knocked something over in another room nearby; the sound of footsteps. With unexpected swiftness Immina wiped her hand on the inside hem of her gown and meandered unsteadily back towards the fire. She glanced back at Donna once and smiled, a grim, sad, frightened smile. Donna found she was shaking. A drop of Immina's blood had fallen on the tooled leather of the desk and she wiped it away with a piece of blotting paper so that it made a large brown stain among the black ink blots. Donna took several deep breaths, trying to grasp her situation. It was clear enough that Immina was being kept somehow pacified and trapped within her brother's chamber, but why? Did it have anything to do with the dragon tattoo?

The sound of footsteps grew louder and closer. Donna bent her head in the appearance of concentration and began to transcribe the text before her with an uncertain hand. The icy draught from the open window chilled her face and her mind with it; she was frozen by uncertainty. Hers had never been a life of action, only of obedience. She had never had to act decisively before. What should she do?

Immina had begun to play an old popular song on her elaborately decorated lap-harp. The sound of the music of Donna's childhood in a world which had become bereft of it brought tears to her eyes. She wiped them away with her hands – it would not do to dampen her work with tears. Immina stopped playing when the Doctor Esteemed Melagiar entered the room. He appeared distracted and only glanced briefly at Donna as she worked.

He walked over to a handsome bureau of dark polished wood and began rifling through the drawers, throwing rolled parchment on to the floor all round him. He was muttering while he worked and Donna strained to hear him, while at the same time appearing to concentrate on her work. She caught only the words 'Blasted worm, Harfoot', and then a tirade aimed at his sister to the effect that she should tidy the mess of scrolls he'd made, as he marched back towards the curtained doorway through which he had appeared. Donna tried to watch him from under her lashes. Unfortunately, his eyes met hers. She tried to look away, but his eyes were very dark and penetrating and they held her in a gaze of such intensity that she found it difficult to look away.

'Do you know my colleague, the Doctor Esteemed Harfoot?'

She shook her head, unnerved both by the question and by the power of his regard. Something about him was very compelling, charismatic.

'You have something of the look of one of his

scribes. Some of his papers are most infuriatingly missing, just as I have most need of his learned discourse. Even an inferior talent may have its uses.'

Donna could think of nothing to say, merely nodding mindlessly as he turned and left the room the way he'd come. Perhaps it was the heat of the chamber and the still lingering fumes, but she had felt terribly exposed under his gaze, almost as if he could see into her very soul. Immina let out a kind of a whimper when he had gone and began to reorganise the scrolls back into the drawer from which he had flung them. Donna was afraid to approach her because the vague look was in her eye again. She observed her carefully, trying to understand what was happening to her. Immina began to order the scrolls neatly and then stopped to drink from the elaborately decorated goblet and pitcher that were placed nearby on a small circular table. With each drink Immina seemed to grow calmer and also less orderly until, after all but throwing the remaining scrolls in the drawer, she merely lay supine on the carpeted floor gazing into space.

Donna waited until Immina was quite still and then slipped from her chair and sniffed the goblet. It was sweet and pungent – a concoction much favoured by aristocrats like the ruling Devarras in the time before the Revolution. Ajeebamor – stenk and wine sweetened with honey and spiced with cloves. Donna poured a small drop of the liquid on to her palm – it was a deep purple, the colour of the flower that bloomed extravagantly in the summer months all over Lunnzia.

Immina was almost unconscious, her breathing shallow. Donna had no idea how much she had drunk, but it was a particularly potent brew and Immina was in a stupor from which she was unlikely to recover any time soon. Donna took an uncharacteristic risk and, kneeling at Immina's side, quickly unbuttoned the high-necked bodice of Immina's gown. She had to know if she had been mistaken – had the woman really worn a tattoo of the dragon of Donna's dreams? It was unusual for Donna to question her own memory, but the dragon dreams had disturbed her with their clarity and semblance to reality. Had she dreamed of Immina's dragon too?

The tiny buttons were awkward for Donna's numbed fingers to manage, but she undid them at last and saw that it was true. Immina bore the dragon's image on her pale, thin skin. It was the work of rare artistry – the colour of true gold, not yellow – and glowed like a living thing, as if a real miniature beast coiled around Immina's pale white skin. Donna fumbled a little in her haste to redo Immina's buttons – she ought to have used a button hook. She was uncomfortable leaning so close to the stupefied woman, smelling the sweet corruption of ajeebamor on her breath. To make up for violating her privacy, which Donna still considered wrong, although the desire for privacy was a sin according to the Arkel, she made an effort to place Immina in a more comfortable position, and tidied up the scrolls in the drawer herself. She stoked the fire to keep Immina warm, then returned to her seat by the window.

Immina slept heavily and her colour was deathly white, but there was nothing that could be done for her until the ajeebamor lost its potency. It would be many hours before she regained awareness. Donna forced herself to return to her task, calling on all her considerable self-discipline, and worked steadily and automatically until the day ended. She could not imagine why Immina bore the dragon tattoo – the obvious explanation that she was a member of some cult or secret society seemed implausible. Her mother had made her familiar with the major secret societies from the days before the Revolution, and there was no cult of the dragon that she knew of. Not for the first time she felt uneasy with the strangeness of the Doctor Esteemed's opulent rooms and the decadence which should have been swept away with the Sumptuary Laws.

Immina still slept. How could she, Donna, misfit oppidan and useless daughter of a Low Lady, help anybody? She hurried back to the refectory. She tasted the smoke of averaine in her mouth, a foul bitterness that she longed to be rid of. She needed more information before she could help Immina. Pride would not allow her to run to her mother again with a less than perfect grasp of what was going on.

It was with relief that she spotted Capla performing his serving duties with quiet efficiency. He gave her a bowl of thin gruel and she knew by the look in his eyes that he expected her to have a question for him.

'Oppidan Donna?' He bowed and whispered in a low voice that only she could hear, 'If you need me I'll be outside when all the bowls are emptied.'

Donna did not allow a flicker of emotion to cross her face as she murmured, 'I will talk with you then.'

Chapter Eight

'I don't know, Rej, you're such a frakking innocent,' Scrubber sighed.

'What do you mean?' Rej felt himself bridle at the criticism. 'I do fine down here.'

'No one takes on a blood oath any more – you know nothing about this oppi. Believe me, Above they're not so sentimental. Trust me, you're going to need your wits to stay alive, not to play revenger.'

'I'm not playing – I'm serious. My mother –'

Scrubber's voice softened. 'Yeah well, no doubt your mother would have approved.' There was a silence between them then. Scrubber did not need to point out that his mother's view of responsibility had got her killed.

Rej broke the silence first. 'You suggested it yourself before – why've you changed your frakking mind?'

'It's one thing to run to safety, another to try some half-lit, scrottle-headed idea of revenge. You don't know the rules Above.'

There was a pause before Rej said doggedly, 'So, you'll lead me through the tunnel?'

'I frakking said so, didn't I?' she snapped. Rej knew Scrubber well enough to know that she was worried, and that made him worried too.

'You'll need to bathe.'

'What d'you mean?'

'The catacombs smell. I'm not saying Above smells much better but you'll be known as a comber from fifty lengths. Don't look so frakking forlorn. I know somewhere where you can wash, I'll get you some clothes too. How much d'you remember of what your mother told you?'

'Almost everything.' Rej could not keep pride from his voice as he said it. He knew he remembered every word of her every story.

'Forget it. It's all different. The war with High Verda is going badly. The oppidans live more like slaves than free men working for the Council of Ten. The Arkel has expelled all the aristocrats and merchants, or bankrupted them, and his interfering priests, the Redmen, are everywhere, whining about the duty of self-sacrifice and the religious duty of sharing while they – well, never mind what I think about the Arkel and his Redmen. The oppidans all sleep in rows in the old palaces and work at whatever the Arkel thinks needs doing, while real craftsmen weed gardens and sweep streets with the slaves.' She sounded terse, angry, more upset than was usual for Scrub. She paused as if to calm herself and took a deep breath. 'I've still got a network. There's a woman I know who might help you, though Arché knows she's got enough frakking problems of her own.' Scrub kicked her kitbag on the floor in frustration. 'Frakk me, but this whole place is going to destruction faster than I can keep up.'

'It'll be all right, Scrub. I'll be fine.'

The face she turned to him was bleak and sad and

more careworn than he had ever seen it. There was something suspiciously like tears shining in her eyes.

'You're an innocent,' she said. 'Arché love you. The odds are stacked, Rejivar. They're stacked against you, and it's a crooked game.'

Rej found himself unexpectedly moved and frightened by her response, though he couldn't help but be annoyed that she rated his survival skills so poorly.

Scrubber gave him what she could spare of her food and led him through the darkest parts of the combe. He had followed her since he was a boy and was well used to her swift, neat movements and her ability to climb any expanse of rock. This time she led him to the very edge of his known world, through a series of ghost tunnels and up the all but sheer walls of a kind of pipe. Spikes of metal protruded from its smooth, man-made surface to form foot and handholds. In the darkness Scrubber lit a small candle and rested it on one of the ledges. From somewhere about her filthy person she produced a metal key. In the meagre light Rej was able to see that the pipe was blocked by a heavy wooden door, bolted and padlocked. Scrubber unlocked the padlock in one deft motion, blew out the candle and returned it to her pouch. She balanced her weight on two footholds placed on either side of the pipe and bent her back so that the wooden door lay across it. Using the strength in her strong back, she pushed the door outwards. It landed silently as if into some kind of padding; then, for the first time, Rej tasted the clean, cold night air of Above – the air of his parents' former world, the air of the city of Lunnzia.

Scrubber said nothing, merely lifted herself up on to her wiry arms and scrambled out. A second later her wrinkled face grinned down at him and a scrawny hand was extended to help him up. He did not need her help but he took it as a gesture of kindness and clasped her arm. It was frailer and more bird-like than he had remembered and for the first time in a long while he was suddenly aware of Scrubber's advanced age.

The stars distracted him, dwarfed him, turned him into a speck of near nothingness. The vast blackness of the sky was like no blackness he had ever seen, and the pin-pricks of light shone with a pure, white beauty that made him forget to breathe.

'For Light's sake, Rej!' Scrubber whispered harshly and he pulled himself together and emerged from the tunnel like a maggot from its egg. Scrubber pushed him aside and re-secured the gateway to the combes. From Above the entrance was almost unnoticeable – a circular piece of wood painted in streaks of grey and brown like the land around. Surrounding them there were stones and pieces of discarded rag, a terrible muddle of objects – an unimpressive entry to this world.

Rej couldn't immediately get his bearings. He was giddily disorientated; there was no frakking roof! Nothing enclosed him, nothing held him in. He had always feared the closeness of the stone walls of the combes, but without their solidity keeping him safe he felt naked, insignificant, vulnerable. He could not bring himself to straighten out of the hunched, crouching position he had automatically adopted.

Scrubber held him firmly by the shoulders.

'Get a hold of yourself, Rej. Don't be half-lit. It's only frakking space, like the Light Hall without a roof. Look! Head for that wall there and rest against it while I tidy up here.'

Her voice was kinder than he deserved. He hated himself for the shivering, cringing fear that unmanned him. He lurched towards the comfort of the dark, black shape that was the wall and shut his eyes so as not to look at the stars. They made him feel about the size of an insect crawling in ignorance across the wall of the combe – in the instant before it was crushed.

He had managed to calm his breathing and open his eyes by the time Scrubber joined him.

'Frakk, Rej, I didn't think you'd be prone to the space queasy.'

'The what?' he managed to answer, pleased that he could speak normally.

'I was raised up here but I still notice it when I first come Above.' She opened her arms wide. 'All this space and air can make you feel scrottle-headed.'

It was darker in the shadow of the wall. There was light from somewhere, light of an unusual quality he hadn't known before, but here in the shadow of the friendly wall all he could see were the whites of Scrubber's old eyes gleaming in the comforting darkness.

'I'm fine,' Rej lied.

'We'll rest here and then I'll take you where you can wash. Wait here and don't move. Don't make a sound. People round here don't worry about the green death – the militia all carry blades of good steel – so don't make a frakking sound.'

It was hard to judge how long she was gone. He wondered if she'd left him alone in order to give him time to adjust to the vastness of the open sky and the strange salt smell of the air and the water he could hear running not far away. The dizzying, sickening sense of his own insignificance was beginning to wear off, and he tried to focus instead on the purpose of the many dark shapes that littered the ground: Above was not what he had expected.

When Scrubber returned she carried a bundle of clothes and a flask.

'My friends are good to me.' Scrubber grinned and for one horrible moment Rej thought it was the sweetness of stenk he smelled on her breath, but it was some other thing. She handed the flask to him. 'My friend, the Poison Lady, says this will help. Don't worry, we were girls together. She will not harm you.'

Rej sniffed the liquid in the flask tentatively. It smelled like spiced wine. He had tasted wine once or twice, usually from Scrubber. He sipped it cautiously; it warmed him and his nausea receded.

'Come on then, you frakking moon-sick boy. Let's get you clean.' She said this without irony, as if unaware that her own particularly noxious scent was well known throughout the combes and might have cost her friends had she not been so well respected.

She led him to the banks of a river not far away. The light, he now realised, was moonlight, and, reflected off the glossy blackness of the water, the ripples of shimmering silver held him transfixed.

'I never thought it would be so beautiful.'

'What're you frakking on about, Rej? This is the Liberty, the old estuary dockside, the stinking armpit of Lunnzia, where we dregs and dross of renegades flit between worlds. I've never heard it called beautiful before.'

But he knew by her voice that she thought the river lovely too. To understand Scrubber, Rej had learned long ago, you had to listen to the quality of her silences, not the content of her words. He stripped down to his undercloth and launched himself into the iciness of the water. Scrubber tossed him a small vial of oil.

'Rub it into your skin – all over – and into your hair.' Rej did as he was told and forced himself to duck face and hair under the water. The oil smelled strongly but he did not know of what, except that it was something pleasant and unknown in the catacombs.

'Then scrub away with this!' Rej only just caught a small piece of light stone that Scrubber threw him. He obligingly scrubbed at his skin until he felt raw, half frozen and freshly made, a new creature forged in the moonlit water, tempered in the biting cold. Scrubber would not let him dry himself on his own clothes but gave him a length of new cloth to wipe himself with, though his teeth were chattering so much she threatened to do it for him.

The clothes she gave him were of plain, bleached, coarse fabric, no better than the cloth they were granted by treaty in the combes. There were fewer layers than he was used to and no woollen undervest, steeped in fat, to keep out the bitterest cold. Maybe it was warmer Above. He could not stop shivering. There was no belt pouch for his flint and other necessaries, but he found a way of thrusting his knife in the girdle of his short robe.

'My Poison Lady is otherwise engaged tonight, but she has said you may get warm and eat in her hide until morning. After that you are on your own.'

Rej nodded gratefully and followed Scrubber into the darkness of an old and decaying building. It was hard to make out much but he was glad to be inside, away from the terrifying space outdoors. There was a fire there as large as the one that always burned in the Light Hall. He sank beside it and allowed it to thaw away the chill. Scrubber gave him bread to eat and pungent cheese and after he had eaten he slept on the floor beside the hearth, curled up like an animal.

'An innocent,' sighed Scrubber, and prepared herself for the long night's watch.

Chapter Nine

Donna did not leave the refectory immediately. She was drawn, rather against her better judgement, to a group of oppidans at the far end of the long trestle table. She had chosen to isolate herself – or maybe she had not chosen it, but she had not known how to behave with the other oppidans who had been together since nursery and never known the care of a Poison Lady. She felt lonely, a little lost, and the bright faces of the young women were the warmest thing in the cold hall. One of the men in her detail, Belafor with the twisted leg, was talking in a low, intense voice, and she was intrigued enough to listen. They stopped as she approached. Why would they trust her? She had never shown any interest in their existence before.

Donna found herself saying, 'If you were speaking of that which is better unspoken, it is wiser to do it in a normal voice; you will attract less suspicion.' She spoke conversationally as she tore at the thick shoe of unrisen bread that was today's meal.

There was a silence before Gayla said hastily, 'We were not talking about you, only about the bread and the lack of a fire. Surely the war cannot be going that badly.'

The Redman on duty patrolled the trestles with his staff shaped like a dragon's claw. It was Hilmarne, one of the most unforgiving ones. He was intoning the hymn of Arché in a low rapid mumble, his ears and bright rat's eyes alert for misdemeanours. Like all priests, he carried a whip with several tongues – the Scourge of Arché. Donna was not the only one to have tasted its bite.

'What do the war notices say?' Donna asked in an exaggeratedly bored voice. She never read them, they made so little sense to her – they mainly talked of the Verdans' imminent defeat following an engagement at some place she'd never heard of: the imminent defeat never came. She could not now remember why they were at war at all.

'Oh, victory is imminent – the usual thing, but there has been no word from my brother at the front for months.' Belafor spoke conspiratorially and Donna started to giggle as if he'd told a joke, which won her a suspicious look from the assembled group. 'For Arché's sake, don't look like you're plotting – do you want to be arrested?'

She risked a glance at the prowling Redman: Hilmarne, the Most Blessed. The well-bred oppidans looked at her in disbelief. It was clear that for all her mother's concern for her there were others in the city even more innocent than Donna. They did not know that punishment did not end with the Scourge of Arché; they must have been ignorant of the opponents of the Council imprisoned to die a lingering death in cages along the dockside. They had not watched the flesh stripped from the prisoners' bones, shred by bloody shred, as the scavengers took them.

Innocent they may be, but not stupid. One by one they too smiled inappropriately at what Belafor had said and when they spoke it was more naturally. They argued about the cause of the poor quality food and the lack of fuel. It was low key, but it was the first time Donna had ever been aware that others were dissatisfied with the way the Arkel and the Council of Ten arranged things, tired of the futile war and endless privation. It was also the first time she had ever really engaged with others in her detail. She had been solitary for so long she had almost forgotten that anything else was possible. She listened and was warmed by the company of others. It made her feel like someone else – not like Donna at all. For a time she almost managed to forget the image of Immina with her stump of a tongue and her bloody message – *Help me!* Then she saw Capla slip from the hall with a meaningful, rapid glance in her direction. Fear returned, but her new sociability made it difficult to leave the table unnoticed.

'I have to visit my aunt, who lives at the Barracks of the Wise.' She pulled a face. 'I promised.'

It was a worthy excuse – all oppidans were supposedly committed to service and respect for the old, and Donna's 'aunt' was a ruse she had used before; the fact that Donna had no aunt was of no consequence. But then Belafor rose and with an expansive gesture offered to escort her there – it was long past the time when he should have visited his mother at the barracks, he said, and it was best it were done quickly, before the curfew. Donna had little choice but to accept his escort.

After they had cleared their absence with the deeply suspicious Redman, Donna saw that Capla was waiting outside, his back against the wall of the building in the sheltered place between the buttresses, chewing something – berenslip by the smell. He made no sign of having seen her, though she knew that he had. In spite of her urgent need to find out more about the dragon tattoo, it was surprisingly pleasant to allow Belafor to chat inconsequentially and to pay her the attentions that once might have been part of a normal Lunnzian life. They shared a single lantern and moved as quickly as possible through streets deserted but for the old men of the Watch. The cold made it impossible to linger, though Donna would have liked to, not least because she was not at all sure of what she was going to do when they reached their destination.

In the end she needn't have worried. The entrance to the Barracks of the Wise was marked by a large red painted cross and the ground beside the large, stuccoed building was dug up.

'Plague,' said Belafor, shortly, his voice tight.

There was no one around to ask so Donna rang the bell pull and a grille in the door was opened. An inhuman face looked out. Donna almost screamed until Belafor raised the lantern and she could see that the face belonged to a man in an elaborate leather plague mask, shaped like a bird's beak.

'What is it? The Doctor Esteemed Garvell diagnosed an ague and no one is to come in.'

Belafor was pale in the lamplight. 'Do you know the names of the dead?'

'Who are you asking about?'

Belafor murmured his mother's name and the masked man shouted back at someone unseen.

'She's not on my list of the dead yet, so you can take some comfort from that, I suppose,' the man said at length, glumly. 'Now leave, before you carry the pestilence away with you.'

Donna was suddenly grateful for her mother's irregular life in the ramshackle Liberty.

'You did not ask about your aunt.' Belafor's tone was accusing.

'I ... I feared to know,' she answered, thinking quickly. 'She is old and I fear none too strong. I think it likely that she would have succumbed.'

Belafor patted her clumsily on the shoulder and she was ashamed at her display of faked feeling, but she needed to seek out Capla and the curfew hour was close.

'Please, Belafor, would you leave me here alone for a moment – I can't face our barracks just yet.'

He offered her the lantern and made a fuss when she rejected it.

'I will be safe here with the Watch on patrol. Please, Belafor, I am fine.'

She felt very alone when he'd gone. The moon was bright and the deserted streets seemed bleak and forlorn. There was no music or laughter or wild gaiety of the kind that had once made the streets of Lunnzia as brilliant by night as they were splendid by day. The Arkel did not even permit the religious parades which had once marked the seasons with feast days and celebrations and music. How she missed the music!

His was a grim, dark faith. Unfortunately, she could not blame him for the biting cold – though according to her mother's theories cold was a blessing in time of pestilence. She shivered and prepared to return. There was no sign of Capla.

Brisk footsteps clipped the cobbled ground like a hammer on an anvil; Capla wore no shoes and the Watch were all old or lame and marched with difficulty. Donna flattened herself into the shadows of the wall and tried not to breathe, but nonetheless her breath froze in the air like the smoke that was the breath of the basilisk: it would surely give her away. A man stood in the moonlight in a thick woollen cloak and waited for the arrival of a second man – Capla.

They spoke earnestly in low voices and then the well-shod man in the dark cloak marched away. Something metal glinted in the moonlight. Donna saw a glimpse of a ceremonial sword and shuddered. It was the Arkel himself, the architect of her misery. She wished she had more courage, but even the thought of him made her afraid. She did not dare speak to Capla until she was sure he was out of sight. Capla carried no lantern so she chose the moment to emerge from the shadows. He did not seem surprised to see her.

'I couldn't get away earlier,' Donna said.

He nodded; the scent of berenslip was strong about him and his eyes burned so that she did not want to meet them. She wondered whether to mention the Arkel but dismissed her disquiet as foolishness. Capla was the Arkel's slave – why would he not meet him to give instructions? It was unexpected and oddly clandestine, but there were other things to think about.

She needed to know what the dragon tattoo signified, needed to know more about Immina and her situation before she dared to help her, dared to take her to the Liberty, with all the risk that entailed for her mother. She needed more information.

'I saw something yesterday – in a scroll I was working on – the form of the holy dragon in gold,' Donna began without preamble. 'There was a suggestion – in the text – that it might be worn as a tattoo for a secret purpose. Do you know what that might be?'

Capla's face changed expression minutely. 'The Basilisk's Breath,' he murmured, almost to himself, then, suddenly aware that he had spoken aloud, he clamped his mouth shut and began to chew maniacally at the berenslip root; a pale trickle of yellowish spittle ran down his bony chin.

'The Basilisk's Breath? What's that? A secret society?' Donna took a step towards him in her eagerness and he stumbled back towards the barracks wall, shaking his head violently. Physically the man was as wrecked as any of the poor degenerates sleeping rough in the Liberty. She reined in her impatience.

'I need to find out more. I will do what I can, Oppidan – for a price,' he said. He was breathing heavily and Donna doubted that he had strength for many more days' life unless his lot improved. She was moved by sudden pity.

'What price?'

Capla smiled suddenly – a death's head smile that stretched his green-dyed skin taut across his bones, so that his flesh reminded her of the soft dyed leather of the Redman's gloves tightening across his bunched knuckles in the moment before he had whipped her. It was not a helpful memory; her pity evaporated.

'It is dangerous to ask questions about holy symbols these days. The Arkel grows ever more watchful for the crime of profanity – I would need to be paid in more than bread, though bread too is needed.'

He was not so far gone, then, that he did not realise his sense of well-being was an illusion. Donna nodded. 'What had you in mind?'

'The Doctor Esteemed partakes of the purple dreaming water – it could be of use to me.'

Donna swallowed hard, though she knew her face retained its mask of serenity. He could only mean ajeebamor. To take that from Melagiar would put her in grave danger, put her tenuous security as an oppidan at risk. The daughter of an illegal ought to be more careful.

She nodded again more firmly, as if he had asked her merely for bread. 'Tomorrow then, here, just before curfew?'

He bowed an ironic acknowledgement.

'And ...' she hesitated for a fraction of an instant, 'for such a high price I need to know something more about Melagiar. You warned me about him before – why?'

'I have heard rumours, but I will enquire further, Oppidan, as you will it.' Capla smiled again, making her stomach lurch, and turned back towards the barracks. Feeling oddly foolish, and more than a little afraid, Donna followed a little way behind. It felt as if she were the slave and Capla – Capla felt to be in control. She did not like the feeling.

She liked the note that waited for her in the barracks even less. It was from her mother, written in her unmistakeably elegant hand. It was supposed to be from her mythical aunt in the Barracks of the Wise.

My dear, in spite of the ague which so provokes us, I am well. I cannot meet you but I will be at my window at noon.

The letter had been marked with a 'P' for plague house – so no one attempted to read it over her shoulder and even the porter, employed for his insatiable curiosity, was only prepared to hold it at arm's length. Donna did not pause to wonder how her mother knew about the plague so swiftly – she would have been more surprised if she had not. The aunt and her window was a code her mother had used before. It meant that there was a message for her at the twelfth warehouse in the wharf on the edge of the Liberty. She would have to find a way to get away from Immina at around the hour of the noon breakfast and meet someone, probably Grimper. She feared it must be bad news.

Everyone else seemed to assume the same thing and left her alone. Only Gayla spoke to her and looked suitably stricken when she said that her aunt was in the Barracks of the Wise where plague had struck. It was a word to strike fear into all of them. If death did not get them in the guise of hunger or disguised as the High Verdan army, it haunted them in its familiar form as plague, the black ague: it was not a good time to be a Lunnzian.

Chapter Ten

Rej dreamed of the dragons again and woke, disoriented, to unimaginable brightness. His eyes streamed and ached with it. It was several moments before he could look beyond the narrow rectangle of light and remember where he was. It was many more minutes before he could see Scrubber sitting by the fire watching him. He blinked repeatedly to clear his eyes of the tears that had formed there.

'It's too bright,' he whispered.

'Well, you're done for then, you twazzock, because this is early morning winter light and feeble enough by Lunnzia's standards. Rej, I've come up with a plan. It isn't a very good one, and my friend thinks I'm linny-minded, but she's agreed to help. She will forge an entry into the Book of Oppidans on your behalf. Without a registration you can't eat or find a bed. Once you're registered you can then join a work detail. My friend will make it known that you're unable to speak and a general prallock-head following an accident – scouting for the army, probably. She will contact her daughter who can maybe show you what to do and – Royal Flush – you're one of the masters of Lunnzia.'

Rej weighed this rather extraordinary idea in his mind. He felt slow and genuinely prallock-headed; there had been too much change too fast.

'Shouldn't I be with the militia if I'm of fighting age?' He felt rather proud of himself for remembering that the Abovers were at war and that they used conscripts in addition to their small standing army: many combers would neither know nor care. The war had little impact Below.

'You'd be exempt if your head got scrottled in a scouting accident for the militia – you don't need to play the prallock-head yet!'

He ignored her sarcasm. 'I thought I'd hide on the fringes – I didn't think I would try to be something I'm not.' This wasn't quite true, as his first thought had been to pose as the murdered Harfoot, but he had abandoned anything so ambitious the minute he realised he couldn't even stand up straight in this world without experiencing a bizarre kind of giddiness.

Scrubber wrinkled her face. 'Well, that was my first thought too,' she said grudgingly, 'but they can't hide you here. There are few enough people left in the Liberty and they're under pressure. Besides, the man you found was an oppidan and a scholar – you won't find many of those in the Liberty.'

'You do think there is something going on then – that Abovers murdered the Doctor Esteemed Harfoot?' Rej couldn't keep the eagerness out of his voice. Now that he was here, he was worried that he was on a fool's errand. More than that, his secret hope that dragons really flew in the skies above Lunnzia seemed childish, moon-witted beyond belief. He did not want to admit that he'd ever considered it possible.

Scrubber spoke cautiously, thoughtfully, as he'd not heard her speak before. Scrubber was not given to political pronouncements.

'I think their war with High Verda is going badly – I know you don't think it matters – but it is going so badly that the Council of Ten might turn their attention to something closer to home to distract attention from it and to keep the oppidans on their side. The treaty which has sustained us for so long was only ever supposed to be a temporary solution, a respite for us rebels until we were strong enough to reclaim what is ours, or, from the Abovers' point of view, until we'd all died of bad air and worse water. The Arkel might actively want someone from the combes to break the treaty and come here – as something more than illicit stenk traders. They've long turned a bind eye to that trade. The Council could have set up Harfoot's murder – to provoke a response and give them an excuse to invade us.'

Rej thought about this. 'You don't think I should be here?'

Scrubber sighed. 'Rej, I don't know. Nothing stays the same for ever. I've lived underground for twenty-odd years and I never thought things could go on like this. The Abovers don't like us – don't want us and are scared witless by us. There's an army of us underground – at any time we could undermine their buildings, enter any citadel from below. They've tried to poison us before now, but we smashed the treaty lights and the fumes permeated their city. They've tried starving us and we broke into the Council Chamber and threatened three of the Ten. They want rid of us more than ever now, Rej. People are growing hungry – they have to give us precious food their own citizens need to keep us sweet. I never thought we'd last twenty years.'

She wiped her filthy hand across an even dirtier face. Rej shut his eyes while lights danced under his eyelids. He had never heard Scrubber talk so much sense with so few expletives. The strangeness of everything made a kind of hard stone of discomfort in the pit of his stomach.

'I don't think I can leave this place,' Rej said at last. 'The light burns my eyes, I'm space queasy as you put it and I don't know if I can pretend to be an oppidan. I don't know anything about this place. What if the Council use me as an excuse to attack the combes?'

Scrubber looked at him intently. 'You're an innocent,' she said, in that same steady, grave voice. 'But you're brave and sharp and a quick learner. My innards tell me our days Below are numbered. We can manage with the air and the water but we're a festering sore to the Abovers – well, to the Arkel and his ilk, anyway – and they're not going to tolerate us much longer. Everything I've heard from my friend confirms it. Someone needs to find out what's going on. Your mother was a good friend to me, Rej, and I don't want you hurt, but you wash up nice, you don't look like a comber, you can read and write – you could work as a scribe like my friend's daughter. You could listen, and people talk in front of those that can't. Maybe you're the right person to do this, though, by Arché, I wouldn't have chosen you.'

She stood up briskly and wiped her hands on her filthy dress. 'By late morning things will be ready. You will be introduced to the group of primary scribes working at the university – Harfoot was from the university. My friend thinks there's something happening there. It's as good a place as any to start. Her daughter will help you.' She sighed with a kind of exasperation. 'Now we're going to go outside and practise not being scared and blinded by the light. You don't need to stoop here – you can't bang your head on the frakking sky. Stand up straight, you great twazzock, for frakk's sake.'

Rej was relieved by her change in tone – when Scrubber got responsible he knew things must be very bad. She threw him some bread and he gnawed at it as he followed her into the unknown spaces beyond the hide.

By mid-morning Rej was sweating and shaking with distress. Although Scrub kept pretending it wasn't bright, he was finding it very difficult to adjust to the light and was desperate to find some proper dimness to ease his sore eyes. Scrubber was getting impatient.

'Frakking Light, Rej, by Arché's bollocks you've got the same eyes everyone else has – you've got to be able to cope with ordinary daylight.'

He struggled on and eventually his eyes streamed a little less. Scrub let him back into the dark interior of the hide to eat. Compared with the bright outside, the room in which he'd spent the night seemed comfortingly dim. He had relaxed into the almost familiar gloom when footsteps set his heart beating wildly again. He flung himself into the darkest shadows, clutching his knife. Scrubber let out a little squeal and Rej saw only the back of the most enormous man he'd ever seen outlined against the narrow window. He launched himself at the figure.

'Let go of her, rat-turd – I've got a knife,' Rej said, his voice low and threatening, as if he was back home. He would have an advantage in this darker place, he knew, though that would be all he was likely to have against this huge adversary.

Scrubber's voice sounded amused and pleased. 'Don't worry, Rej, this is my twin brother, known as Grimper. Grimper, this is Hara's boy, Rej.'

Someone lit a lantern and Rej saw Scrubber's twin. The man towered above Scrubber and if they were truly twins then he must have taken much of the height and weight that should have been hers. He wouldn't have fitted into Scrubber's niche, let alone been able to use her ghost tunnels. Grimper gave Rej a hard, appraising look, and his small, bright eyes were as calculating as Scrubber's own.

'I'd put the knife down, boy. I could kill you before you had time to notice.' Grimper's voice was not threatening, but Rej saw the small throwing knife glinting in his hand and judged that he might not be exaggerating. Rej slid his knife back into his belt.

'You favour your mother, boy,' said Grimper and his expression was not unkind. 'She was all that was best about old Lunnzia. Yes, you have her look about you, though you're a good deal lankier.' He exchanged an unreadable look with his sister. 'You can read and write and you can keep your mouth shut?' he asked Rej.

Rej nodded.

'Say your goodbyes then, Venetia, and we'll be off.'

'Venetia!' Rej echoed with a mixture of amusement and disbelief.

Scrubber winced. 'Scrubber to you, linny skull, and don't frakking forget it.'

Rej ignored her scowl and gave her a swift, unexpected embrace. 'I owe you, Scrub. I won't forget.'

'I'll see that you frakking don't. Do as Grimper says – he knows the ways here. May Luck, that fickle frakking bitch, smile on you, Rejivar. Stay clear of the Redmen. You can find me through Grimper if you need to.'

She waved casually over her shoulder and disappeared and Rej knew by the way she held her shoulders that she was upset. She was the only one in the combes he relied on, the only one anywhere he would trust with his life. He straightened up and found to his surprise that the giant Grimper's eyes were level with his own.

Grimper doused the fire. 'We've registered you as Oppidan Rejivar Consolia.'

Rej nodded; his mother had come from a minor branch of the Consolia house so it was near enough the truth.

Rej followed Grimper into the bright light and the wide sky. He tried to look only at what was directly in front of him, to hug the line of crumbling buildings of the wharf. He tried not to experience too much of the journey, in case the wonder of this frakking Light-benighted Above ground space made him giddy again or he lost his footing. Sweat stood out on his forehead with the effort of self-discipline, but a man who could brave a ghost tunnel was not a man to falter in deving daylight. Grimper did not look back to check that he was following but kept up a swift pace, though Rej noticed that he never left the shadow of the dockside. Rej allowed himself to glance up once or twice, but his vision was overwhelmed and he had to sort through his impressions later. He thought that there were fishing boats and people unloading fish – the salt distinctive smell was strong in the air – but Grimper did not stop and he dared not hesitate in following him. He focused down on the task ahead of him and would not let himself be seduced by the scents and the sounds of this new world.

It got busier as they moved further away from the hide where he had spent the night. They moved from dirt paths to cobbled streets and Rej saw several people sweeping the streets and chatting. He even saw a man in an elaborate flame-coloured robe. His eyes drank in the colour from afar, hardly able to believe that such a beautiful colour could exist outside his dreams. A Redman, Rej thought, if that eye-searing colour could be called such a simple thing as 'red' – a priest of Arché under the Arkel's order. Rej noticed that all conversation between workers ceased at the priest's approach.

Grimper hurried on with an air of businesslike purpose. He finally stopped in the doorway of a huge towering building of yellow stone. Rej strained his neck, trying to see what it was, but its walls were sheerer and higher than the highest rock face in the combes. He was afraid to lose his balance and show himself up as a scrottle-skulled fool in front of Grimper, so he stared at the floor.

'You've not got the space queasy, have you lad?' Grimper asked, watching him.

'I'm fine,' Rej said, willing it to be true.

'Listen, the oppidan is coming here. She's a scribe. She will help you. Treat her with respect or you'll have me to answer to, and remember you cannot talk. What you don't say can't get you or anyone else in trouble.'

It was at that moment that Rej saw her. He struggled to keep his mouth closed and his wits from wandering too obviously. He felt a jolt almost of recognition, though he had never seen her before. She was beautiful, more beautiful even than the water by moonlight, lovelier than the manuscripts he'd pored over in delight as a child when his mother taught him to read. She was dressed inadequately for the cold of the day in a long plain wool dress of dark grey, paler where the sunlight touched it, and her long-lashed dark blue eyes dominated a perfect face. She wore no cloak or shawl. She looked at him with some surprise and he saw something flicker in her eyes too.

'Who is this, Grimper? Why are you here in full daylight? You've taken a risk. Is my Lady mother all right?'

'She is fine, Donna. This is Rej. He's lost his wits in an accident and no longer has the power of speech.

Your mother wishes you to introduce him to your work detail and keep an eye on him.' Rej watched relief, quickly followed by disdain, flicker across the girl's face. She nodded.

'If that is what she wishes, Grimper, but if he has lost his wits, how can he write?'

'Oh,' said Grimper with a gesture of impatience, 'it's more his memory – I think he still works well enough.'

Donna's large eyes examined Rej more closely. Her expression was unreadable but her astonishing eyes were shrewd. He felt himself blush.

'Send my mother my good wishes,' she said formally, before hugging Grimper warmly. 'Tell her I'll do what she wants, but I wish she trusted me a little more – and Grimper, for Arché's sake, don't take such risks.'

Grimper's smile was like Scrub's, though his teeth were in better condition; it turned his dour face into something loveable. 'Pray to Arché that you never know the meaning of the risks I take, sweet one. Here, take Rejivar's papers.' That smile removed any sting from his words – he thrust the scrolled parchment into her hand and then he was gone.

The beauty turned to Rej. 'Follow me, Oppidan. I don't know what my mother is up to, but if you are witless I'm Queen Regan of High Verda,' and with that she led him away from the shelter of the shadows into the open street, the harsh midday light and the terrible emptiness of Above.

Chapter Eleven

Donna's work detail were all labouring in what had been a university lecture theatre. They were copying the Arkel's own *Prayer Book for the Common Man* for distribution to the troops of Lunnzia, fighting their unseasonal, incomprehensible war. She indicated that the strange man should follow her, and strode off towards the theatre.

Donna was worried. She didn't know what her mother was plotting but 'Rej' was no more witless than she was. True, he looked unusual and a little bewildered. His hair was dark brown and curly, tied back in a pony tail in a style that she had not seen since before the imposition of the Sumptuary Laws. Almost all men Donna knew wore their hair short or even shaved – it kept the lice down. All the men she knew were also injured or maimed in some way, or else old; the whole and the fit had been sacrificed to the army and the military efficiency of the High Verdans. This youth looked whole and well made – as tall as Grimper but probably less than half his weight, with a marked tendency to stoop. He was preternaturally pale, paler even than Immina, so that his intense dark eyes burned like fires in the snow. He had a gash on his cheek, as though he had been in a fight. It was curious, but as their eyes had met she had felt a brief and instant affinity with him. It shook her. She had never experienced that before. She supposed that if anyone had asked her she would have been obliged to call him handsome – in a gaunt and undernourished way.

She was very aware of his eyes focused on her back and the stiff tension with which he moved as she led him through the streets. As they neared the quadrangle and the looming presence of the university building Donna sensed Rej relax slightly. Once through the doorway and into the dark stairwell he leaned against the stairs and breathed deeply. It was not in her nature to ask him why.

He followed her to the light, well-proportioned room with banked rows of chairs. It smelled damply of unwashed bodies and ink and it was very cold. They all looked the same, Donna's fellow oppidans – pinched and pale, bent over their scrolls, watering eyes squinting. Donna's heart sank: at least working for Melagiar was better than this. The Redman, the Most Humble Servant Martrin, was dictating the words of the Arkel's prayers in a flat toneless mutter so that his audience of frozen workers strained to catch his words. Donna walked the exposed stretch of board floor from the door to the lectern at which the Redman stood, conscious of the rapid, curious glances of all present. Martrin made her wait until he had finished a long tedious section about the joys of service to the Humble Way while Donna fought the urge to sneeze.

When finally he permitted her to step forward and

explain, she found herself unaccountably fearful.

'This man is a former soldier – suffering for our noble cause. He was injured – in the head – and his wits are affected,' she began. 'I was requested to bring him here as he is to join our detail.'

Martrin's bright eyes glinted maliciously. 'And why were you selected for this task of introduction, and by whom?'

It was acceptable to look frightened – it was what he wanted. She rarely gave him the pleasure but now, fearing that otherwise she might fail her mother, Donna allowed her mouth to tremble, allowed herself to swallow hard and to speak with her head lowered in the pose of supplication.

She stammered, 'I do not know, Holiness, but here are his papers. The official who gave them to me requested that he work with me in scribing for the Doctor Esteemed Melagiar.'

She prayed that Martrin would not pursue the issue further, would not check. She made sure that she appeared humiliated before him, biting her lip as if to keep back tears. He smiled, apparently satisfied that she feared him and that she was therefore honest.

'Walk the Humble Way, Oppidan.'

She bowed her head again, further than was required, but not too far – she did not want to overdo things. The youth, Rej, bowed his head too, copying her with a jerky, awkward motion like a badly-worked marionette. It was clear to her that he had never bowed to anyone before. That was not normal – she needed to get him away from the Redman fast, before more questions could be asked.

She led him to the foot of Melagiar's staircase before speaking to him directly. His eyes, insofar as she could see them in the shadowed hallway, were not the eyes of a fool, so she did not treat him as one.

'I shouldn't really bring you here. This is my apportioned task, this season – to scribe for the Doctor Esteemed Melagiar. I will tell him I needed additional help – I have no doubt that he will be angry. Are you sure you can write with a good hand?'

The stranger nodded firmly in the dimness.

'It is unusual here – they don't heed the Sumptuary Laws, and the room is scented with things you might not have come across in the rest of Lunnzia, but don't make a fuss about it. Just act as normally as possible.'

Again the stranger, Rej, nodded. Satisfied, Donna mounted the steeply spiralling stairs ahead of him. She could feel his warm, steady breath on her neck as they climbed. She stopped outside the door of the Doctor Esteemed's rooms. She could hear thudding, the sounds of a violent struggle and wild muffled screaming, an inhuman babbling that she knew had to be Immina. Rej heard it too – she could tell by the way he tensed and curled his hand round the weapon in his girdle. Oppidans did not carry weapons – had Grimper forgotten to disarm him, or he had he another more sinister motive for letting an armed soldier into the city of Lunnzia?

The stranger waited for her to make the first move, to lead the way, but she did not know what to do. There was a crash as if some heavy object had been overturned, and the tinkling of shattering glass. Rej looked at her expectantly. Trying to appear more confident than she felt, Donna knocked tentatively on the door and, on receiving no answer, gently pushed against it. The door was not locked as she had expected and the inner door was ajar. She was shocked by what she saw. The place was in chaos. An inlaid table was on the floor and the pitcher of ajeebamor had spilled over the floor and stained the patterned rug with purple poison. There was blood too, crimson against the cream watered silk of the wall hanging, and it was smeared by that other curtained entrance to Melagiar's private rooms. The inks and quills on the work table were in disarray and one of the chairs was broken. Immina was gone. It took Donna a moment to realise that Melagiar had not. He lay, groaning, in a pool of blood by the fire.

Reluctantly, Donna went to him. Like a dutiful oppidan, she sacrificed the hem of her dress to staunch the blood and knelt beside his prone form to tend to his wound. She did not want to touch him. He frightened her, her instincts recoiled from him for no real reason she could name. Rej glanced around the room, his eyes unreadable, and, finding the blood stain on the wall by the curtained doorway, was through it swiftly and silently into Melagiar's own quarters before Donna could stop him.

'Doctor Esteemed Melagiar, can you hear me?' Donna asked.

The Doctor grunted and spat a thick gob of congealed blood on to the exquisite blue and golden rug. He seemed to have lost a tooth. He was also bleeding profusely from a slice to his upper arm. Donna, the assassin's daughter, knew at a glance that the wound was not itself serious, and was unlikely to be fatal unless it had been poisoned. There was some ajeebamor left in the pitcher, enough to be of use. She poured it over the open wound. Stenk had some limited antiseptic qualities, as long as it wasn't mixed with spittle, and the alcohol would cleanse the cut until a physicker could be called.

Melagiar winced and slapped her hard across her mouth. 'You stupid bitch! What did you do that for?'

Donna reeled back in shock from the blow. 'Sir, I did not know if the wound was poisoned – ajeebamor will wash it and inhibit any poison until a more permanent treatment can be administered.'

'What do you know about ajeebamor?' Melagiar grabbed her upper arm in a savage grip; his bloody spittle flecked her face.

Donna answered without hesitation, while pointedly and fastidiously wiping her face with her hand. 'I have completed a work tour with the apothecaries, Esteemed Sir. Its colour is quite distinctive. Would you wish me to call someone?'

'No!' He struggled to his feet, using Donna as an unwilling support, as if she were an inanimate object or a conquered, green-stained slave. She wished she had not bothered to help him; he deserved to be sliced with a poison blade. Her cheek stung. Melagiar pressed the makeshift bandage against his upper arm.

'Pour me a drink,' he said.

There was no ajeebamor left in the pitcher. 'I ...' she began.

'There is more in the armoire, there.'

Donna opened the armoire and suppressed a gasp at

the rich assortment of ornaments and crystal hidden there. There were also two decorated glass flasks – one of green wormwood wine and one of violet ajeebamor. She poured Melagiar a generous glass, one that would have laid low one not accustomed to its effects, and handed it to him. If she had her mother's skill she would have palmed a dose of glorabind and dropped it in his drink as revenge for that slap – glorabind was tasteless, and lethal when combined with stenk. But she was not her mother, and had not her resources, so instead Donna merely closed the door of the armoire and watched Melagiar as he drank.

Rej had returned unnoticed. He bore a fresh scratch over his eye. His face was closed, watchful, but he did not seem afraid or ill at ease.

'This is Rej.' Donna waved in his direction. 'I was going to ask your permission to use his assistance. He is mute and moon-witted, but he writes with a fair hand and I fear that there is enough work here for two.'

Melagiar, drinking deeply of the ajeebamor, scarcely looked up. His penetrating gaze was dulled already by the stupefying drug. His speech slurred slightly, as if his tongue had relaxed just beyond his control.

'Immina is unbalanced. Her humours work against the serenity of her soul – she is more than moon-witted. She stabbed me. I who have brought her here to share in this luxury when I could have left her …' he waved his arm vaguely, 'elsewhere in less salubrious surroundings. I could have left her to her purple dreams, and how does the wild wench repay me? She is as deranged as our beloved mother – long may she shine in memory. Fear not, she will be punished, but when the madness is on her ...'

He did not finish his sentence but handed Donna his goblet for a refill. Donna was suddenly glad of Rej's quiet presence. She had only just met him but, even if he had not been sent to her by her mother, she would have trusted him. She met his eye and gave him a warning glance. Ajeebamor was known for its aphrodisiac properties if taken in the right quantities. Melagiar's eyes were greedy and she felt them on her as she refilled the goblet. The wormwood wine was very potent. She carefully tipped a small quantity in the glass and hoped he would not notice the slight muddying of the violet colour. It would make him sleep, at the very least, and it might make him ill. She could not be sorry. Even her mother did not strike her any longer, now that she was grown.

'Doctor Esteemed, do you wish me to continue with my work?' She kept her voice pleasant and level, as her mother had taught her.

'For now,' he said, with the strange blurring of his vowels that ajeebamor produced. He took the goblet from her hand and caressed her fingers, so that she had to suppress a shudder of revulsion as she quickly removed her hand. She was aware that Rej moved closer.

'My dear and unexpectedly lovely Oppidan, would you join me in a glass?'

She was given no choice – he thrust a second goblet into her hand and she filled it with ajeebamor. She ran through her mother's instructions in her mind. She took a small sip. Melagiar's long hands were at her throat, forcing her to swallow. She swallowed.

'There, my dear,' he said. 'Isn't this nice.'

'Let me stoke the fire,' Donna said thickly, and staggered to the fireplace. As she piled fresh logs on the dying blaze and stoked them she spat out the venomous liquid, which hissed on the stones. She had some tolerance of most of the major poisons – her mother had fed her minute doses in carefully controlled conditions since she was a small child. She hated the slight numbing sensation in her mouth. Rej was watching her, waiting some signal. She did not give it.

She busied herself for a moment longer and when she returned to Melagiar's side he was sleeping with his mouth open and snoring gutturally. She had no intention of waiting for him to awaken.

Donna signalled to Rej that they should leave. As he moved to the door she paused for a moment to take two small crystal vials from the armoire and fill them with the remains of the liquid from Melagiar's goblet. She had an old linen pouch pocket of her mother's which she wore under her tunic, attached to her waist by a thin leather belt. She turned her back on Rej and slipped the crystal vials inside. It was time for her to *think* like a Poison Lady, if nothing else. They would have to slip away somehow and avoid the Redmen, but at least she now had the means to pay Capla.

Straightening her skirts, she crept down the dimly lit staircase and whispered to Rej, 'Did you see a lady – finely dressed, and very pale and thin – when you went through that doorway?'

He nodded. She couldn't see his face in the darkness but was somehow aware of his intent gaze. He followed her out of the small door that led back to the quadrangle and did not stray from her heels as she led him at a near run through the cloisters of the priests of Arché to the small temple dedicated to the Sacred Dragon's First Egg.

The temple was an ugly, squat building that was rarely visited, except by Donna, for whom it offered a haven of peace and solitude. It was empty during the day when the Redmen were overseeing the oppidans. Donna found a seat by one of the narrow arched windows that let in light, stained purple as ajeebamor by the coloured Lunnzian glass. She regained her composure and at length asked, 'Was she all right, the lady?'

Rej's dark eyes were fixed on her face. She felt as if he were weighing her soul for a long moment and then he made his decision. He spoke.

'She seemed quite mad. I tried to approach her and she scratched me. She did not speak, but she gave me this and shooed me away.' He handed Donna a torn piece of parchment on which a design had been clumsily drawn in a shaky hand: the sign of the dragon.

Donna didn't say anything. So the stranger could speak after all!

He looked at her with his direct look and added conversationally, 'I have only ever seen a dragon like this in my dreams.'

Donna let out a little involuntary cry of surprise. How could two people dream the same dream?

Chapter Twelve

Rej was not at all sure he had done right by speaking, but he could not keep up a pretence with this girl in front of him. She had called him mute and moon-witted; he did not want her to believe that he was either. The frakking mad woman in the corridor had frightened him more than he would have liked to acknowledge. She was probably a stenk-head – that much was familiar. She had been wild, out of control, but in passing on the scrap of parchment she had also tried to communicate with him, as if she was caught between three contradictory responses – fight, flight and friendship. The look in her eye as she had scratched him while thrusting the drawing into his hand had been of desperate appeal. It was that which frightened him most – the sense that there was a rational, suffering creature marooned in stenk-fuelled madness. He could not rid himself of the thought.

Donna looked at him with her habitual hauteur; she kept her feelings locked away behind all that cold beauty. Her voice was as expressionless as her face. 'You can speak then?'

He nodded, temporarily unable to – he didn't know what to say.

'What do you mean about … dreams?' There was emotion in her voice now. She faltered, hesitant. 'I mean … do you dream of dragons?'

She looked at him. She might have been blushing, but it was hard to tell in the tinted light. He should not trust her. Scrub had called him a frakking innocent, but he was desperate to share the strangeness of his dream experience. His mother, of an old mercantile family, used to say that you had to speculate to accumulate. It was perhaps as true of friendship and the search for answers as anything else. He felt as if he were leaping from a rock face in the combes, taking the wild risk that his feet would find some purchase and that he would not fall into the foulness of the Styx.

He took the same deep breath which always preceded an abandonment, and began.

'For the last few months I've dreamed that I've seen dragons flying in a clear blue sky. They looked like this one and they were the most beautiful things I'd ever seen. They made me feel happy and full of hope.'

It sounded stupid now that he'd said it; a child's fantasy, no more, but Donna was nodding, her huge eyes shining and glistening with an unexpected moistness, her whole body leaning towards him in conspiratorial intimacy.

'I have seen them too, and believed that I was one of them – a dragon, no longer earth-bound, free.' Rej could tell that she instantly regretted the eagerness in her voice by the way she snapped her spine suddenly erect; it felt like a withdrawal, a retreat.

'I have never heard of shared dreams before,' he

said, and wondered if that were true. Stenk-heads dreamed all right – Scrub had told him. He shuddered – surely they did not dream of dragons. He tried to remember Moon's tale of his oppidan alchemist cousin, or whoever the frakk he was, handing out potions which might have had an effect on dreams – could this be what he'd been talking about? You never knew with Moon – he was right more often than Rej's bets. 'I mean, could there be some potion that might make two people share a dream?' he said out loud.

Donna shook her head. 'None that I know of, and I know something of poisons. Besides, I have taken nothing. Ajeebamor is believed to increase the potency of dreams, but I do not drink it.' She coloured, and Rej wondered if it was at the memory of the way that man, the Doctor Esteemed, had looked at her when he'd made her drink it.

She seemed suddenly less confident when she added, 'But the treatise I'm copying talks about dreams and – it was difficult to follow – but something about dreams being between life and death, between the world of the soul and the world of matter: a special sphere of being, neither creative nor destructive, but with the potential for both.'

'I'm not sure I know what that means?' Rej sounded more abrupt than he had intended – frakking metaphysics was not what he needed at that moment.

Donna shrugged coolly, as though it were of no importance to her whatsoever. 'I did not claim to understand it, but if dreams are not figments of the mind but perceptions of another place, then surely two or more people could share them. There was something else too – about the power of dreams to influence the humours, to bring joy and desire and ambition, or fear and self-loathing.'

'Is that important?' Rej had to remember to keep expletives from his conversation – it was easier to remember not to speak. He was not uneducated, thanks to his mother, but Donna's confidence in talking of arcane things was as strange and unnatural as anything he had yet encountered Above. He knew he sounded hostile, but the dreams mattered to him, for frakking Light's sake. He forced a smile to show his goodwill.

Donna ignored both the aggression and the smile. She was concentrating on answering him honestly. He admired that. 'It felt important when I copied it,' she said slowly, 'and that dream – of the dragon – well, since I had it I've thought of nothing so much as seeing that dragon, having that feeling again, that wild, soaring freedom, and that doesn't make sense, does it?'

She was vulnerable in her uncertainty, and Rej's antipathy melted. Rej wanted to touch her, to reassure her that he shared that unaccountable feeling, but he did not know if such intimacy was permitted between Abovers. He cleared his throat nervously.

'No, it doesn't make any sense. But,' he added quickly as her face grew colder, 'but I've had that feeling too.'

'I will pay more attention when I work.' She spoke flatly and Rej waited for her to go on. It was getting very cold in the small temple and he longed for the warmth of the fire in Melagiar's chamber. It was not for him to suggest a return.

'Why did Immina give you that picture?'

'I don't know.'

'She has a tattoo of that same image across her breast.' Donna said the words grudgingly, keeping her eyes lowered, while she twisted the coarse fabric of her dress. She seemed to find it difficult to confide information, unless, of course, such reticence was a general feature of the oppidan way and he was too ignorant to know.

She glanced at his face anxiously. 'I wondered if it meant something, but I don't know what, and she is too mad to ask.'

'Is she?'

Donna shook her head slowly, 'She drinks a lot of ajeebamor – it is not well known for encouraging sanity – and her brother burns other befuddling herbs on the fire. I don't know what else is given to her, but she has seemed clear-minded on occasions. She asked me to help her – she wrote down "Help me." But I don't know what to do. Did she know you would recognise the dragon – how could she know that? What did she mean by it – did she mean anything by it? It makes no sense.'

Rej was beginning to wish she would stop talking so that he could move around – he had never been so cold. He hugged his arms around his waist and tried to control the chattering of his teeth. She did not seem to notice and if she was cold herself she did not show it; these Abovers were tougher than he'd expected. Rej could not answer any of her questions and he had a few more to add to the list. Though he wanted to learn about the dragon, he needed to know who had killed the Doctor Esteemed Harfoot – that was why he'd come to this frakking corpse-cold place. He was beginning to feel dizzy with fatigue and the strain of it all. Nothing was quite as he'd expected.

A short savage slap to his face roused him. His face stung.

'Hey, what the frakk?' He thought the words but nothing emerged from his mouth. Donna was standing above him, her eyes blazing.

'Get up and move!'

'What?'

'It's the cold – move!'

She half supported, half dragged him back to the Doctor Esteemed's rooms. His legs were leaden and all he really wanted to do was sleep, but Donna's slender frame belied a steely strength. The door to the chamber was still not locked and she thrust him into the room and the dying fire. There was no sign of Melagiar or the chaos that had reigned. The furniture was restored to its proper position and the spilled ajeebamor had been cleaned. Donna hesitated only very slightly before she banked up the fire, found Melagiar's abandoned sable-lined cloak and wrapped it around Rej's shaking shoulders. She made him sit so close to the fire that his face felt scorched on the one side. He was vaguely aware that in doing these things she was breaking rules he did not understand, and was grateful.

'I am sorry. I hadn't realised that you weren't used to the cold.'

Rej's tongue still felt heavy and difficult, but he

managed to shake his head weakly.

Donna poured steaming water from an elegant kettle that he had not previously noticed into a goblet. He sniffed it; it smelled of spice, the perfume in the room and of strangeness.

'It's just hot water and carga leaves. Nothing more. It is wholesome and restorative,' Donna said impatiently, and he sipped it carefully to avoid it scalding his tongue. 'So, where are you from?'

He could not answer at once. It was another of those moments of choice. He had been Above less than a day and already told this stony beauty more than he had ever told any other living soul. He seemed quite unable to keep his own council. Scrub was right. He was an innocent and he should never have come.

Chapter Thirteen

Donna stared at the white face of the youth. He had stopped shivering at last. The cold of this winter season was insidious and, in the inadequate clothing which the Council of Ten had distributed, more than a few of the street labourers had died, as well as the young girl, Gracia, of her own work detail.

Something was wrong with this Rej. He did not seem like the other oppidans; there was a strangeness to him, an earnest watchfulness. He was afraid all the time, just like she was. She felt it and, more than that, he dreamed of dragons. He was weighing her again with his eyes. In the firelight the angular planes of his face were exposed, sculpted. In his way he was as exotic as Melagiar's chambers.

She should not have come back here. Strictly speaking she should have reported to Martrin that the Doctor Esteemed was – what? Indisposed? Unable to oversee her work? She was in a situation for which neither her mother nor the Humble Road had prepared her, and had taken the risk of returning to Melagiar's rooms, thinking only of the stranger's need for heat. She was trembling and she felt enfeebled by fear at the thought of what would happen if anyone found the ajeebamor in her pouch pocket. She steadied herself and Rej finally broke the silence that had opened up between them. He broke it with a whisper that she had to strain to hear.

'Do not tell anyone, but I am from the combes.'

She recoiled; she could not help it. The combes were the home of all criminals and aristocratic and other degenerates expelled by the Council of Ten in the Great Cleansing at the beginning of the Revolution. It was home to the stenk caves and a million other poisons. Her mother, she knew, traded with combers, but would not speak of them, so that for once Donna had taken her lead from the Redmen, and their evaluation of the combes had become her own.

Rej was looking at her, waiting for some kind of response. None was forthcoming – none was necessary. Donna could hear footsteps from behind the heavy curtain that covered the entrance to Melagiar's private chamber. The moment for conversation was over. She pulled Rej to his feet. She did not want to find out what would happen if they were found luxuriating in front of the illegal fire, drinking carga water from a gold goblet of the late Brandaccian period and not at work. She took no notice of his grunt of surprise and propelled him towards the desk while taking up her quill and an expression of scholarly concentration at the same moment. Rej had the wit to appear busy – she would give him credit; he was not stupid. She dared not remove his borrowed cloak in case the cold torpor should return. He looked rather fine in the deep emerald velvet, and the illegal, sumptuous dark fur gave him an air of aristocratic distinction, while lending his white face an almost greenish cast. They would have to hope Melagiar would not notice.

But it was not Melagiar who emerged from the hidden door; it was the Arkel himself. Fear almost paralysed Donna, the daughter of an illegal, companion to a man so illegal he could start another war. She tried to keep her mask of serenity as her mother had taught her. There were tricks to being a Low Lady and there were skills, but most of all there was discipline. She called upon it in her desperation and managed a sober smile, curved high enough for welcome but not for invitation, with the sidelong look from under demurely lowered lashes that her mother called 'the smile that is humble and in awe'. It may have worked because the Arkel seemed to study her for a heartbeat's pause with quiet approval before speaking. Donna could not help but notice that the Arkel's own cloak was also a thick, wine coloured velvet, lined not with illegal fur but with lamb's fleece, so that *his* risk of suffering from the cold torpor was small. When he spoke his voice was deep and resonant, as befitted a man who had turned Lunnzia on its head with his preaching.

'You have just arrived?' he asked.

Donna nodded. 'We did not start as early as we should, Holiness; we were delayed elsewhere.' Donna's voice sounded pathetically insincere to her own ears, and she prayed inwardly that he would not check her claim but take her at face value.

The Arkel did not even appear to be listening. 'The Doctor Esteemed Melagiar has been taken ill. You are to remain here in this room until the end of the work period. You are to continue with his work here until further notice. I wish to be assured that you will not discuss what you do here with any other oppidans.'

He inclined his head in acknowledgement of Donna's murmured response and Rej's emphatic nod and swept from the room, two Redmen in attendance. It did not seem to occur to him that his will would not be respected. Donna saw with a shock that his hand on the hilt of his ceremonial sword hilt was crimson and that under his cloak of office his long, dark robe was also smeared with a slime-like stain of fresh blood. Donna gave no sign of having noticed, but her quill pen shook like she had the palsy.

Rej didn't say anything but got to his feet and strode decisively towards the hidden door. Perhaps if he had not done so Donna might have obeyed the Arkel's order. Oppidans did not disobey the Arkel. She did not stop him; instead she followed him fearfully through the small door that led, she presumed, to Melagiar's rooms.

It was dark and cold in the narrow stone corridor, but Rej walked confidently into the next chamber, apparently recovered from the early symptoms of the torpor. Donna followed him and gagged, unable to stifle her body's response. Melagiar lay upon a carved bed, his eyes open and lifeless. That in itself was not so difficult to deal with – Donna had seen a lot of death – but the blood flow seemed to her excessive. It bloomed like the dark petals of some scarlet flower across the delicate green of the embroidered silk bedspread. There was some sign of a struggle and two of Melagiar's menservants, slaves by their dye-stained faces, were also dead. A third one was being helped to a semi-upright position by Rej.

'What has happened here?' Donna's mouth and throat were dry, and it was a stupid question anyway; it was quite clear what had happened.

'The Arkel came to see the Doctor Esteemed and found him unwell. He had drunk too deeply of ajeebamor and the Lord Arkel became enraged. He said that he could not wait at Melagiar's pleasure.' The slave's tone was hysterical. 'He said that Melagiar had been given a fair chance and had achieved nothing. The Arkel said he had found another who could better serve the cause – then he went mad. He was like a man possessed. No one had time to react.'

The slave's purple face worked convulsively and Donna's early training took over. A Poison Lady could not afford to be squeamish. She was careful to avoid the blood and gore that pooled on the polished wooden boards of the chamber but she managed to examine the slave with firm and steady fingers. She found his wounds: a vicious slash to the upper thigh and a number of deep cuts to the arm. The man might live. Rej handed her his knife as if they shared the same thoughts as well as the same dreams. The slave's eyes widened in fear.

'I need to bind these wounds,' Donna explained as she cut strips of cloth from the clothing of the nearest corpse and fashioned a tourniquet. Rej did not speak but supported her shaking patient.

'The Arkel is going to murder me too,' he moaned.

'I think he thought he already had,' said Donna,

gradually becoming aware of the import of what was going on. The Arkel, High Priest of Arché, leader of the Council of Ten, had murdered one of the Esteemed of the city with his own hands. What would he do now?

'We need to get him away,' said Donna. 'He is a witness. We must pretend we know nothing of this. The Arkel will send Redmen or militia to clear this up.' She could not keep panic from her voice. They would be killed too if they were involved in this scandal. Maybe he would have them killed anyway. He might guess that they had found their way to Melagiar's private rooms, though she doubted that any of her work detail would have done as Rej had done. Oppidans were meek and obedient and she found that she was more an oppidan in her heart than she had realised. Whatever else the Arkel was, he was universally regarded as the mouthpiece of Arché, at least in her creator's aspect. It seemed that he had taken it upon himself to act as the hand of Arché – as the basilisk, the divine destroyer. What would the loyal oppidans think? What would the Arkel's most pious, loyal Redmen say, or did they know already? She could not imagine having the courage to tell anyone of what she'd seen, but then it was unlikely she would be given the chance. Bile rose in her throat. She remembered the dying in the cages by the dock and her mother's poison pin worn to escape deaths worse even than theirs. She must think like a Poison Lady, not a frightened oppidan. Think!

Rej spoke. 'I doubt we'll have long. No one would want to leave all this.' He gestured to the bodies abandoned where they lay, all broken and bloody, and so recently dead that the warmth of life had scarcely left them. The purple-faced slave looked anguished.

'Don't leave me!'

Rej looked at the slave, his expression anxious. 'Perhaps we should have let him die.'

It was her own thought issuing from Rej's mouth. Donna glanced at him in surprise, shook her head and handed him his knife. Her mother might have the strength for such decisions, she did not. Rej sheathed the knife. He was not prepared to kill the slave either; she was glad about that. For an assassin's daughter she was perversely reluctant to approve of murder.

'Is there anywhere we can hide him?' Rej looked at her expectantly and she was ashamed that she could not answer him. She did not know anywhere but the Liberty and she dared not bring trouble back to her mother. The slave himself came to her rescue.

'There is a bride's hole,' he gasped. 'It is a dire risk to take for a slave but I will find a way to pay you back, by the power that made me!' His voice sounded raw and desperate; his face was shiny with sweat. He reminded Donna irrelevantly of the glazed plums her mother had given her as a treat in the time before.

'A bride's hole?' Rej sounded bemused.

'Years ago when Lunnzia was at war with Borrodimo, Prince Givane the Mad promised one hundred of the city's most beautiful virgins as a peace offering, to seal a treaty. Those who couldn't afford to bribe the officials hid their daughters, but the soldiers came every day for a month and some of girls starved or suffocated in their holes – at least that is the story.'

Donna knew the stories if nothing else.

'Where is it? Let's go!' Rej was on his feet and with unexpected strength lifted the slave, as if he were a small child.

'Through there.' The injured man pointed in the direction of an opening covered by a thick green curtain, which led them still further from the main room, their work and their small hope of walking away from this situation alive.

'Let me stand.' The man's breathing was laboured and, though he struggled to walk, he staggered unaided through the curtain and into a panelled chamber, empty of furniture and musty with lack of use. He groped his way to one of the panels, panting with the effort of movement and pain; he seemed to collapse against it. There was an unpleasant creak and the panel opened like the badly-oiled door that it was, to reveal a small stone-walled, windowless cell.

The slave appeared to have used up what little strength he had remaining and continued to lean against the door, unable to move. 'Help me in!' he rasped.

Rej pushed him inside none too gently. 'We'll come back,' he said in a voice that lacked conviction. The man smiled weakly by way of reply and folded himself within the tiny airless space.

Donna followed Rej almost blindly back to the main chamber. She tasted blood in her own mouth; perhaps it was the taste of terror. She allowed the stranger to lead her back to her place at the window desk, allowed him to check her clothes and hands for any stray spatters of blood. She even let him thrust the quill back into her hand. He smiled then.

'You are brave, Lady,' he said.

She did not reply, because there was a clatter of footsteps and armour in the stairwell and whatever words she might have uttered died in her throat.

Chapter Fourteen

Rej checked his knife surreptitiously. He did not know why Donna had saved the slave; it was dangerous and somehow she had seemed too calculating to take such a risk.

She was his kind of gambler – one who bet consistently on the losing hand. Frakk. He couldn't let the man die either, but even with his limited grasp of current Lunnzian politics he knew that they were in trouble. He was not in much of a state to fight, what with the space queasy and the cold torpor and his general, probably terminal innocence; Light, he was almost certain to end up dead himself. He glanced at Donna. She was as impassive as ever, coolly pretending to write – frakk, maybe she was writing, for all he knew. He would defend her whether she wanted him to or not; he had no choice about that. He knew it like he knew that darkness followed light. He waited.

Five militia men marched into the room in good order. Their sallets shone and each wore the gold embroidered dragon and basilisk motif that was the symbol of the city on their dark blue brigandines. He had never actually seen men in that uniform before, except in his mind's eye. He was momentarily awed by the sight, by the keen edge to their weapons; their well-maintained, brutal-looking fauchards and the knives they carried at each hip. What would he do if they attacked? His heart began to pump, he felt that familiar internal tautening as he readied, then steadied himself – they may not attack him, may not attack Donna, if he looked like he had a right to be there. He gripped his quill rather than his knife and tried to look imperious. He noticed then that they marched stiffly, awkwardly even, that the hair that escaped their sallets was grey and that the faces beneath them were gnarled and no longer young. He cursed himself as a scrottle-headed, moon-witted, half-lit rat-turd – all the young men were on campaign fighting the High Verdans. He felt a rush of relief. The odds were still five to two but the five were old, and though he knew well enough that all the most dangerous men in the combes were old, he took comfort in that fact.

Donna arched a questioning eyebrow at the leader of the men, who wore a violet silk scarf tied around his upper arm as a sign of rank. He ordered the men not to linger on the 'unholy opulence' of the scene, then stopped in front of Donna.

Rej tensed, looking furtively for something he could use as a weapon – to supplement his belt knife.

'Oppidan,' the leader said briefly with a half bow. 'I was told to give you this.'

It was a note. Donna took it and read it without comment. Her colour was high, but she breathed calmly and managed a gracious nod to the militia man. He admired her poise.

'The Arkel has requested that I perform some tasks in the university library,' she said briskly, and swept from the room. Rej followed her as quickly as he could, almost knocking over the heavy carved chair on which he had been sitting. He was reluctant to leave the warmth of Melagiar's cloak behind and so left it where it was, slung nonchalantly around his shoulders as though he had a right to wear it. No one commented and he managed to turn his back on the guards without imagining the long slaughter-man's blade of the fauchard cleaving a chunk from his back. He forced himself to think of something else, of the purple-faced man bent almost double in the bride's hole, and wondered if he and Donna would be able to reach him before he died. It would be worse than a ghost tunnel in the bride's hole – at least the fetid air of the combes could still flow where no man could walk.

Silently he followed Donna down the steep, twisting stairs to the icy quadrangle; he bit back a confession of his worries. It was wiser not to share them anyway – Donna already thought he was a frakking twazzock.

Donna broke the silence herself. 'The note was not from the Arkel, but from another slave, Capla. He helped me. I was going to meet him later but he wants to meet me outside the library.' Her whisper sounded uncharacteristically nervous and uncertain. She met his eye. 'You cannot wear that cloak in the open, you know – it's against the Sumptuary Laws. I don't know how we are going to get the slave out from that hole.'

Rej said nothing. He did not feel it was safe for him to speak in the open; besides, he had no advice to offer the girl in front of him. She looked vulnerable, young. The quality of her beauty was ageless, in her very bones, but she was probably no older than he was, for all her self-possession.

She did not remain indecisive for long, but led him towards an enormous circular building faced with white marble that gleamed so brightly in the sunlight that Rej was quite unable to look at it. His eyes streamed and his head hurt and he longed to scuttle like an insect for the dark shelter of stone.

It seemed a long walk in the piercing cold and eye-searing light. They passed other oppidans and other people without slave markings who were sweeping the ordure from streets that seemed clean enough to Rej; they were poor-looking, dressed in layer upon layer of patched and ragged clothing that combers would have shunned to wear. Maybe there was warmth in the multiplicity of layers or maybe they were all as tough as Donna for none wore a cloak, though a few glanced at his borrowed finery before looking quickly away. Rej tried not to squint against the light, for no one else did, and he tried to stand tall though he longed to crouch like a frightened rat, to hide from the glare of the winter sun and the glances of strangers. He felt giddy, unsteady, and desperate not to look a linny in front of Donna.

A solitary figure stood by the entrance to the building – Rej did not see the man's face. Donna guided Rej inside with a hissed, 'Wait for me – I'll not be long.' Then she moved back outside to talk with the stranger.

Rej walked into the vastness of the library quite

alone. Nothing had prepared him for what he saw there. He tried not to stand open-mouthed like a frakking moon-witted prallock at the row upon row of bound books behind cases of fine rose-tinted Lunnzian glass. Light streamed from narrow windows to form shards of pale gold that striped the boarded floor of the vast domed hall. There were more books than he had ever seen before – many hundreds, hidden beneath the reflecting glance, like treasure under water. He was worried that his obvious awe might make him conspicuous, and backed towards a wall, any wall, to get his bearings. It was then that he saw it. A curse died on his lips and he almost ran, almost called out in shock in spite of the heavy silence in the room and the atmosphere of reverence that he had recognised instinctively the moment he had entered the vast vaulted space.

Above him soared the dark basilisk of Lunnzia, stubby wings unfurled, talons extended, fire flaming from its black eyes. It looked to be in mid-dive, hurtling towards the very spot on which he stood. He felt his breath escape in small frightened panting gasps, and then his uneducated vision recognised the sight as no more than a fantastic image, a likeness of the beast, painted with inhuman skill upon the dome and walls of the building. He clutched the wall behind him for support and, as he turned to look back the way he'd entered the building, he saw a second version of the beast: broad and graceful wings outstretched, a golden egg nested in the almost finger-like talons. He understood now. The library celebrated the dual aspect of Arché as dragon – creator – and as basilisk – destroyer. The two enormous figures, one dark green and one gold, each dominated half of the dome, which he could see now was intended to symbolise the egg from which the Creator Arché herself was hatched, from the eternal, self-existent, uncreated One. It was an awesome sight. The high arching of the room made him dizzy, and confused his positional sense. It almost felt as if he was above and the dragon and basilisk below and that at any moment he might fall.

Donna's steadying hand was suddenly on his shoulder. The contact was unexpected and his hand strayed towards his belt knife reflexively.

'The frescos are incredible, aren't they?' she whispered.

He nodded, remembering not to speak.

Donna whispered, 'Capla – the slave – said that Melagiar was trouble.' She pulled a face. 'As if we didn't know that! I told him Melagiar is dead. I don't know if that was a mistake.' Donna looked at Rej for reassurance, a furtive half-glance, and Rej felt obscurely pleased. His heart was still beating like a trapped rat's but he hoped it didn't show. He tried to look reassuring. Donna leant towards him casually so that her lips almost brushed his ear. 'Move towards that place there – the Arc for Quiet and Reverent Contemplation – and look holy.'

There was a small area beneath the talon of the basilisk where a curved screen cordoned off a teardrop-shaped area of the vast hall. The screen was formed of intricately carved basilisks making the form of the eternal circle, their poison fangs biting their own scaled tails symbolising the futility of conflict which eternally harms the aggressor. Rej knelt on the step provided for the purpose and Donna knelt beside him, her eyes downcast.

'Capla says that the dragon tattoo and the dragon Immina drew were once signs of a secret society called the "Basilisk's Breath".'

Rej risked a look at her face as she spoke. She was suppressing her feelings with difficulty. Her face in the burnished light from the high windows was the most beautiful thing he had ever seen, and he struggled not to stare at it.

'Capla also said,' she continued, 'that the society had something to do with exploring the realms of dreaming.' There was triumph in her voice which Rej would have liked to have shared, but he could not see how it helped him. 'I had to pay Capla in ajeebamor. I think he knows more than he is telling me. He said he would find out more.'

Rej did not think he ought to speak, even behind the screen, but he raised a questioning eyebrow.

She seemed to guess what he meant. 'He is a friend – he tried to warn me about Melagiar – but you know the old saying, "If you buy from a Lambrugian one day you'll be bought by a Lambrugian another", so I didn't tell him about the slave. If anyone finds out that we know the Arkel killed Melagiar ...' Her voice tailed away and Rej noticed that she was trembling. The loss of control was momentary. 'Look, I've seen a contact of my mother's here. I don't think he's legal but he swore the paper oath so long ago that he is well trusted, and he knows things.'

The look on Rej's face must have registered his confusion.

'You don't know the paper oath – you have never sworn it?' She looked almost as horrified as when she had seen Melagiar's bloody corpse. 'You cannot come in here without the oath – *To bring in no flame but the light of Arché's creation, no knife but intellect's sharp blade, and no fluid, only thirst to know the wisdom of Arché.*'

Rej would have liked to know what the frakk she was talking about. This was not the time for lectures on library etiquette.

Donna looked haughty. 'Stay here,' she said shortly, and walked off, her head bowed, the very picture of humility, and yet Rej received the very strong impression that she had marched off, cross as a crooked-back comber taking the hump.

He was not sorry to be alone for a moment, to drop his guard. It was peaceful there – not as silent as he had at first thought. There was a background level of sewer noise – the sounds you only heard when you listened hard – scholars scratching their quills on parchment, clattering their wooden line-markers against the glass viewing cases that housed the precious books, and murmuring in secret whispers as they copied from the paper treasures of Lunnzia. Rej was grateful to kneel behind the carved screen, to listen and to watch. He was less exposed to the vastness of the high vaulted dome, less vulnerable to the black eyes of this monumental dual image of Arché, huge as the sheerest cliffs of the combes. He liked the solid stone wall of the building at his back and he could view the library through the tracery of the basilisk's wings, delicate as the branches of the tree from which they had been carved. He could still see the giant Arché in her creator aspect above him and he had to fight not to tremble.

The bright light from the high arched windows that ringed the base of the dome made his eyes tear. His vision must have been playing tricks on him because he thought he saw something that could not be there. He watched Donna walk, straight-backed, through the aisles of scholars. He had to be wrong, but he thought he saw the massive bulk of Barna hunched over the glass viewing case of a scholar's dark study desk, talking with Donna. Had he become so disorientated and afraid in this new Abover's world that he had to conjure frakking Barna, as if the reality of the place were not bad enough all on its own?

Chapter Fifteen

Donna was worried. She did not know what she was doing, trusting an ignorant comber because he dreamed of dragons, involving herself in illegality and risks that disturbed her oppidan training more profoundly than she wanted to admit. She was ridiculously glad to be rid of at least one of the flasks of ajeebamor. Not that it made much difference, she still had the second vial, and if she needed a reminder of the risk she took she could feel it thud heavily against her hip as she walked. Capla had taken the first vial from her with greedy, eager fingers: he had not struck her as an addict and to her mind no one touched ajeebamor who did not risk addiction.

There was something subtly different about Capla this time. She could not define it exactly but in some way he seemed surer of himself, less desperate. It was hard to believe his claim that until recently Immina had been as much of a force in Lunnzia as her brother, and that she herself had demanded that one of Capla's fellow slaves – a craftsman of the distant city of Terpero – tattoo her with an elaborate image as a sign that she was to reinstitute the long disbanded secret society of the 'Basilisk's Breath', originally founded by her mother the Lady Melagiar. It was just possible that Immina's madness was the desperation of a strong woman whose will had been subverted by the subtlety of the poisoner's art, but to Donna's inexperienced eyes Immina seemed more victim than anything else; she had surely not cut out her own tongue? Donna was glad she had not asked Capla about the slave. She had given him too much power over her already by telling him about Melagiar. Capla no longer smelled of berenslip, and she wondered why.

Barna would know somewhere to hide a half-dead slave. Her mother depended on Barna; had met with him often in the days when Donna still lived with her, and she was sure that he was not a client. The Low Lady Estelle had numerous techniques for flattering and welcoming clients – she used none of them with Barna.

Barna was less than helpful. She spoke to him surreptitiously while he allowed his words to dribble from the corner of his mouth, grudgingly, as if he resented speaking to her at all. He was unmoved by what had happened.

'The city of Lunnzia is no worse for the lack of another Doctor Esteemed, believe me. And as for the Arkel – if Melagiar's was the only life he'd ended he would be a holy man. He has the blood of more men on his hands than I have hairs on my head. Listen to your mother, girl. I don't know how a child of the foremost Low Lady of old Lunnzia could be so ignorant. What did you expect of the Arkel – the righteousness he preaches about?'

As she *had* always believed the Arkel earnest in his

faith, Donna tried to ignore her own embarrassment at yet another failure of understanding and persisted with her questioning. 'And if you were to believe it worth the effort to free the slave from the bride's hole, what would you do?' Donna whispered as she searched the floor for an imaginary lost quill.

'My advice would be – forget it. There is nothing to be gained in getting involved with this. It stinks of the Council's business. Murder is a tool of the state and a particularly blunt one in the hands of amateurs – you should know that. I'll not tell you not to rescue the slave – if you think it's your selfless duty.' He had looked at her mockingly so that she felt her face heat again. 'If you are so much a fine, upstanding oppidan of our new Lunnzia you will do what you must, but I will not help, nor would the Low Lady or Grimper. A good gambler risks only to gain – there is no gain in this.'

Donna walked around the library a little after that, pretending she had some business there, waiting till her temper cooled and she could be calm enough again. The Redman on duty smiled at her and she responded with a shy smile. She kept coming back to the same thought, as she always did: she would not be so ignorant, so ridiculously oppidan-like in all the wrong ways if it were not for her mother's policy towards her. Even now she was asking advice, waiting to be told what to do, always wanting help. She dragged Rej away from the library without explanation before the Redman could approach her. Rej wisely stayed as silent as if he had been truly mute.

On their return to Melagiar's rooms the door was locked and they could not get in to continue their work as the Arkel had requested. Donna lodged a complaint with the Redman who was overseer to the secondary scribes, and fully expected to have the key and most probably a personal overseer by morning.

She stormed back to the refectory with Rej following discreetly behind her. It was time for the last, sparse meal of the day and all her fellow oppidans working at the university were also making their way to the barracks. It was colder than ever. Donna was so distracted that she only remembered to make Rej remove his cloak at the last minute. She did not want to give the Redmen an opportunity to use the Scourge of Arché on the unsuspecting Rej. She made a kind of a bundle of the cloak and pushed it under the bushes at the door.

'Remember not to speak, and look moon-witted!' she hissed at Rej.

He already looked, if not moon-witted, uncertain of what to do. She kept forgetting that he was new to Lunnzia, not just to this particular barracks. It would have been easy to take his arm and guide him to her own accustomed isolated place at table, but that would have aroused comment. Instead, she walked just a little ahead of him, trusting that he would follow and that he would deal with the curious looks and the supercilious scrutiny of the Redmen in his own way.

Rej gazed at the ceiling vacantly and ate his food with all the finesse of a pig snuffling for truffles. Even Belafor avoided her – though he smiled a shy welcome

– because to sit with her meant sitting too close to Rej. Madness and indeed any other kind of non-conformity was an offence against perfection and self-dedication; it was rarely allowed to flourish unhindered.

Donna could not take Barna's advice and forget the slave; the Redmen spoke of compassion and she believed in that, even though the Arkel failed to exhibit it. She was sure too now that Immina and her society of the Basilisk's Breath had something to do with her dragon dreams and perhaps even with Melagiar's murder. She felt compelled to learn more. Perhaps that first breaking of the Arkel's command had begun to undermine her habit of obedience. She was much less afraid than she should have been, quite calm and quite determined. She would do what Barna would not: rescue the slave and question him. How else was she to learn?

'Excuse me a moment.' She bowed to her fellow oppidans as was customary, sparing Rej a direct and warning glance, then padded out of the hall along the labyrinth of corridors and work rooms to the small glass-panelled room belonging to the backstairs Watch, the night porter. She undid her hair in the shadow of the wall and shook it loose as she slipped the scrap of fabric with which she'd bound it into her pouch. The porter gazed morosely at the servants' door, a pitcher of ale at his side.

He turned the moment he heard her. 'You should not be here. This is slaves' and servants' territory, Oppidan. You have no right to be here.' He bristled officiously, grateful to have something to do.

She flicked her hair beguilingly over her shoulder so that it fell like a dark, glossy curtain almost to her waist. She had thick, heavy hair that all the men she had ever met wanted to touch.

'I'm sorry, it is just that I lost the linen ribbon from my hair, outside, yesterday, and I had heard that things like that are often brought to the Watch. I wondered if you might perhaps have seen it? It isn't a possession, not really,' she added quickly, forestalling the inevitable lecture on the evils of ownership among oppidans, 'I need it or my hair keeps getting in the way.' She tossed her head and sent a ripple of hair to brush the Watchman's neck and hand; he shivered when it skimmed his skin, and was captivated. She giggled as her mother had taught her and as he reached out to touch her, she flicked the dark mane away and while he was distracted, deftly poured a small quantity of ajeebamor from the vial remaining in her pouch pocket into his pitcher. It would taste odd, but in times of shortage ale was made of anything that would ferment, so he would drink it. She gave him her most dazzling smile, the one even her mother claimed was enchanting.

'No, Lady – I mean – Oppidan. I have found nothing,' he breathed, his self-importance forgotten.

'Well, I'll come back tomorrow, anyway, to see if the ribbon turns up.'

Once out of sight she gathered her hair up into one thick hank and twisted it tightly before tying it in a loose knot out of her way. She had learnt how to flirt well enough from her mother – but that was all she had learnt. The daughter of the foremost assassin, spy and intriguer in Lunnzia had to rely on a slave for her information. She tried to ignore her impotent anger. There was still time to meet Capla as they had agreed, before curfew.

Donna marched back through the kitchens, trying to look as though she had some right to be there, and slipped out of the main door to wait shivering outside the refectory in the shadow of the wall to meet Capla where they had met before. She waited until the temple bell tolled its doleful reminder that the hour of curfew was upon them, but he did not arrive. Donna had no way of finding him, knew no one to ask about his whereabouts. She did not wish to draw attention to herself by breaking the commonly accepted taboo and speaking to a slave who served them in the refectory. She had paid him already – perhaps, as a Lambrugian, he saw no point in continuing their association. She was worried nonetheless. She had perhaps placed too much trust in Capla.

She returned to the ranks of the oppidans sitting in rows at long trestle tables. As a sign of the times few of the wall sconces had been lit so that each table was illuminated only by one meagre candle and the vast vaulted ceiling was lost in a depthless sea of darkness. A small gaggle of girls from Donna's dormitory were taunting Rej, who was maintaining a resolute silence.

Donna pushed herself into the place on the bench beside him and whispered, as she tried to make herself comfortable, 'Make a fuss when they come to take us to the dormitories.' She needed him near her if they were to rescue the slave that night. He gave no sign of having understood.

'What are you saying to him, Donna? Making an assignation? I thought you had your eye on Belafor!'

There was more of the same and Donna hoped that Rej would not be shocked by the girls' remarks. She did not know what girls were like in the combes, but since the introduction of the Humble Way the rules had changed Above and all the girls coupled freely. It had not always been so or her mother would have been out of business.

When the Redmen began the evening chant to Arché, one of the lantern slaves handed Donna the key to Melagiar's rooms, and, as Donna stepped into her place with the rest of the women to be escorted to their dormitory, Rej howled wordlessly like an animal at being separated from her and cowered away from the men's line.

'I'm sorry, I think he's afraid,' Donna said awkwardly as Rej threw himself to the ground and began to beat his fists on the cold stone. 'He's not violent, I don't think. He is calm with me.'

'Oh, let him stay with you then,' said Gayla with a raised eyebrow.

'But Gayla, he might be dangerous,' said one of the other girls.

'He has been through a lot – scouting for the troops,' Donna said quickly, having to shout over Rej's inarticulate roaring. 'I think he is harmless.'

'So you say,' said Gayla with a meaningful look. 'Let him stay with you, Donna, and afterwards we will want a full report.'

Donna smiled in just such a way as to allow Gayla to believe that her suspicions were confirmed and placed a calming hand on Rej's shoulder. He fell silent at once as she whispered in his ear, 'That's more than enough. You will be locked up if you carry on – they don't tolerate noisy madness here.'

Donna fell to the back of the line of laughing women, just in front of the second escort slave who traditionally held the lantern at the rear of the women's line. He too bore the green stain of Lunnzian slaves. She could have asked him about Capla, there was plenty of time as they shuffled along the icy stone-floored corridors, but Donna had lost her nerve.

Chapter Sixteen

Donna had not intended to sleep but only to wait until the steady breathing and gentle snoring of the women indicated that it was safe for her to leave. She placed the dead Gracia's bed roll next to her by the door for Rej and then as soon as she lay down the dreams came.

She was flying high, high above the city, so that it looked below her like a flat tapestry of stone among the green and blue cloth of the land and sea. The air was warm as summer and smelled of attar of damask rose. Her wings beat strongly and around her she saw two other dragons flying whose wings shone like burnished gold in the sun. The sky was a colour she had almost forgotten and she had never felt as free or as happy until she noticed the dark basilisk perched high above the city on the pinnacle of the former Devarra Palace, the seat of government. A cloud appeared from the west, black and thunderous, and all she knew was fear as the lightning flashed and the cold wind blew, tearing at her wings, unsettling her control, making her fall …

She woke with a cry – swiftly muffled by a hand – Rej's hand. The whites of his eyes shone in the darkness – it was all she could see, but his touch was soft and calming. He pulled her gently from the sleeping companions and into the corridor.

'I dreamed,' she said, still breathless and disoriented from the dream.

'I know,' he said, 'so did I.'

She struggled to put into words her fear of the dark cloud and the lightning. Her heart was pounding as if she'd been running very hard and she was drenched in sweat that was cooling far too quickly and making her shiver. She felt shaky as if she had really been flying and then thrust suddenly back into an unfamiliar body to which she had not yet adapted. Rej held her hand. She did not take it away.

'It's all right now. It was just a dream,' said Rej.

She must look as shaky as she felt. She did not like her feelings to be so easily read. She stiffened. 'Was it?' she answered thickly, from a dry mouth. She was not sure. She did not believe that dreams were shared. It felt as if she had been somewhere else.

She led Rej towards the back exit from the barracks; she was still disoriented and unsteady. 'We should go now if you still want to rescue the slave,' she said, then added, 'you know we could be hanged – if we are found out after curfew. You are sure you want to come with me?'

She could not see Rej in the darkness but she sensed him move as if to shrug. Perhaps he thought he had nothing to lose. For herself she was still not sure why she had accepted this course of action. Perhaps she was tired of being 'protected' by her mother and kept in ignorance of what was truly going on in Lunnzia. In the cold, dank darkness, when the danger suddenly seemed more tangible, that seemed an inadequate reason for risking her neck.

Rej shivered; she would have to retrieve Melagiar's cloak when they got outside or he would risk the cold torpor again. She was better used to the cold. He dropped her hand as if he was embarrassed by the intimacy of the gesture, and it felt colder without his warmth. Donna folded her arms and led Rej towards the servants' entrance, the way Capla had shown her the night she'd visited her mother, the way she'd followed hours earlier to adulterate the Watch's ale. It seemed very different in the post-curfew darkness, without the flicker of candlelight and the noise of the ever-present slaves. The stone floors of the old palace were icy under her feet and the fear of her dream still haunted her. The palace was silent but for the soft pad of Rej's feet behind her, the sense of his presence shadowing her. She tried to reassemble the components of the dream, to try to understand what had happened to so shock and frighten her. She remembered the joy of flight and the scent of attar of roses and the terror the dark basilisk engendered. Why should Arché in her destroyer's aspect suddenly haunt her dream?

Donna needed to focus on the moment, now, on moving silently through the old palace and rescuing the slave from the bride's hole. The key to Melagiar's chamber and the remaining ajeebamor were still in her pocket. If she got her chance she would refill the vial and take what she could of the other potions. There was power in such things, and she needed to feel a little less powerless.

Donna listened intently; there was no sound from the other dormitories. The palace was a huge one and most of its fine rooms were now empty. They had been used for storage at the beginning of the war but now there was nothing left to store. Donna and Rej did not use the sweeping stone staircase that led down to the refectory but the small back stairs that led to the kitchens and the cold stores, the stills and the pastry ovens. It was warmer there. Though the fires that once would have burned all night had been allowed to die, the thick stone walls still held some heat, and Donna was glad of it. They crept past the sleeping scullion slaves huddled together in the small straw-filled loft above the scullery, and down the dark and narrow corridor that led to the servants' door. The night porter was snoring loudly; his face looked grey in the moonlight and dribble flecked his chin. Donna hoped she had not given him too much of the ajeebamor, but his breathing was regular enough. Silently she lifted the bar of the door and was out in the stillness of the night. Donna picked up the cloak, still bundled where she had left it, and handed it to Rej.

'Take it, please.'

He was going to argue but then shivered. He placed it reluctantly around his shoulders and then, by unspoken consent, they ran towards Melagiar's rooms as if speed alone could save them from the Watch and the risk of the cold torpor. It was a freedom almost as pleasurable as the soaring flight of their dreams. Donna made almost no noise as she ran, though her hair tumbled wildly around her shoulders and she had to resist the hysterical urge to laugh. Rej matched her pace easily, though he stayed close to the shadows of the university buildings – the wiser course. In any case, no one saw them.

Donna's exhilaration died when they reached the staircase. The wooden door at the foot of the stairs was shut and for that door she had no key.

'There must be a back way?' Rej said hopefully.

'I don't know where.'

They walked along the front of the university building. The pale stone reflected the moonlight and Rej pulled Donna into the shadows. The windows were all shuttered to protect the precious mullioned glass behind. Then Donna remembered that the window at the back of Melagiar's study had still been open as she had left it when the militia had arrived. She led Rej via a series of narrow roads and back alleys to the walled kitchen garden which Melagiar's study overlooked.

Rej's long limbs made him look like a spider as he climbed the garden wall. Donna was much less sure. It was an old wall of the dry stone variety, made without mortar so that there were many hand and footholds, but climbing had never been much a part of her education and she did it awkwardly and anxiously. She was worried that she might smash the crystal vial in her pocket against the wall. She was worried that she would fall. She was ashamed of her feebleness and refused Rej's proffered hand, choosing instead to jump down. She jarred her knee in the process and grazed her hand. She was grateful that Rej made no comment. She could see a casement window slightly open on the third floor. It seemed impossibly high, and the facing stone of the building looked smooth and without purchase.

'Give me the key and I'll try and unlatch the staircase door from the inside. Will there be Watchmen?'

'I don't think so – I don't know – maybe. But you can't climb up there!'

'Yes I frakking can. I'm a comber, remember.'

Donna flinched slightly at the expletive – it was rarely used except in the Liberty. It was a reminder of Rej's otherness. He was so much a stranger, even though he appeared to share her dreams.

He didn't wait for a response, just held his hand out for the key, which she gave him because she had no better idea. It was very dark and very clear. The air felt like a razor in her lungs; she was not used to running. Rej gave her the precious cloak and without a word loped towards the building. He could indeed climb. It was hard to see him in the shadows but before she had time to become concerned she saw his tall, lanky figure reach inside the casement, push open the window and then somehow fall inside. She was glad he was not there to witness her clumsy attempt to climb back over the garden wall. She skinned her knees and made her finger ends bleed before she got over it. She was glad of the cloak, which at least gave her a semblance of dignity and necessary warmth. The ground sparkled with frost where the moonlight caught it, and even the sound of her soft shoes striking the earth had a bell-like clarity. By the time she had made it back round to the front of the building the door was open and Rej was waiting for her, an oil lantern in his hand.

'I thought we might need this,' he said, and she nodded. She ought to have said something graceful about his climbing skill but the words wouldn't come. Perhaps it was as well that she was not destined to be a Low Lady, because she found it hard to manage well-earned compliments, let alone the extravagant flattery that was part of the job.

She smoothed back her hair from her face and Rej noticed her cuts. His pale face in the light looked concerned.

'You should bind them,' he said, anxiously.

She wiped her hand on the underside of her skirt and shrugged. 'They're nothing. I'm just clumsy at climbing. You're very good.' There, she'd said it.

'I'm a comber,' he said again, without bravado. 'That's what we do. I haven't seen any guards. Shall we go?'

He leaned past her to relatch the door. The soft candlelight made his face a strange landscape of planes and hollows. What was she doing here with him? They hadn't talked about what they would do once they had rescued the purple-faced slave. She clutched the cloak around her shoulders for comfort rather than for warmth. Rej lifted the lantern high and she followed his strange elongated shadow up the staircase; she did not know why.

Chapter Seventeen

Rej suppressed a shiver as he climbed the narrow stairs. His first task on entering Melagiar's rooms had been to stumble around in search of light. He had thought about going to rescue the slave on his own and saving Donna the trouble, but he doubted that she would have thanked him, so he had kept his word. He felt an odd affinity for the girl, in spite of her cold aloofness. Donna and he shared dreams. That must mean something, though he had no frakking idea what.

Although it was only a matter of hours since Melagiar had been killed, his rooms already had an abandoned air. As far as Rej could tell nothing had been moved, but the hearth was cold and the place, though still crammed with furniture, seemed as empty as a disused hide in the combes. He led Donna through the door to Melagiar's private chamber. The corridor smelled of pilchin-water, the strong astringent herb that was used even in the combes to scrub away serious filth; it was surprisingly evocative of home.

The bloody chamber was clean again, the counter-pane of green silk had been removed to show the fine wool blankets beneath. Rej touched one. In this cold openness of Above such a thing had to be worth more credits than he had ever won. He would have taken it, but was not sure that Donna would approve. He wanted her to approve of him. The stink of pilchin-water was even stronger in this room, catching at the back of his throat. It was a smell redolent of corpses and childbirth, as it was used liberally for both.

Rej moved on to the bride's hole. He found the place easily enough, unable to prevent the slight tightening in his stomach. Would he find another corpse? Donna did not wait for him to gather his courage – she ran to the panel and pressed it. It slipped open to reveal the hunched and unmoving form of the slave. Rej swung the lantern but it was hard to tell whether the man still breathed. Donna shook him but could get no reaction; his skin was cold to the touch.

'Is he dead?' Rej's voice rasped in his throat. Poor frakking loser to die with rescue on its way.

Donna shook her head. 'He might just have the cold torpor. We won't know if he's dead until we thaw him out.'

'But if we light the fire we'll be seen, won't we?'

Donna's face was as expressionless as the pale stone of the university buildings. 'If we don't, he will die, even if he's not dead already.' She paused. 'I'd like to save him if I can.'

Rej did not ask why. He supposed she wanted to save the slave because she was that kind of person, the sentimental kind like himself, the kind his mother would have approved of – another frakking innocent.

Donna wrapped the fur-lined cloak around the man and Rej helped her lift him from his hiding place.

Though he was not a small man he was lighter even than Rej himself, malnourished, so that Rej could feel the bones of his ribs when he moved him. Rej carried him alone in the end, it was easier that way, and Donna built the fire up in the main room. It was very surprising that the wood still remained where it had been left; fire in Lunnzia was a rare and precious thing.

'We must warm him slowly or he will die – the body's heat has to be coaxed back along with his soul. He is far gone in torpor.' Donna's movements were swift and competent. 'We could get the blankets from the bed but it would be good if we could give him our own body heat.'

Rej fetched the blankets and they heaped them on the slave and then lay down beside the near-corpse, close to the fire. Rej felt uncomfortable lying so close to another human being; he had slept next to his mother when he was very small, but in the combes even couples kept to their own niches most of the time. It made him feel a little as he had in the ghost tunnel, as if he might not be able to breathe. He did not know whether Donna knew that privacy and isolation were treasured in the combes, whether she was able to guess at his profound unease at lying there, but she spoke to him in her cool voice and he felt less disturbed. She spoke impersonally – about the cold torpor mainly, and how since the war there had been insufficient fuel. She had a way of speaking that was oddly comforting. Something about her formal tone discouraged intimacy so that, even lying huddled next to the body of a stranger, he felt that she carried her own private niche with her, like the shell of the tortoise he'd seen once in a picture. If she could do that then so could he. In the combes they kept themselves apart from one another, but knew each other as intimately as brothers. Here oppidans slept together like puppies in a litter but surrounded themselves with an extra skin of formality, or at least Donna did, so that people did not seem to know each other at all.

Somehow Donna talking like that made it easier to bear the closeness of the slave. He lived, it seemed, for his shallow breath was on Rej's neck, making his flesh crawl. Under the warm wool of the blankets he felt the slave become less cold, less corpse-like, and Rej began to feel warm, the first time he had felt entirely warm since he had arrived Above. In spite of the danger and the uncomfortably close presence of the slave, Rej felt his own awareness slipping away and was powerless to stop it. The combes seemed very distant and he was as weary as he had ever been. His eyelids grew too heavy to lift, and once again he dreamed.

He was no longer flying, though he knew that he was still a dragon, but a frightened dragon, a dragon becoming angry. He cowered in a cave as the rain lashed and whipped against the cave and the wind howled like a motherless infant. Fork lighting ripped through a sky the colour of granite and the rumble of thunder was deafening. He feared that the roof of the cave might fall, as he had feared that the roof of the combes might tumble in when he was a child.

He was filled with terror and woke with a start, utterly disorientated. It took him a moment to work out where he was. The fire still burned in the grate. Someone gave a muffled squeal. It was Donna – she sat up. He could see her in the firelight, wild-eyed and flushed, frightened and confused.

'It was another dream?' she asked.

'The storm and a cave?' Rej asked, his own voice less steady than he would have liked. She nodded. He did not know what possessed him, but he reached for her hand over the body of the slave. She squeezed his hand with surprising firmness. Her hand was hot and sticky; he could feel her racing pulse.

'What do you think it means?' she asked, all the coolness and distance gone from her voice.

'I don't know – maybe nothing.'

'Could it be real? It's like being someone else and yet feeling frightened and panicked as if I were still me.'

He understood what she meant, in spite of her incoherent explanation. The man between them moved suddenly and groaned. Donna untangled herself from the blankets and checked that there was still water in the kettle by the hearth.

'I will make him some carga – it may revive him.'

'Are you all right?' Rej spoke to Donna, but it was the slave who answered.

'I am alive, which is more than I had expected. You came back – my heartfelt thanks.'

Nobody said anything for a moment. Rej was still fighting the after-effects of the too vivid dream and the slave was not up to conversation. When the kettle boiled Rej helped the slave to drink the steaming carga while Donna opened the armoire and clinked glasses out of sight; she seemed to be looking for something.

The slave drank deeply and eagerly. He was weak, but in better condition than Rej had expected. When the goblet was empty he spoke.

'I have to get away – the Arkel may recognise me as the Doctor Esteemed Melagiar's body slave.'

'I can't see you going anywhere for a while,' said Rej. 'How are your wounds?' Rej saw that the makeshift bandages Donna had made were caked in blood.

'I am alive and lucky,' the man said shortly. He looked about him, taking in his surroundings for the first time. 'By the breast of the goddess – this is Melagiar's room. This is risky.'

'We know,' said Rej shortly. Donna came back to the fire. She still looked flushed, but she had smoothed back her hair and seemed composed.

'Could he not go underground?' she asked Rej, ignoring the slave, as the other oppidans had ignored the serving slaves at the refectory.

'He could,' said Rej carefully, 'but he'd die of the green death within days, with those wounds, if he didn't start a war first. Abovers are not allowed Below any more than combers are allowed Above.' He looked at her warningly. His secrets were his own; he hoped she was not about to spill them.

'Why could he not stay here?' Donna asked suddenly. 'If anyone noticed he'd gone, it would be the last place anyone would look for him. I have a key – we have been told to carry on our work – why not? As long as he stays away from the overseer, who will surely watch us work tomorrow, he should be safe enough.'

The slave looked uncomfortable. 'I don't think it

will be safe here now. Someone will come eventually to remove all of this.' He indicated the opulent furnishings. 'Melagiar only managed to keep them because he'd convinced the Arkel that he could win the war for him. He can't do that now that he's dead.'

Rej looked around the chamber, at the richly coloured furnishings glowing in the golden arc of firelight, at the dark sheen of the highly polished wood reflecting the flickering flames. He loved the beautiful things in the room – he loved the colour and the texture and the smell of it all. It was as far from the minimal comfort and filth of the combes as it was possible to be, and he delighted in it. His senses had been starved of such variety. He had not known the poverty of his experience until he had seen these riches. He was not envious of them, but he was glad that they existed. He felt only regret that it was all to be destroyed, but he put such indulgent thoughts from his mind – he was getting frakking moon-witted – it was not his most important concern.

'How was Melagiar going to win the war for the Arkel?' Rej asked the obvious question, but did not expect an answer. The rescued man was a slave – why should he know his master's business?

'He was working on some weapon of great power, along with the Doctor Esteemed Harfoot.'

'What kind of weapon – a ballista?' Donna asked in surprise. She had not thought the Doctor Esteemed Melagiar the practical, warmongering type. The slave shook his head. Rej was stunned into silence. He had not forgotten his oath to avenge Harfoot, but he had been so distracted by the strangeness of everything that he had not had time to give much serious thought to his avowed task until that moment. That Harfoot and Melagiar were colleagues was not even that unexpected or surprising, and yet he had not expected it and he was surprised.

'Did the Arkel kill Harfoot too?' he said. The slave's purple face seemed to colour pink, though it was hard to tell, what with the heat of the fire and the lurid stain of his slave mark. He looked nervous and surprised.

'How do you know of that?'

Rej turned away and brought Harfoot's ring from its hiding place in the folds of his undercloth. The slave looked sick when he saw it.

'Did the Arkel kill the Doctor Esteemed Harfoot?' Rej repeated.

'No,' the slave said reluctantly, in the heavy accent of a non-Lunnzian, 'that was the work of Melagiar, or rather of his servant.'

'What do you mean?'

There was a pause, before the slave seemed to make a decision. He met Rej's eyes and Rej, who prided himself on reading the intent in a man's face, found it impossible to work out what he was thinking. The man spoke in a near whisper.

'I killed the Doctor Esteemed Harfoot, and I very much hope that he was not a friend of yours.'

Chapter Eighteen

Donna was bemused. She had heard of the Doctor Esteemed Harfoot – she was sure Melagiar had mentioned him – but why should Rej know of him and why should he have been murdered by a slave? She noticed that Rej took a moment to recover himself after the slave's revelation, that he looked disturbed, even angry. She saw that he took a deep breath and said, 'Why don't you explain what is going on here? I'd like to know why you killed Harfoot and why the Arkel killed Melagiar.'

He looked as if he wanted to say more but he snapped his mouth shut as if to prevent it. The slave fingered the hem of his dirty robe, nervously, his fingers fidgeting constantly with agitation.

'My name is Filefa,' he began, hesitantly. 'I was captured last year and I told Melagiar that in my own city I too was a Doctor Esteemed. We had met once or twice socially in my home city of Terminoria, as people used to do before the war – my family was of good standing there. They were all killed so I was not ransomed. Melagiar was not …' He paused for the word he needed. 'Well, he was not particularly gifted at his chosen field, while Harfoot was brilliant – well-known for his revolutionary theories on the nature of dreams and their power over the emotions. I had myself done work on the connection between feelings and the humours of the body, such that a man afraid sweats, breathes rapidly, etc. Melagiar wished to use some of that work, under his own name of course, and I was collaborating with Harfoot on a project for the Arkel.' He looked at Donna and Rej in turn. 'Melagiar believed that it is possible to scare people to death. He was developing some kind of contraption to scare a large number of people to death as a weapon of war.' He paused.

It was Donna who broke the incredulous silence. 'But how? I mean, that seems –' She was halted by an imperious wave of the slave's hand.

'It was not a new idea – indeed some people from Lambrugio had also been working on a similar theory. There are, after all, many reports of people dying of fright. Certainly it was commonly said, in my home town, that many a coward died of fright while a brave man tasted the kiss of steel. What is different is this device that Harfoot built – a machine which he believed could make people frightened enough to die.'

'The Basilisk Contrivance,' said Rej softly, and Donna wondered what else this stranger knew about her own world that she did not.

'Indeed,' said Filefa, giving him a sharp look.

'Do you know what and where it is?' Rej asked slowly.

Filefa shook his head. 'Melagiar is – was – very jealous of his secrets. He was afraid that with my background I might steal and take credit for the invention myself – not easy as a slave in Lunnzia. But I believe that it somehow used the power he referred to as the "Basilisk's Breath".'

Donna felt herself become very still, waiting for more.

'And how did you come to murder your former colleague?' Rej's voice was as steely as the blade he still carried. Filefa wrung his robe like a wash slave.

'Harfoot knew I was never a Doctor Esteemed but a wastrel student of his old friend Vespigi – it was his work I was using, claiming it as my own. Harfoot threatened to tell Melagiar if I did not help him sabotage Melagiar's work. I was afraid Melagiar would abandon me if he knew I was not a Doctor Esteemed, or kill me if he realised I was working against the success of his schemes. At times like these when food is short, slaves are the first to die. I was afraid.' Filefa lowered his eyes with what might have been shame, or the pretence of it.

'So, you have not answered my frakking question. Why did you kill the Doctor Esteemed Harfoot – to keep him quiet?' Rej's knife was in his hand; he tested the sharpness of the blade against his finger. Filefa swallowed hard.

'Two nights ago I heard Melagiar and Harfoot talking. Harfoot was an abstemious man, but Melagiar had laced his food with something to make him talk. Melagiar knew something of the poisoner's arts and the Arkel permitted him a supply of many unusual philtres. It was clear from what I overheard that Melagiar thought Harfoot knew the solution to the problems they had been having. Harfoot wasn't making any sense and Melagiar got angry and tied him up and got one of the slaves – who had been a torturer in his home town – to … do what torturers do.' Filefa looked uncomfortable. 'I didn't stay to listen so I don't know what he did – there were tasks I had to do. When Melagiar called for me later, Harfoot had gone. He said that Harfoot had somehow escaped. Melagiar had been drinking ajeebamor and Terminorian Spirit of Fire – he'd probably passed out. Melagiar told me to find Harfoot and to kill him. It suited me to obey.'

Donna glanced at Rej's face – it was as hard and unreadable as Velarian granite.

'Go on,' he said as Filefa stopped to lick his lips.

'Harfoot was badly injured and befuddled with Melagiar's potions. He was easy to find. I caught up with him as he was trying to escape through a floor-door in the Melagiar Mansion. He made so much noise muttering and sobbing I was able to follow him. I thought he would kill himself, the desperate and clumsy way he staggered along the underground tunnels – it was almost dark and I thought I would die too.' Filefa grimaced as if at the memory of the combes. 'The Doctor Esteemed made it to some cave. I heard voices and when someone came out, I went in and stabbed him. It was a release – I think his wits had gone.'

With the unexpected speed of a striking snake Rej placed his comber's blade against Filefa's neck – in the place where the blood pulsed most strongly. Donna started in surprise and the terrified Filefa did nothing but blink like a startled hare.

'I swore to kill you, if you are indeed Harfoot's murderer,' Rej said evenly.

'Don't!' Donna spoke instinctively – she knew with sudden certainty that Rej was capable of killing Filefa. She had told the other oppidans that Rej was harmless and had believed it, but she now realised how little she really knew about him, about what it meant to be a comber. She began to feel the first flutterings of real fear.

'Rej, there are things he could still tell us – about Melagiar and Immina.'

She did not know if her words would make any difference, but she saw with relief that Rej relaxed his pressure on the blade, which now merely rested against Filefa's neck. Filefa's eyes were bulging and Donna was suddenly aware of the rank smell of his sweat.

'So, Filefa, why did the Arkel kill Melagiar?' Rej asked with a chilling calm, worthy of Grimper.

'Melagiar didn't succeed in getting the weapon to work and cost the Arkel dear in privileges – Melagiar became too difficult. He took to ajeebamor because it makes some people dream, and that was important to him for some reason, but he took too much, became too expensive, too indiscreet in his flouting of the Humble Way within the university, and the Arkel – a pragmatic man – found someone who could do the job better, someone more ruthless and less demanding.'

Rej said nothing for a moment. Donna could not guess at what he was thinking. 'And there was no plot to start a war with the combers by breaking treaty?'

Filefa shook his head. Rej released him and Filefa

felt his neck reflexively. 'At least *I* was not involved in one. But you must know that the Arkel would have all the combers killed if he could find a way. I believe that when he gets the Contrivance to work he will use it first on the combers before he puts it to work against our enemies of High Verda.'

'Will he get it to work with Harfoot and Melagiar dead?' Rej said, with such an intense look in his eyes that Filefa turned away.

Donna was growing impatient and increasingly worried with every instant they remained in Melagiar's rooms. 'We can't stay here any longer, Rej. It will be dawn soon. We have to be seen at the refectory, if not at the dormitory.'

'Wait, Donna. I have to know. Filefa, can he get the Contrivance to work without those two?'

Filefa nodded. 'I was not the only helper, there were others – the Doctor Esteemed Garvell has the Arkel's ear. The greater part of the work is done. With the right subject I think it would work.'

Donna broke in. 'Garvell, I know that name – he diagnosed the ague at the Barracks of the Wise!'

Filefa shook his head. 'Rather he poisoned about half the inmates to save on bread, and claimed it was the ague – like I said, a man more ruthless even than Melagiar. The Arkel is having Harfoot's notes copied for Garvell to use and I do believe that with persistence he will solve the difficulties.'

Donna was silenced by the thought of Garvell's callous murder of the families of her workmates. Rej was still paying attention to Filefa.

'But Harfoot destroyed his notes.'

Filefa nodded awkwardly. 'He tried, but they had already been copied. Garvell will succeed. I'm sure of it.'

'Rej, we must go – it will be dawn soon.' Donna did not try to keep the fear from her voice. Rej, unused to the subtle gradations of darkness and light in Above, could not argue with her. He regarded Filefa thoughtfully for a moment and then abruptly sheathed the knife out of sight and in one smooth gesture he threw Harfoot's ring into the fire.

'I cannot kill a slave in cold blood. I have reneged on my oath – the ring should follow Harfoot.'

Filefa's face lost some of its desperation and Donna found that her legs were shaking so that she had to hold on to the wall. 'Go!' said Filefa. 'I will make it as if you were never here and then I'll hide back in the bride's hole.' His voice was eager: he had survived a second close brush with what Donna's mother called the 'Fatal kiss of steel'.

Donna looked at Rej questioningly and he nodded.

'There is just one thing more,' Donna said quickly over her shoulder, as they hurried towards the door. Rej glanced at her curiously, as if wondering what of all the many questions that should be asked she would choose to ask. 'Do you know what happened to Immina?'

Filefa looked sombre. 'The Arkel's men took her as she was trying to escape from her brother. It is my earnest hope that she is dead. It would be best for everybody.'

There was no time to find out more.

Chapter Nineteen

'Work details start at dawn. Many will be awake before then and I don't know how long the Watchman will sleep,' Donna panted over her shoulder as she ran through the still empty street; Rej had to lengthen his stride to keep pace with her. It was good to run – his thoughts were muddled. It was surely a joke of Luck, his wayward Lady, to reveal that a man he'd risked his life to save was the same frakking man he'd risked his life to kill. And what was this weapon that could be pitted against the combes?

His fickle Lady favoured them in that the porter still snored and did not move as they crept past him. They could not take their previous route through the kitchens because the scullions would already be up and working. Rej did not like the darkness but found that if he concentrated, his comber's sense of direction was as good as ever. Donna let him lead her and they were able to slip into the refectory a short while later. Donna had soot on her face from the empty coal store they had run through. He wiped her cheek with the corner of the now grubby cloak before taking it off and rolling it up as he had seen her do. She said nothing while he did this, just watched him with her eyes that seemed too large, too intense.

'What do you think Filefa meant when he said Immina would be better dead?'

Rej shook his head. There were no other oppidans around, only a few slaves sweeping the floors in desultory fashion, but even so he could not answer for fear of being overheard. The Redmen had taken their place on either side of the hall and begun their monotonous, tuneless chanting.

Donna belatedly remembered that he was supposed to be mute. 'I'm sorry – I forgot,' she mumbled. 'I'm not used to intrigue, though Arché knows I ought to have been bred to it.'

Donna sighed and concentrated on eating the food that had been served to them – a thin gruel with flecks of something which might have been raisins or mouse droppings. It was worse food than Rej was used to in the combes. He was beginning to see what the combers' comforts cost the Abovers. Melagiar had lived well, but he seemed to be alone in that.

'I can't see Capla here, either. He should have more information for me. What did Filefa mean by the power of the Basilisk's Breath?' Donna said between mouthfuls. She sounded exhausted and dispirited.

Rej raised a questioning eyebrow – he could not remember who Capla was. Besides, he had more serious concerns – what Melagiar's frakking Basilisk Contrivance could do to the combers. He should get word to Scrubber that they were in danger – only he had so little of use to tell her. Since he had come Above nothing had worked out as he had hoped: he'd failed to avenge the death of Harfoot, and he'd learned that the threat to the combes came not from Harfoot's killer but from Harfoot's own invention – the Basilisk Contrivance. He was no closer to finding the dragons of his dreams, or knowing the glorious freedom that they represented. He watched Donna surreptitiously as she ate her gruel. She glanced at him, aware of his steady gaze.

'Stop it! You don't have to be moon-witted with me,' she hissed. 'We'd better go and check on Filefa before Martrin sends an overseer.' Just then the women of their work detail trooped sleepily into the hall. 'By Arché's breath, I don't want anyone asking me why I got up so early. The girls will think we slipped away for intimacy.' He guessed what she was talking about and felt himself blushing. Women were more discreet in the combes.

What had happened to him? Light! Here he was acting like a right twazzock, too uncertain to take risks. He was a child again and an embarrassed child at that. Was he supposed to have made some move? She'd not given him any sign that she'd wanted him. In the combes it was always up to the woman to give some indication – here he did not know. He shrugged in a non-committal way. She did not look pleased. She surprised him by deliberately walking towards one of the men who had entered the hall at that moment.

'I need to tell you something,' she whispered to him, just loudly enough for Rej to hear. The man, who was lame, showed unexpected presence of mind and pretended to lose his balance, and, in the confusion that ensued with his stick getting caught in Donna's skirt, she whispered, 'Belafor, there was no plague at the Barracks of the Wise – the people there were murdered!'

Rej saw the shock register on the face of 'Belafor', but there was no disbelief. He nodded, apologised for his clumsiness and moved on. Rej could not ask her why she had told Belafor that, but followed her outside, with the vacant air which came to him a little too easily. It was a grey, cloudy day, less painful to his eyes than the previous day, and warmer too. He managed to walk the distance to Melagiar's rooms with his back straight and his head high. It was good to know that he would not hit his head on anything, good to smell clean air.

He knew at once that things were changed as soon as he entered the stairwell. Donna opened the rooms with the key. He found himself reaching for his knife again. The inner door swung open on an empty space stripped of furniture, denuded of rugs, tapestries – everything except for the empty grate, a table and two chairs. They had only just avoided the Watch or whoever had cleared the room of all its opulence and much of its beauty.

It was still a large, well-proportioned room, but their footsteps echoed hollowly on the bare polished boards.

'It was fortunate we left when we did. They took it all,' Donna said forlornly. There was an unexpected moistness to her eyes. 'Like they took all Mother's things. I don't understand the Sumptuary Laws. What is wrong with beauty?'

Rej wisely said nothing. Donna walked to the table where the tools of her trade and the manuscript she had been copying lay. She seemed distracted, worried, even a little lost.

Rej followed Donna through Melagiar's now empty chamber to the bride's hole. He could not have said why he was unsurprised when Donna opened the secret door and screamed.

Filefa lay crouched in the shallow space, quite dead. His throat had been cut. Donna reflexively turned away, her voice catching as she said, 'Who could have done this?'

'What do you mean, Donna? Anyone could have done this! How the frakk do I know who did it? This Arkel maybe – one of the Watch or whoever came to clear the room. If you want my opinion we should get out of here – fast. It is not a place where people live very long.'

'But we are supposed to be working here. This is the manuscript I've been copying.'

'It is the one Filefa was talking about, isn't it?' Rej asked, looking at it with distaste. 'Harfoot's notes.'

'Though Melagiar passed them off as his own,' Donna added.

'Oh, for frakk's sake, let's take it with us then. Do you really want to stay here and copy the frakking thing while the Arkel is plotting to make some kind of weapon to kill everyone in the combes? Light, but you're as imprisoned here as I ever was Below. Meekly eating food the rats would turn away, being marched off to bed – never daring to wear a cloak to keep you warm. I don't understand why you don't frakking do something, all of you!'

'That's why not!' Donna shouted. Her face had

drained of all colour at Rej's obscenities and she pointed angrily at the bloody corpse of Filefa. 'That's why not, you insensitive, arrogant comber. We do what the Council of Ten says or we die – like Filefa, like Melagiar. What else can we do? We have nothing to fight the Arkel with – we haven't even the clothes we stand up in – they, like us, are sacred resources of the city.'

Unexpectedly she started to sob. She tried to choke it back and turned away from him, but her whole body shook in silent, quaking convulsions. Rej found himself resting an uncertain hand on her shoulder.

'Donna, I'm sorry. I didn't mean to upset you.'

She turned on him angrily. '*You* haven't upset me – this has. I don't know what it's like for a comber, but I don't like seeing men murdered.'

He patted her shoulder awkwardly and ineffectually. 'I'm sorry. Maybe I should just deve off, back home – find Scrubber. She'll help me find Melagiar's Contrivance – maybe we can destroy it before he has a chance to use it. Why didn't we ask Filefa where it was? I can't believe I could be so frakking moon-witted.'

He wasn't trying to make her feel guilty, it was regretfully what he felt. He would not even have to confess his failure to kill Harfoot's killer – Filefa was dead. He had found out what he had come Above to find. There were no dragons – only dreams and the promise of death.

'No,' Donna spoke firmly. 'I don't think you should "deve off". I should help you find the Contrivance. I'll help you. I'm all right now.'

She wiped her face on her stained clothes. Her nose was pink and swollen, along with her eyes; crying did not suit her. She twisted her hair back into the loose knot and stepped away from him. He let his hand fall to his side. What was he supposed to do now?

'I'm sorry, that was self-indulgent,' she said with lowered eyes.

'Is that what he'd say – your Arkel?'

She nodded. 'Yes, it's the beginning of the confession of the Humble Way – but in this case he may be right.' She straightened her rather grubby dress and smoothed her hair. 'You might be right too. Everybody's right but me! We should take the notes, quickly, before the overseer comes. I don't know why, but I always seem to do what I'm told.' She smiled rather weakly up at him and then resolutely closed the panel door of the bride's hole on the unfortunate Filefa.

Rej led the way back to Melagiar's study. The dark corridor could easily hide an assassin and he found it hard to believe that their part in saving Filefa was unknown.

'They might have found him when they came to get the furniture,' Donna said, as if in answer to his thoughts. 'Maybe he'd been at the ajeebamor and lost track of time. It doesn't mean that the Arkel was watching this room.'

'No,' Rej agreed shortly. 'I don't understand why they let us copy Harfoot's notes if they are so important.'

'Why would we know they were important? I've been copying the manuscript for hours and most of it didn't sound important to me. It was all I could do to stay awake. Anyway, as you've already noticed – we oppidans do as we're told. Most of us never gave up thinking for ourselves because we never started. I should have known better.'

'I can hide the manuscript in the combes if you like. No one would find it there, and we could burn your copy.'

'Shouldn't we read it first?'

Rej frowned. 'But where? Not here.'

'No. The temple?'

Rej shrugged. It seemed crazy to sit down and read when they were in danger, but it was Donna's world; she was supposed to know best.

There was a tinder box left near the oil lamp on the table of the otherwise emptied room and he carefully burnt Donna's painstaking copy of Harfoot's work in the grate. The sudden flare of heat reminded him briefly of Harfoot's own demise.

'Let's go, then,' Donna said, expressionlessly, when her hard work was nothing but ashes.

They walked stealthily down the stairs together, expecting to hear the tread of the anticipated overseer at any moment. Rej eased his knife from his belt and tried to work out how he could defend them while still carrying the bulky weight of the manuscript, but his Lady was going to make him pay one day soon because she favoured them still. Donna marched confidently towards the small temple, never flinching when three Redmen passed them. Rej kept his eyes downcast. He did not know what expression to wear so he'd rather keep his face shadowed.

It was cold in the chapel and the filtered purple light was too dim to read by with any ease.

'It's in chapters,' Donna said quietly. Her voice echoed a little in the empty space. 'I don't understand most of it, and there are lots of philosophical symbols and things which my mother omitted from my early education. I've copied the first half already – you read those pages and I'll try to make sense of the rest.'

Rej had always treasured the manuscripts he had read in the combes. Each moment he'd spent with them had been precious and they had all been committed to memory long before the poisonous vapours of the combes destroyed them; but now, he felt like action: he felt like a fight. It took all of his self-control to sit meekly and begin *A Treatise on Dreams* by Nikris Melagiar, Doctor Esteemed of the University of Lunnzia.

Chapter Twenty

It did not take long for Donna to realise that neither she nor Rej were likely to make much progress in unravelling the mystery of Melagiar's Contrivance from the document in front of them. Her eyes strained to read the cramped writing on the parchment. The ink was of poor quality and had faded and much of the work had been written hastily so that there was little to distinguish one letter from another. She worked silently for a while, forcing herself to concentrate, and finding it necessary to reread many of the passages several times because they were either illegible or incomprehensible. She found only one interesting passage:

It has been speculated, most notably in the work of the Elandrian philosopher Resephus, that the soul in dreaming enters that place between life and death in which all manner of creatures are made manifest. These creatures are capable of being apprehended only by those organs of sense and feeling that come into their own when the body and thinking parts of a man are dormant. The reality of such beings can scarcely be denied, as many men at many times have described similar dream experiences; so that if we accept the existence of material objects we must surely accept by the same proofs the existence of these immaterial ones. Whether man might be capable of apprehending these creatures in his wakeful state and what the impact of such creatures might be upon the waking soul is for the moment a subject only of conjecture.

Donna pointed the passage out to Rej, who squinted at it without interest.

Rej rubbed his eyes. 'I don't think whoever wrote this plague waste was fair-witted.'

He was jiggling his knee impatiently and it did not take much sensitivity on Donna's part to recognise that he was in no mood for calm study.

'What is it?' she asked, as his fidgeting became impossible to ignore.

'I think this Contrivance needs to be destroyed, that's all.' He banged his open hand abruptly on the sturdy darkwood pew so that it shook. 'And I can't see the point of sitting here reading Harfoot's half-brewed sewer scum either.' He took a deep breath.

'I came here, Above, partly because I wanted the dragons to be real and I thought I might find them here. Now I'm not sure that it matters any more. I have friends down there,' he pointed emphatically downwards, towards the combes, 'and I don't want the Arkel using this new weapon against them. That's what matters now. I think the dragons are just a dream. Let it go, Donna.'

'Even though we both shared it?'

'I don't know. I'll worry about it when I've

destroyed the Contrivance.'

'But what if the Basilisk Contrivance is a machine to bring the dream dragons here and let them loose on the Arkel's enemies?'

Rej looked at her sharply. 'What, let loose Arché?'

'Do you think one of the dragons was Arché?' Donna was surprised. She had always been taught that the dragon–basilisk was only a symbol of the creative and destructive forces of nature, and that it was the folly of the ignorant to believe that Arché truly was a dragon or a basilisk, but merely a metaphor for the creative and destructive power of God beyond All. Donna unerringly believed what she was taught.

'Well, what do you think they were?' Rej's tone was aggressive.

'Well, I never thought they were a holy vision,' Donna said, suddenly horrified. 'I was taught that Arché was symbolised by a dragon in her creative aspect and by a basilisk in her destructive aspect. I suppose I assumed that somewhere there were real dragons and real basilisks and that I was dreaming about them.'

Rej did not seem to be listening to her theorising. His face was if anything paler than before, insofar as the coloured light permitted her to tell.

'What would happen if a dragon was let loose?'

'I don't think it would hurt anyone, do you?'

It was Rej's turn to shake his head. 'But if it became like the basilisk in the library …' Donna did not expect the sudden fear she saw in his eyes.

'Maybe Immina knew that was what Melagiar was trying to do using the power of the Basilisk's Breath –

whatever that means. Maybe she was trying to warn you – with that picture! I have to find Capla – I'm sure he knew more than he was telling me. As a slave no one notices him – he sees more than we do and I believe he has many more contacts. We can't let this happen.' She was surprised by her own certainty.

'I know we can't,' Rej agreed, standing up, but Donna was still thinking aloud.

'Filefa was talking about the Contrivance making people die of fear. A real basilisk would terrify me.' She stood up too, suddenly purposeful. 'It doesn't matter how the Contrivance works, does it? We have to destroy it. You were right.'

Rej nodded. 'I need to go now – warn Scrubber and the combers that something is planned.'

'I think we should tell Grimper first,' Donna said decisively. The moment for struggling alone with the mystery was over. Her mother might be able to help them. 'Grimper and my mother, they know things – they find out what's going on somehow. Lots of people owe my mother and she is ...' She paused – how did she explain her mother's ruthless non-conformity to Rej without appearing to criticise her? 'Well, she might know what to do – she might even know where the Contrivance could be,' she finished lamely.

Rej was already thinking about practicalities. 'Well, I can go there first – Scrub said to find her through Grimper anyway. The Liberty's on the way to the combes. Will I find Grimper where I first met him?'

'If you head for the Liberty, the dockside, he'll probably find you first. You don't sneak up on Grimper.'

'I'll tell him what we've found out – a rat's nest of nothing much though it is, and then find Scrub. She will think that I have truly lost my wits if I tell her I fear the Arkel is to let loose a basilisk in the combes.'

'But she will believe you – won't she?'

'I can't imagine why. I have no proof – nothing to take to her but this frakking manuscript no one can understand and a wild woman's drawing.'

'But you do think that's what the Arkel was doing, don't you?' Donna spoke earnestly. Her face remained carefully expressionless but she knew that her voice betrayed her; she sounded desperate, frightened, even to her own ears.

Rej looked thoughtful. 'Those dreams were different from anything else I've known – do you think other people have shared them? Would we know? Why have we never had such dreams before? There are too many things I don't understand. I don't understand how this Contrivance might work – does it make people dream? Or does it bring the creatures of dreams here? All I'm sure of is that something bad is going on and that the combers are in danger.'

Donna had nothing to say to that – she felt she understood even less than he did. 'I'll see if I can find anything out from Capla. If my mother can't help, maybe he will know where to look for the Contrivance. Someone must have seen it or heard a rumour, and if it is a big thing slaves will have carried materials, made food for Melagiar when he was working on it. Someone must know something!'

'Unless the Arkel has killed everyone who had a hand in building it.'

'Why would he do that? If people believed he had a weapon that could win us this interminable war against High Verda and bring back our men from the front they would be even happier to follow the Humble Way.'

'You're right. I'm sorry – I've seen too many corpses of late. I'm getting overly suspicious.' Rej smiled bleakly. 'Where shall I see you? Are you going back?' He indicated the direction of the university buildings with his thumb.

Donna shook her head. 'No, I don't think I can go back there. I'm not keen to feel the bite of the Scourge of Arché, which will be the least of my punishments when the overseer finds I'm not at my post and neither is the Arkel's precious manuscript. I think I'll stay with my mother. I need to talk to her myself. I will see you there.'

'I'm sure she'll be grateful to find a comber on her doorstep.'

'You're my friend – she'll cope. Besides, she helped you to start with.' Donna smiled back equally grimly. 'You're right. I have always done what the Council of Ten said unquestioningly. I've just accepted it all. I thought it was my duty, but perhaps it was cowardice – I don't know. I saw enough corpses myself when I was growing up. Maybe it made me too cautious, too fearful of ending up the same way.'

Rej seemed surprised, though whether that was because she'd claimed him as a friend, seen corpses, or admitted he was right, he did not know.

'So, I'll see you at your mother's hide then?'

Rej picked up the rolled manuscript and stuffed i

into his tunic. If he covered it with the cloak it might not look so bad. He hesitated for a moment as if he was going to say something, but then thought better of it. He bowed, no more than a slight inclination of his head, and left, murmuring to himself. Donna only just caught the words, 'May that bitch – Lady Luck – run with you.'

Chapter Twenty-one

Rej did not want to leave Donna. He wasn't sure that she should pursue this slave informer of hers but he had been unable to think of a rational reason why not. His bones told him it was a bad idea – time to leave the game. He could not explain that feeling to Donna not least because his own gambling instincts had failed him so spectacularly lately. In the combes a frakking major loser didn't give advice.

He made himself walk confidently across the quadrangle and along the main street towards the docks. He still felt exposed, but the space queasy was a good deal better. The desire to throw himself under the nearest wall had all but disappeared. He carried the manuscript under his tunic as though he were on an errand and smiled to himself and at anyone who looked his way; in Lunnzia smiling was a certain qualification for madness, and consequently all passers-by kept their distance. The broad streets of the University Quarter were quiet and subdued. There were people around, of course – slaves carrying baskets of laundry and vegetables, oppidans in their thin clothes hurrying, shivering about their business and the extravagantly scarlet-dressed Redmen with their long elaborately woven beards heading somewhere more important, but he had seen nothing of the vast grandeur of the place as his mother had remembered it and as he had dreamed of it in the cramped crepuscular world of the combes. He was not sure that he would ever have another chance.

The West Tower of the university was little more than that, though once it had housed a silver bell that could be heard across the whole of Lunnzia. It was of the same white stone as the library, but decorated by rings of dark granite so that it was striped as the mythical Zebra of Coraville. In spite of the pressing need to carry the news to Scrubber Rej could not resist trying the heavy wooden door at its foot, only to find it opened easily on to a dark flight of dusty spiral stairs. It was no part of his task to view Lunnzia, but he needed to see it once for himself as he thought he had glimpsed it in his dreams. If he'd dreamed true, never having seen the city from the heights, why then perhaps Donna was right and the dream was real. But that was only an excuse, and he knew it. The boy who had longed for the wonders of Above could not resist the call of curiosity: he just wanted to see the city of his mother's memory and his own childhood fantasies in all its glory.

He raced up the five hundred stairs until his heart beat faster than his running steps and he was bathed in sweat. There was no door at the top; the stairs opened on to the viewing platform around the arched apex of the empty campanile. It was many times higher than the highest cliffs of home, and the white expanse of cloud, high above and around him, made him want to cower somewhere close and covered for protection. The sky was huge, an infinity of empty space; he felt dizzy and would have fallen but for the decorative iron railings that still surrounded the platform.

He leaned against them and stared giddily down at the panorama – the city of Lunnzia, the jewel of the West. He could see as far as the city wall and the docks of the Liberty outside it, spilling around the delta of the river Stan and beyond that the silver sea. He could see the few streets he had so far explored – the quadrangle at the front of Melagiar's building, the walled garden behind, and beyond that street after street of stone-clad buildings, some in the famous Provian white marble, others in soft golden sandstone. The painted tiles on the many bell-tower roofs were bright, even on such a grey day. For the first time Rej understood why the Blue Quarter was so called – the azure-blue glaze of the tiles shone like sapphires on the roof of every building of note. Further away at the very outskirts of the city, by the distant wall, he could see the smaller emerald glass tiles, round as bottle bottoms and dark as algae, that graced the roofs of the Green Quarter; while to the east, the gilded temple domes of the holy Golden Quarter shone like lesser suns. For the first time Rej understood that it would be impossible to find the Basilisk Contrivance just by looking for it. The scale of the city made him almost as dizzy as the open sky and he began to tremble. It was much as he had seen it in his dreams, only bigger and more daunting. So what did that mean – his dreams were real?

Directly below him a horse-drawn cart flanked by armed militia men clattered through the street and Rej hoped wildly that it might contain, against all the odds, the war Contrivance, but unfortunately, he could see that it was merely a solitary grain wagon heading for the oppidan scribes' quarters. His Lady Luck was not going to bless him so generously; this was going to be a long game. The thought reminded him of what was missing from the streets of Lunnzia: there were no street gamblers, no hawkers, no peddlers, no masquerades, no traders of any sort, no street musicians, no tradesmen or craftsmen going about their business. The jewel of the West had lost some of its lustre – it looked abandoned, in spite of the slaves endlessly cleaning the streets with their inset treaty lights and scrubbing the stone steps of the fine buildings. It seemed that there was nothing to trade, nothing to sell and no one to entertain or be entertained.

Rej hurried back down the precipitously steep stairway and back on to the broad street. There were too few people, too little noise; he felt exposed and too visible; he did not see another man under thirty-five and of the few men around almost all struggled under some disability. He was grateful to reach the docks for, though it too was comparatively deserted, the buildings were closer together, there were small alleyways and hidden yards, fishermen still worked the estuary and women sat on the dockside gutting fish under the supervision of a couple of militia men who ensured that all they gutted ended in the baskets. Rej supposed the fish would be sent to the Doctor

Esteemeds and other notables of the town. He wondered who got the guts. He grinned broadly and gesticulated at the militia and, though the women nudged each other, no one met his eyes – they did not want to see him and that was his best disguise.

It was colder yet out of the sunshine in the dank alleys of the Liberty. From the tower it had been clear how the sprawl of dark brick warehouses and ill-made cottages had bridged the city wall, a foolish error for a city at war. From the ground it was much less clear what was part of the crumbling city defences and what was not. The wall simply seemed to evaporate, as tunnels had been excavated through it, buildings constructed alongside it and adjoining rooftops spanned it. It had something of the negligent, make-do air of the combes, something of their damp, fetid quality. He had not paid a lot of attention those few days ago when he had first arrived, bedazzled by the sunshine and his space queasy – now he could see that the Liberty was a ramshackle rat-hole of a place. His neck prickled with the awareness of other eyes upon him as he picked his way along the corrupted remains of a cobbled road, where grass grew and where the earth smelled of fish. Overhead the sea birds cried raucously. A rusting cage, large enough to imprison a man, hung from a broken chain on an unbroken expanse of faced stone that might once have been part of the city wall. He pulled his knife out of his tunic as surreptitiously as possible.

He was ready when they came from the shadows, and they did not take him easily. Someone came from behind him – it sounded like a big man with a heavy tread, not subtle at all. Rej flung his head back and knew he made contact with his assailant's nose – he felt it; there was an audible crack and the man grunted, but he did not let go of Rej's chest and, by Light, he had strong frakking hands, big as spades. A second figure attacked him from the front. Rej cut him, felt the wet blood on his hand and the flesh part like the gutted fish as his knife slashed. He kicked out hard and with good aim into the other's groin. Even in the Styx-scum thin oppidan's shoes the blow hurt and that man groaned. He may have sliced the third man too, but then someone smashed him hard in the face with a broad fist and something else thumped down on his head and his ears rang and his vision blurred and a warm stickiness was trickling down his face.

Someone had tied him so that he couldn't move. Something coarse like rope bit into his flesh and chafed and it was the frakking green death for him, that was certain. He hoped it wouldn't take long because when the flesh went black and that smell began he'd rather not live through it – if he had a choice.

He woke to the smell of food, the awareness of pain, and the bitter metal taste of blood in his mouth, like he'd swallowed a knife. He opened his eyes, or tried to – one stayed resolutely shut. He could not touch it to check, but he imagined it was puffy and swollen, though it didn't hurt as badly as his head. He tried to move his head but quickly discovered that was a frakking bad idea. It was dark, but he felt the coldness of damp stone behind him, smelled the stench of stagnant water and decay. Somewhere water dripped on to stone and the sound echoed like the ticking of the clock in Melagiar's study. Through the smoke, he could see two figures in the hazy firelight.

'Will he be all right?' one said in a low voice.

'Depends how hard his head is. He put up a fight, anyway.' The deep but feminine voice sounded approving.

'It hardly helps us. Terrandorr will be days recovering from his wound and he broke Bagin's nose. Couldn't you have spoken to him?'

'I got there too late to stop them. Scrub is going to have some hard words as it is – don't you start as well.' The woman's voice sounded irritated.

Rej thought he recognised the other voice, the man's voice, as belonging to Grimper, Scrub's brother. Donna had said Grimper would find him – he hadn't expected it to be quite like this. If it was Grimper at the fireside Rej ought to speak to him. He remembered that he had something important to say about the Basilisk Contrivance, but the pain behind his eyes made it difficult to formulate sentences, even in his head. Anyway, he wasn't sure it was Grimper – he had met him only once and he had been disoriented then and was hardly less so now. If it wasn't Grimper then he might be better off pretending to be mute and moon-witted – not that to do either posed much of a challenge at the moment. He decided to keep still and silent until he had a better idea of what was going on, until his eyes adjusted to the light. Rej blinked his single functioning eye to clear it of smoke. Someone moved towards him, a dark shape blocking out the light. Rej had the impression of a huge presence and the smell of fish and wine.

'You all right, combe-mate?'

He did recognise the voice and it was not Grimper and Rej wasn't all right. His eyes had finally adjusted to the smoke and the darkness and, as he looked into the small, calculating and malevolent eyes of Barna, Rej was suddenly overwhelmed by nausea and was violently, extensively and exhaustingly sick.

Chapter Twenty-two

Something had happened to Donna in the brief time since she had met Rej. She had stopped thinking like an oppidan. It was a new, braver person who left the Temple of the Sacred Dragon's Egg, someone who could no longer pretend that the Arkel and the Council of Ten were motivated by noble intentions. It chilled her to recognise that it was the Arkel who was her enemy. She wished she was able to share the new insight with Belafor and Gayla and those others who were themselves beginning to question the wisdom of their masters. Was there a way to put Belafor in touch with the rebels of the Liberty without risking his life or their security?

In her new spirit of recklessness she elected to take a further enormous risk. Away from the bell-ringing and prayer-intoning of the overseers it was more difficult to gauge the hour, particularly on such a dull, clouded day, but she estimated that it must be almost time for noon breakfast. She walked purposefully towards the refectory and waited unobserved by the outer wall. She heard the Redman's chant as they approached the refectory. Belafor was towards the back of the column of scribes being escorted to the hall, on account of his twisted leg. She murmured his name as he passed her and he dropped back behind the others to readjust his badly worn and slipping shoe.

'What are you doing?' he hissed. 'I heard overseer Jenta tell Martrin that you were not at your appointed task.'

'I'm not coming back, Belafor. I can't do this oppidan Humble Way any more. I can't believe in it now. If you want to get out too, make your way to the Liberty and tell whoever finds you that you want to speak to the Lady – they'll know who you mean. Tell her that you're a friend of mine.' It was hard for her to read his thoughts in his sombre expression.

'Arché keep you, Donna,' he said, before hurrying inside.

She had no idea if she had behaved well or foolishly. There was no one to obey now but her instincts, and they were untried and possibly flawed. But she had chosen her path.

It was good to walk the streets of Lunnzia, free at last from the mental and spiritual burden of trying to be a good oppidan. There were not in fact that many Watchmen and Redmen around – not enough to keep track of the every movement of all in Lunnzia, just enough to make everyone feared that they could.

Donna was not sure of the exact location of the Arkel's slave compound. She knew that the Arkel occupied the former Devarra Palace in the Golden Quarter, but that was all. The streets became busier as she left the University Quarter behind. There were many more Redmen around and they were very obvious in their finery. It was odd how the Sumptuary Laws did not include their warm garments of scarlet and gold. Surely a priest ought to provide an example rather than a burden he was himself unprepared to bear? She felt herself stiffen each time she saw one of them.

In addition to the Redmen there were many more slaves carrying baskets of vegetables and other goods covered in muslin – cheese perhaps, or fruit. Donna almost salivated at the thought, and when she passed a working bakehouse and the smell of newly-baked bread she felt light-headed, dizzy with desire. She almost stopped to try to beg a loaf. Why was there grain here when elsewhere oppidans struggled on war-grain bread, thick and harder than shoe leather? She felt her anger grow. She had not travelled these streets around her former home for a long time. The rigorous work schedule she and all the oppidans followed left little time for movement outside the narrow confines of workplace and barracks. She had not realised that the Golden Quarter remained such a haven of privilege. She smelled wood smoke more than once and the savoury smell of spiced meat. She found herself peering through the unshuttered window of a house well furnished with chairs, table and sideboard and saw a slave mending the quilted surcoat of a priest there. From this she surmised that those Redmen serving the temples of the Golden Quarter still lived in private dwellings with slaves and other possessions of their own; priests and Doctor Esteemeds were both exempt, then, from the obligation of communal living and shared deprivation

She wondered if Belafor and Gayla and the others of her work detail knew that and whether they would approve. She did not.

The buildings' exteriors were no finer here than in the University Quarter – apart, that is, from their peeling gold-leafed roofs – but the feel of the place was quite different, and Donna felt self-conscious and untidy in her drab oppidan's dress; that irritated her too. She had, until very recently, followed the Humble Way dutifully, if not enthusiastically – she should not feel out of place in the religious centre of the city. She quickened her step so that she marched in tune with her temper.

She was almost at the broad stained-glass gates of the outer courtyard of the former Devarra Palace when her eye was suddenly caught by the doorway of the building to her right. It had once been the city residence of some aristocrat probably swept away in the Revolution of the Ten. Its great door was double height, massive and rectilinear, in contrast to the graceful arches that characterised much of the city's architecture. Although this was notable in itself, it would not have been enough to arrest Donna's attention if it had not been for the carved stone lintel that dominated the doorway. It was painted and gilded and elaborately worked, but it was clearly the model for the hasty sketch that Immina had thrust into Rej's hand. When Donna saw it she experienced a jolt of recognition, a certainty that this place meant something to Immina, that this place was significant to her quest. She was not prone to such insights but she accepted this one; she knew this place was important like she knew her dream was real.

Donna glanced behind her. Four green-stained slaves were arguing over a spilled basket of vegetables and were gathering a small crowd of onlookers. No one was watching her. There would obviously be no entry through the great doors, but she remembered that every former grand mansion had several entrances – it was only a case of finding one which might admit her. She tidied her hair, smoothed her threadbare clothes and walked purposely around the building to a second square door of more modest proportions, though it too was surrounded by an elaborately carved and gilded lintel, this time of a scroll, bearing the defaced and now illegible coat of arms of the aristocrat house that had once owned it. To the right of the door was a gong niche – Donna had not seen one of those for a long time. She struck the gong with the stick attached to it by a tarnished silver chain and the sound reverberated through her bones. For some unaccountable reason the sound made her shiver and she was afraid that she might regret this boldness. It was a small concern compared with her overriding conviction that this place had something to do with Immina and with the Basilisk Contrivance. There was no logic to that belief, but belief kept her rooted to the spot.

She waited and tried to think of a plausible reason to be permitted entry to a building that could have been used as anything from a laundry to a court house in these post-revolutionary days. She regarded her ink stained fingers without inspiration. It was a long time before anyone answered the gong, but eventually narrow portion of the door opened; there was an inner door cut into the larger wooden one. An old man in an antique breastplate and a lethal-looking glaive appeared and eyed her speculatively.

'I am the scribe that was sent for,' she said quickly, hiding her stained hands in such a way that the gatekeeper noticed her inky fingers and nodded. Donna hid her relief – it was a courtesan's trick to pretend to hide that which you most wanted to be seen.

The gatekeeper indicated for her to enter the dim hallway. It smelled of stale urine and damp, and the fine plaster walls had been much defaced with revolutionary slogans.

'He'll be wanting you to take confessions, no doubt,' he said, grimly.

'I – I wasn't told,' said Donna quietly, conscious of a growing disquiet.

'They should have sent someone older,' the old man said, not unkindly. 'It's not a job for a young lady.'

Donna smiled thinly. 'I'm an oppidan – I go where I'm sent.'

The man grunted. 'I'm sure they should think a bit harder about who they send to the House of Melagiar. I should stand guard – sometimes the poor bastards get as far as the door. Follow the corridor – the Inquisitor is there – you'll hear where.'

Donna went very cold, remembering Immina's stump of a tongue and her strange desperation. By Arché's breath, had she been tortured here, in what was once her family's home? There seemed no alternative but to go where the gatekeeper had directed. She almost told him that she'd made a mistake and was perhaps needed next door instead. She was sure the old man would have let her go, but somehow the words wouldn't come.

There was a strange keening cry coming from the room at the end of the corridor. It sounded bestial, but Donna knew that it was not the sound of a beast. Her legs were drained of strength and all the virtue in her blood leeched away until she felt as pallid and enfeebled as if water flowed from her heart. It felt as though someone other than herself knocked on the dark wood door and feet that were not her own propelled her forward when two armoured men opened it.

The room was lit by many candles, a wealth of candles in Brandaccian decorative sconces around the elegant vaulted chamber. A fire blazed in a vast marble fireplace and a small, pale rag-doll of a figure was strapped to a heavy chair in front of the fire. The animal noises came from that throat, and that throat and pale, terrified eyes belonged to Immina. That was Donna's first shock. Donna gave an involuntary, feeble cry of horror and surprise when she saw the woman she had agreed to help in such a condition. Immina's clothes were torn and she was drenched in sweat so that both her skin and the sinuous dragon tattoo gleamed in the firelight. For a moment it looked as though a true dragon writhed on the poor woman's breast, but it was only a trick of the light and Immina's convulsive trembling. She strained against her bonds but the movement was instinctive because there was no reason left in the wild eyes. The room stank of rank fear and excrement and the sickly sweet aroma of bergensalve. Donna held the corner of the door for support.

'Someone sent for a scribe,' she said, as assertively as she could manage. Her instinct had been right; she had found Immina, but the discovery gave her no satisfaction. How could it? A black-robed man, who by the insignia embroidered on to his dark velvet cloak was the Inquisitor, turned slowly at her voice. He was not a large man, and his face was hawkish, cadaverous and slightly pink as if he had spent too long too close to the fire or as if he had had the green stain of his slave status painfully and painstakingly removed by the application of astringent creams and scrubs. The room seemed to darken and Donna struggled to remain conscious as she recognised the man as the slave, her almost friend, Capla.

He started when he saw her and sketched her a deep courtly bow.

'How ...?' Donna began, her voice little more than a whisper.

'Only those who have never known slavery wonder at what others will do to escape it.' His tone was brittle. 'Oh, don't wonder, I have every right to wear the Inquisitor's robes. I was Master of Secrets, as we call the Chief Inquisitor in my homeland. Indeed I was the Overmaster of Secrets to His Excellency Prince Javed of Lambrugio before the conquest. I had only to prove my usefulness at information-gathering, first to Melagiar and then to the Arkel, to regain something of my old status. I tried to warn you away from Melagiar, Oppidan Donna. I fear that my warnings did you no good.'

'I tried to meet you.' Donna's throat and mouth were suddenly too dry for the words to come easily; fear had sucked saliva from her mouth as it had sucked red, courage-bearing life-blood from her heart.

'I am afraid I had found information of value to the Arkel which involved me in absence from my usual duties. And of course the death of Melagiar left a vacancy for someone of my superior gifts. '

Donna felt a sudden rise of panic at the memory of the night Grimper had escorted her home and Capla had surprised her outside the barracks. Pray to the Creator that he had not seen Grimper. She knew her fear showed in her eyes and that he would read it there, professional that he was.

'I was able to let the Arkel know the hideout of some of the more successful outlaws of the Liberty.'

Donna made herself carry on breathing and reminded herself that, if all else had failed, her mother would have used the last exit. Donna would not cry. He was toying with her, it may not even be true. Her mother might be dead but she would not walk willingly into an Inquisitor's hands – and Grimper? Maybe there had been poison enough for Grimper too.

'Anyway, while you are here you may help me – no, you need not look so sick. You were a friend to me of sorts and I will not ask you to act violently, if it is not in your nature to enjoy it. I had not thought to ask for a scribe, but now that you are here you may note down some of my thoughts. You may find them interesting – you were interested in Immina, weren't you? She is an unusual case – an enigma. Of course, her foolish brother has botched the job of breaking her, and made it harder to work out what is going on in that head of hers. Cutting out her tongue – what an ill-conceived bit of melodramatic foolishness that was. Bring up a chair – the cold has made you pale. Have you materials with you or shall I send for some?'

Donna could not take in all that he said. She was too shocked to respond. She walked on thin ice over a lake of grief. If her composure cracked she would drown. She walked across the glass mosaic floor to the chair by the fire, next to Immina. The arms of Immina's chair were splintered and scratched, stained red with blood from her ruined fingers. Donna could not look at her face. She fought the rising of her gorge. Her face burned from the proximity of the fire and something else – fear, hate? She was too shocked to know. She sat down and waited, despairingly, for whatever would happen next.

Chapter Twenty-three

The smell of vomit scarcely improved the stench of the Liberty or Barna's temper.

'What the frakk?'

The woman hurried to his side and shone a lantern into Rej's face. He blinked in confusion.

'Don't make a fuss, Barna – there's water in the barrel. If your henchmen bludgeon friends about the head you can expect these consequences.' She sounded amused. Rej felt terrible. The woman gave him water, clean water to swill his mouth and drink. He accepted it cautiously, but found himself better for drinking it. Barna, to Rej's astonishment, began to clear away his mess.

'Can you stand?' The woman's voice was patient but cool. With her help he was able to stagger to the fire. She waited for him to settle himself before speaking again. 'So, you are Scrubber's protégé?'

Rej nodded, wincing at the sudden headache the movement caused him. 'Scrub is my friend. I came here to find her and her brother.'

He did not want to give too much away, but as far as he knew there was no antagonism between Barna and Scrub, though Scrub was certainly afraid of him and this woman must be a friend of Scrub's, judging from her previous comments.

'Grimper?' The woman looked surprised. Rej was very conscious of the looming bulk of Barna a few feet away, listening. He got the impression that a lot depended on what he was to say next.

'I promised a friend that I would find him.'

'Ah,' she said, 'you have a message for him?'

Rej licked dry lips. His mouth tasted sour and he was afraid that fear might make him sick again. He did not know who this woman was, and her association with Scrubber was no guarantee that she was to be trusted – Scrubber cultivated many people for her own ends to whom Rej would not show his back.

'Do you know where Grimper is?' he countered.

'This is the Low Lady Estelle – don't play games with her. It is she who gave you clothes and shelter when you broke the treaty and came Above.' Barna was angry and it was not good to anger Barna.

'I am Donna's mother,' the woman said calmly, ignoring Barna's outburst. 'Tell me, was your message from her?'

Rej was surprised, not least because he had no idea that Donna's mother was also a courtesan. He took more notice of her appearance. In the pink firelight she looked too young to be Donna's mother, though there was a marked family resemblance between them. She wore nothing to indicate her trade, for she was simply and warmly dressed in tunic, cloak and leggings – masculine clothing. She was much shorter than Donna, but her eyes were harder. She was looking at him quite coldly now, waiting.

'Yes, in part,' he said cautiously. 'She wanted you to know that the Arkel is making a weapon of war. I think it is designed to be used against High Verda eventually, but he is going to test it on the combers.' He explained as briefly as he could what they had discovered from Filefa.

Barna waited until Rej had run out of words before he spoke. Barna did not laugh or ridicule Rej, as he had expected. Instead he simply asked in a voice raw and taut with emotion, 'And where is she now? Where is Donna?'

'We agreed that I would warn the combers and Grimper. She went to find out more information from a slave she knew; she thought it all had something to do with a woman, Immina. She met her when she was working for the Doctor Esteemed Melagiar.'

Barna exploded in a tirade of inventive comber curses. The Low Lady Estelle did not move a muscle – her stillness was uncanny.

Rej did not think he had explained things very well and yet neither the Low Lady nor Barna asked him anything else for several seconds. Barna quietened down and merely glowered at Rej angrily, as though the Arkel's plot was Rej's own.

'What was the name of this slave?' the Low Lady asked at last, very quietly.

'I think it was Capel or something like that.'

'Capla?'

'Yes, that was it. He had helped her before.'

'Frakking Arché's arse!' Barna said and banged one fist into his open palm in a gesture of frustration. 'He's got her too!'

The Low Lady closed her eyes for a moment. She hardly seemed to breathe. Rej glanced at Barna for explanation but Barna gave him a hard, unfriendly stare.

'Capla offered his services to the Arkel,' Estelle said, flatly.

'Yes, isn't he the Arkel's slave?' It seemed to Rej as though he would have had little choice.

'He was also Lambrugio's best Inquisitor,' Barna snapped. 'Somehow he found out the whereabouts of the Low Lady and Grimper. He led the militia to the hide and they took Grimper prisoner. Fortunately the Low Lady was meeting me at the time and we saw them leave. Estelle recognised Capla at once. Did you not dine with him once in Lambrugio?' Barna addressed this last to Estelle.

'He was a business contact,' she said softly. 'He was a deal younger and plumper then. Anyway, by this action he was probably able to convince the Arkel that he could be trusted with a job that better utilised his skills. He was boasting about it to the Watch. I pray Grimper retains his pin.'

Rej was bemused by this last remark and it obviously showed on his face.

'Capla will torture Grimper – his poison pin would bring him a quick release. He is a double danger both as a resistance leader and as the head of the Devarra family – the last hereditary rulers of Lunnzia,' Barna explained shortly, his eyes on the still face of Estelle.

'What?' Rej could not disguise his surprise that Scrubber's brother and thus Scrubber herself was a frakking aristocrat.

'Well, where did you think the aristocrats went after the Revolution? In spite of the Arkel's best efforts he couldn't kill them all. Your mother was a Consolia, her best friends were Venetia Devarra and her twin Leopold – universally known as Scrubber and Grimper. Estelle hopes he has the poison pin with him which will allow him to kill himself before Capla extricates all the details of the resistance out of him.'

The Low Lady spoke sadly. 'Leopold is the bravest of men, but Capla uses both pain and poisons to destroy reason and restraint. He has no chance of keeping silent. Capla will unman him, and it will not be his fault. We spoke of the efficacy of certain draughts, long ago. He had knowledge of many poisons and philtres even I had not heard of at that time. Lambrugio was more advanced even than Lunnzia in the knowledge of such things. Better that Grimper chooses his own final exit.' Tears glistened in Estelle's eyes but her voice showed no trace of emotion. Tears ran down Barna's brutish face unchecked.

'Does Scrubber know?' Rej felt sick again at the thought of Scrubber in pain.

'She knows,' Barna sighed. 'She has not taken it well.'

'She's not gone back on the stenk?'

Barna acknowledged the fact with the slightest inclination of his head.

Rej felt his stomach churn. Scrubber was his only family – he could not bear for her to come to any harm. She was all he cared about – apart from Donna, of course. He did not know quite when that 'of course' had happened.

'Capla wouldn't hurt Donna, though – I think they were friends?' He said it quickly as an assertion to reassure himself, but it came out as more of a question. As he asked it he felt his fear and sense of foreboding grow.

Estelle shrugged. 'I don't know. If he tries to use Immina he will try to use Donna too.'

Rej felt his heart turn cold. 'What do you mean? You know something about Immina too?'

Barna and Estelle exchanged a glance.

'Tell me!' Rej forgot his fear of Barna in his concern for Donna.

'It may be nothing ...' Estelle began.

'Tell me!'

The Low Lady sighed and rested the lamp that she was holding on the ground. 'Long ago, in the Days of Decadence,' she began, as if telling some fable, 'when we were young, there was a group, a society led by the Lady Melagiar, Immina's mother. I knew of it – as I knew most of the people involved – through my work. It was called the "Basilisk's Breath". Actually, at the time, the priesthood of Arché was in decline; it was before the spiritual revival and the institution of the current Arkel. The Arkel – or plain Pavenos as he was then – was a young man then and, along with many others, practised a form of deep contemplation – they called it spiritual breathing. Some of them came to me for philtres which would help them lose themselves more deeply in this contemplation. I never knew exactly what happened, but I provided them with a number of different potions, many of which were stenk-based.

'The rumours started soon after. There was talk of spiritual possession by Arché, of members of the society being driven mad by visions, not just of Arché but of other things. Anyway, people said that Immina's mother was the source of this strangeness. She was a powerful woman, wilful as well as rich. One night when six of the group died suddenly and unaccountably in their sleep, Immina's mother was blamed. Pavenos denounced her, the Basilisk's Breath and their practices – the Lady Melagiar was executed for murder. That was what started Pavenos off – he went on to denounce all stimulants, aphrodisiacs, strong liquor and "herbs with the power to distort and confuse the senses of a man". It was the beginning of his rise to power – he joined the Council that overthrew the Devarras, and, when he had cemented his position, he imposed the Sumptuary Laws. In the beginning they only presented the consumption of "poisons", but by the end they outlawed all personal possessions.'

The Low Lady paused and Rej scowled. He did not see where this was going.

Barna took up the story. 'The Arkel's in trouble – the war is a disaster. He has lost all of his popular support – you have seen for yourself what Lunnzia has become. Unless he can win this war he won't survive the return of the army, and that's a comber's gamble. Some think that's why he keeps them away from the city, in the winter when no one fights. He may be desperate enough to use the power he so despised, the power that Immina's mother apparently had in such abundance: the power to conjure visions through her dreams. There have been rumours, and what you've said only confirms them. This Contrivance that was being developed may be connected with this power. Immina was, until recently, a very forceful young woman. I believe that she wanted to reinstate the society of the Basilisk's Breath just as much as her brother did. She had her own body tattooed. I did not think she would wish harm on others, though. She was wilful but never cruel, but anyone can be made to do anything – it is a question only of pain.'

Rej risked a look at Barna – the bleak expression on the man's hard, immobile face frightened him. 'You think Immina has the power to kill through her dreams?'

'Very good.' The Lady Estelle looked at him approvingly. 'I never got to the bottom of what happened when the Lady Melagiar was accused all those years ago, but some say the meeting room was full of monsters, that she somehow opened a gateway for them into this world and the six who were with her all died.'

Rej felt himself turn cold. Perhaps Donna was right. What if somehow through Immina and the power of Harfoot's Contrivance the Arkel brought the evil of the dark basilisk into the world?

'But why should Donna be of use to Capla?'

The Low Lady Estelle was still a moment, as if weighing the merits of sharing further information with him. She looked thoughtful.

'There is perhaps no reason for you not to know. Do you understand how, when you breed pigs or dogs or horses, the characteristics of the sire and dam often appear in their offspring?'

Rej nodded, even more uncertain of the direction of this conversation.

'I cannot have children. My mother, a famous courtesan, had seven, and lost four of them in childbirth. When I was born she was determined I would be spared that pain. She knew of poisons … anyway, my surviving brother was not so treated and he fathered a daughter on the Lady Melagiar. It would have been a scandal for them – my brother has most distinctive looks – so I pretended pregnancy and took the child from Milla, the Lady Melagiar, as soon as she was born. We told everyone her baby was stillborn.'

'Donna is Immina's sister.'

'– half-sister,' Estelle corrected softly.

'Then Melagiar was …?'

'Her half-brother – yes.'

Rej hesitated. 'Had he this power with dreams?'

'No, though I believe that he tried to produce them through ajeebamor.'

Donna's mother paused and Rej spoke again, a horrible suspicion forming in his mind. 'I think that I have shared dreams too. Does that mean …?'

The Low Lady gave the slightest shadow of a smile. 'I knew your mother and father well and, believe me, you are not related to my Donna in any way. You have come by that gift another way. Perhaps it is not the unique talent I had suspected, merely very rare.'

Rej's mind was still racing, trying to work out the implications of so much new information. 'But Capla doesn't know that Donna is Immina's sister and that she can dream like Immina, does he?'

'No, no one has known until now except Barna and Grimper and, if he is not already dead, you can see just how much we have much to fear from any of Grimper's revelations.'

'Why did you tell me?'

'I should have told her. I have deprived her of her heritage. Once the Council of Ten are gone she may wish to reclaim her birthright. The Melagiars were wealthy once. She has more to gain as the daughter of the Lady Melagiar than of the Low Lady Estelle. I was going to tell her. I arranged for her to work for Melagiar so she would at least meet her half-siblings before I told her, but last time I saw her … I couldn't. She always thought Grimper was her father.' Tears ran down Estelle's face but still she spoke calmly, even coldly. 'But I'm telling you now, because I want you to find Grimper and kill him before he betrays us. It is better that you understand at least one of the reasons why he must be silenced. Barna here says you have killed before. This time Grimper himself would wish it, and so would Scrubber if she were in her right mind. I would ask her to ask you, but it is better that you do not see her until she has recovered herself. It will not be too difficult. I myself will furnish you with poisons and Barna will return your knife, though we will keep the manuscript you had with you.'

Rej looked at her with horror. He did not know which of her statements was more painful to hear – that Barna believed him a killer, that Donna could be tortured, that Scrubber was an addict again or that he was expected to kill the man who'd guided him into Lunnzia scant days ago. He did not know what to say.

Chapter Twenty-four

The walls of the Melagiar Mansion no longer echoed to the sound of Immina's screaming – she had collapsed into unawareness. It was an inexpressable relief to Donna, although it meant that Capla was able to give her his full attention.

He offered her food and drink, and though she was hungry she refused both. Immina smelled pungently of many things – fear, sweat and faeces – but there was the musky base tone scent in her perspiration which suggested bergensalve. It had a spicy quality which made it hard to detect in highly flavoured food or in the warm mulled wine that Capla offered her.

'Why are you doing this?' she asked eventually, after he had offered her wine for the second time.

'You are my friend,' he said sharply, 'aren't you?'

She could not answer that, so she rephrased her question. 'I mean, why are you hurting Immina – what good can she do you? She can't even talk!' Donna tried to keep the contempt she felt for him out of her voice, but it was a struggle and her voice sounded strangulated to her ears. He did not seem to notice.

'Immina has certain latent abilities – her brother believed she could be bullied into using them. I think she will use them when they are all she has left.'

'What abilities?' Donna found his words so chilling it was hard to talk without trembling. Why hadn't she noticed that he was so callous, so cold?

'Immina can apparently send her soul to the place Between – the place between life and death, found only between sleep and waking. It is apparently full of the most unholy creatures as well as the most divine, though why all Immina ever sees is dragons I do not know.'

'You have seen the dragons?' said Donna in honest astonishment, but the minute the words left her mouth she wished them unsaid. Capla looked at her with a strange intensity.

'What dragons do you think I've seen?' he said softly.

'I don't know,' Donna asked lamely. 'I wondered how you knew she only sees dragons.'

'Did you really? Or have you, perhaps, dreamed of dragons soaring over Lunnzia?'

It was becoming uncomfortably hot by the fire. 'I don't remember my dreams,' Donna said as firmly and as calmly as she could.

'You see,' said Capla, taking her hand in his. She allowed it – his hand was cool like a physicker's, and dry. Her own was sweaty and hot. He was concentrating entirely on her, watching her every breath as he spoke.

'The Arkel wants Immina, with a bit of help from some ingenious device of the late Harfoot's devising, to seek the monsters of the phantasmagoric Between realm and cause their incarnated appearance here. I am not up to the metaphysical thinking myself.' He waved his hand dismissively, indicating somehow that he didn't believe a word of it. 'That is not my problem – my problem is that Immina is weak, too mad, thanks to her over-enthusiastic brother, for the task she must perform. I told you Melagiar was not to be trusted. Immina is not working out as well as the Arkel hoped. So you see how someone else with the same gift would be useful to me. Are you sure you have not dreamed of wheeling dragons high in the skies above Lunnzia?'

Donna kept her face as immobile as possible.

'If you were able to help me I am sure there are ways I may pay you back – good ways.' He looked at her very directly. 'You see, the Arkel has promised me my freedom if I help his man Garvell make the infernal contraption they have built function as its inventor intended. The person who helped me could come with me, away from this rat-infested sewer of a city. Lambrugio is beautiful. It is never cold. Fruit you will have never seen in Lunnzia in your lifetime grows in abundance from every bough of every tree in every tree-lined street in Lambrugio.' His eyes were shining and he sounded wildly, unrealistically idealistic. It was hard to believe that moments ago he had been the cause of Immina's inhuman screams.

He picked up Donna's hand and pressed it to his thin lips. His kiss was unexpectedly tender and wet. She had expected his mouth to be as dry as his hands; she forced herself not to recoil. She made herself smile and spoke carefully.

'I'm sure a person who could visit this realm

Between would be useful to you but, alas,' she shrugged dramatically to indicate that regrettably she was not that person. 'Tell me, Capla, can you not visit that place yourself?'

He smiled back at her, but the precise meaning of the smile was hard to read. Slowly he rolled up her sleeve. His touch was gentle. He traced the contours of her arm lightly with his forefinger. She hardly dared breathe. She had never been more afraid.

'Ajeebamor has many uses,' he said. 'Let's just say that if you can allow your soul to explore Between, I will know it. That is, if indeed it is your soul that travels – when we dream of dragons.' His smile was unwavering. 'Did you know that you have a beautiful neck? It is one of the first things I noticed about you.' He traced the curve of it up from her shoulder in a gesture that was part caress and part threat. He loosened the knot of hair at the nape of her neck and her dark hair tumbled to her shoulders. 'Come on,' he said brightly, 'this room stinks. There is another along the hall, which the Arkel has allowed to remain much as it was when the house was the Melagiar Mansion. I'm sure you and I can find much to talk about. I will order dinner for us. I eat well now – the Arkel himself sees to it – and I would like to feed you in return. You don't know how good that bread you gave me tasted, fresh from the ovens of the Liberty.'

So he had followed Grimper, had known where she had come from the night he had guided her back into the university barracks. Had she led him to find the secret she had most wanted to keep: the whereabouts of her mother and Grimper? Her mother was right about her – she had risked everything and everyone just because she had wanted to go home. She tried to keep her face bland, expressionless, as he played with her hair, weaving it between long fingers and kissing it.

'There are Raburgunian body slaves here,' he said, as if she might be pleased to know that. 'I asked for them. I was going to ask for you to be brought here anyway. I long to see you dressed as a woman of your beauty should be dressed. There are garments here that better befit you, left from the days of the old court. The Arkel has not always been so rigid with his Sumptuary Laws. He is a hypocrite too in his way, but why should we care? Don't you long to feel fine silk against your skin, to bathe away the stench of that barracks in fragrant oils? I would like to repay you for giving back my pride to me.' The look he gave her made her shiver with revulsion. 'You are as lovely as any Lambrugian lady. Indulge me, and let me dress you as you deserve.'

He kissed her lightly on the top of her head and helped her to her feet. Terror made Donna unsteady, clumsy. Armed servants she had not known were present took her firmly by the arms and half guided, half supported her through the door and up a sweeping marble staircase to a set of rooms on the first floor. It was only then that she realised that he had not asked her why she was there. Did he know already? She was trembling so much by the time they helped her into the elegant bedchamber that she could do little but acquiesce to being undressed, as if she was in her mother's house in the Golden Quarter, before the imposition of the Sumptuary Laws. Slaves filled the huge copper tub in front of another roaring fire with boiling water and oils from crystal vials. She had no qualm about being naked before slaves, Raburgunian or otherwise – in her childhood, servants had always assisted herself and her mother with bathing and dressing. In spite of everything, she could not deny the pure sensuous pleasure of bathing – the feel of the warm water against her skin and the scent of attar of damask rose. It was a heady scent, insinuating itself into her very pores until all trace of the filth of her everyday life was gone. It was the scent of dreams. She did not think in those moments; she did not think about Immina or her mother or the threat posed by Capla. She separated her mind from her body as her mother had taught her and as she so rarely managed.

She was flying again, but her wings ached and she was afraid. Storm clouds darkened the bright sky, and …

'My Lady.' The slave approached her with a towel and Donna struggled dreamily from the bath. The scent of the oils was suddenly overpoweringly strong. Her limbs felt heavy and it was hard to rouse herself to object as the slaves dressed her in a deep rose-coloured velvet gown, lacing her bodice so tightly that breathing was difficult. The neckline of the gold embroidered bodice plunged deeply, almost to her nipples, and as she breathed, in the shallow panting breaths that the dress necessitated, she was peripherally aware of her breasts' exposure. She felt that she should object, especially when a slave sprayed them with some pungent oil that made them glisten in the candlelight. The same servant also doused her with more of the same heavy perfume that had scented her bath. The woman turned her own head away as she did so and held a rag to her nose, which was strange, because although the perfume was powerful, it was not actually unpleasant. Donna's head felt thick and her thoughts slow and confused. Again she felt that odd disassociation from her body as the slaves dressed her hair in an elaborate high bun, held in place by a net of tiny, pink seed pearls. The two women who had dressed her had to half carry her down the stairs; her legs were weak and she seemed to have forgotten how to walk. They spoke to her, but she found it hard to understand what they were saying. Two militia men escorted her to the room where Capla waited. They held her firmly by the arms and one encircled her waist with a brawny arm. Her feet did not touch the floor, which was fine, because the slippers she had been given were also embroidered with pearls and she would not have wanted to soil them.

The table was laid with the most beautiful vessels of Lunnzian glass and silver which split the candlelight into a thousand sparkling diamonds. The room was warm and the touch of Capla's hand on her arm as he guided her to a place near the fire was pleasantly cool. He handed her a goblet of violet liquid. The goblet was formed of dancing prisms of light and within it the violet liquid glistened like an enormous gem. She sipped the drink slowly and allowed herself to sink into the chair. The silky fabric of the chair felt smooth against the soft, clean skin of her back. Capla touched her carelessly on the shoulder.

'You look as I have always imagined you might look,' he said in a voice that came from a long way away, and Donna giggled. It was clever of him to speak as if he was talking from the bottom of a deep pit. She wondered how he managed it.

He began to stroke her bare shoulder. He held a goblet of the violet liquid in his other hand. It was a beautiful rich colour, as if lit from within. She took another deep draught from her own goblet and a slave filled it again to the brim. Molten fire burned her throat as she drank it and with each sip her body seemed to melt further into the chair. Capla said something and brushed his mouth across her hand, the barest touch. It was hard to remember why she did not want him to do that, though she knew that she had not wanted it – once. She took another long sip of her drink and her spine seemed to liquefy. She closed her eyes – her eyelids were too heavy to do otherwise – and the forms and colours in the room were melding together, shifting like reflections in water, fragmenting and reforming in the gently lapping motion of undulating waves. Everything was dissolving; she was dissolving. It was too much trouble to remember why this was wrong. Everything was fluid; even the chair, moulding softly around her, seemed to embrace her in a silken flow. She was drowning in it, disappearing. Her limbs were boneless, useless. She tried to sit up and could not. This was wrong. She did not like it. She fought against it, but knew with a sudden moment of clarity that it was too late. Capla's lips were on hers. She did not want them there, but her power to do anything had all but ebbed away.

Chapter Twenty-five

Rej checked that his knife was safely secured and for the sixteenth time made sure that the small metal cap remained tightly fixed to the poison pin on the inside of his tunic. According to the Low Lady Estelle, the poison that stained the pin's point yellow-green was fatal within the slow count of six. The thought made him sweat, had made him sweat since the moment she had taken it reverently from inside the bodice of her own tunic.

Barna led him through the crumbling wharves of the Liberty to another hidden combers' entrance. Rej still ached from his beating and one eye was still completely closed. Luck, his vicious Lady, seemed intent on making him pay.

It was darker than his imagination Below and, although he was a comber born and raised, returning to that total darkness was the hardest thing he had ever done. He was instinctively afraid of the absolute blackness, the stale air and the rat-foul stench that made him gag. He was in a part of the underground world that he had not known existed, a part which was accessible only from Above. He followed Barna's bulk cautiously, still not entirely certain that Barna would not kill him from the debts that remained unpaid on his comber's slate. Barna had not mentioned them, nor the frantic chase that had nearly cost Rej his life scant days ago. It was too frakking strange.

Barna had, somehow, learned that Capla was operating out of the old Melagiar residence in the Golden Quarter. It was a kind of irony, though whether deliberate or not, no one seemed to know. Rej knew the location of the Golden Quarter from the vantage point of the West Tower of the university, the Zebra tower; but he did not know how to get there by this route. There were several tunnels, all apparently as narrow as a grave, all of roughly hewn rock, seeping damply with moisture – the rocks' own sweat.

They were underground but not in the combes – not what Rej had known as the combes, anyway. This part of the sprawling city was not built over the ancient catacombs but upon solid rock that had been laboriously excavated to make these lightless tunnels, dark and narrow as ghost tunnels. Barna did not waste words, for to do so was to waste air, but he grunted an explanation before they began. The strength of the combers depended on being able to attack the Abovers at any point at any time. Those buildings not above the combes were less vulnerable to comber infiltration so the combers had built tunnels under each of the major buildings in Lunnzia to remedy the situation – a flaw at the heart of every citadel. The Melagiar Mansion still had such a tunnel, or so Barna believed, and though it had never been used by combers it was probably still intact. This did not reassure Rej; probably intact might also mean possibly caved in, blocked or rerouted to a cage trap for all anyone knew, but he wanted to help Donna. If Donna too was in Capla's hands within the Melagiar Mansion, then that was where Rej needed to be. Something wholly unexpected had placed Donna at the centre of his thoughts, some shift in his mental landscape that had occurred in the few days that he had known her.

There was no sound in the tunnel beyond Barna's grunting, wheezing breath and Rej's own too-rapid breathing. They crawled on, each aware of each minute change in the breathing of the other. It was a timeless agony of laboured movement, unmeasured by external events. Although the Low Lady had given them knee and elbow padding, Rej crawled on old bruises and the soft, tender skin that was only just beginning to heal from previous lacerations. It hurt to move – more than it had before. He no longer thought of dragons to keep him sane, only of Donna and of Immina. Could Capla turn cool, controlled Donna into something as wild and as mad as Immina had been?

Who knows for how long they had crawled when Barna spoke for the first time.

'It's above us now.' He panted a little, struggling for breath. Crawling was not an easy movement for a man of his bulk. Rej was young and light and yet the unnatural position placed great strain on his shoulders and arms and on his neck, which he had to keep lowered for fear of hitting his head on the tunnel roof. It must have been very much worse for Barna.

'How can you tell?' Rej asked, unconvinced. It seemed to him that they passed through an undifferentiated, unmarked blackness.

'There's a marking on the ground and a trap door above.'

'Do we know what it opens into?' Rej said, his fear at the thought of the next stage of his task crystals of ice through his blood. He kept his voice calm, though his breathing was loud and ragged and echoed around the tunnel, which was comparatively spacious at this point. He did not like Barna knowing of his fear, but there was no way round it.

In the darkness Rej felt Barna grope for his shoulder and touch his face with callused hands.

'Scrubber rates you, boy. Don't you frakking let her down. A man like Grimper … ' Barna's voice faltered, revealing more emotion than Rej would have expected – only part of it was suppressed violence. The darkness revealed too much; it was difficult to lie when tone of voice and pace of breath gave so much away. 'Grimper has held us together all these long years – Abovers who wanted change and combers who wanted out. Give him a quick death, a clean death. Give him his dignity.'

The blind shovel of a hand sought his shoulder again, found it and clapped it firmly. 'Light be with you. Be lucky!'

There was an awkward moment where Barna squeezed past Rej to return the way he'd come. 'If you come back this way, take the left fork at the first junction and the second after,' he said, though it was clear from his tone in the honest darkness that he did not expect Rej to make the return journey.

For the first time Rej wished that he'd asked for a poison pin for himself – but if there had been more than one would the Lady Estelle have given him her own? His heart was beating too quickly, the blood was loud in his ears. He waited until Barna was out of earshot, counting slowly to one hundred, trying to steady himself, but continually losing track of how far he'd gone. He did not think that he could delay any longer and, feeling his way in the still all-encompassing dark, he used his knife to score along the edge of the door above his head – cleaning it of nameless accumulated gunk by wiping it clean on his tunic. When he could feel the edge of the trapdoor with his fingertips he found what was probably the mid-point and, squatting down beneath it on his haunches, heaved. The door moved forward easily, landing on hard stone with a clang of steel that should have sent a warning to anyone who might have been listening that something was going on. Rej blinked in the sudden daylight streaming from an unseen window and, carrying his knife between his teeth, lifted himself into the light.

He was in the corner of a large, high-ceilinged room. An elaborate chandelier of fine Lunnzian glass and multifaceted crystal hung over a polished table set as if for a meal. The remains of chicken sitting in congealed fat seemed the most appetising thing Rej had ever seen. No one arrived to check on the sound, so Rej carefully replaced the trap door. To all appearances it was of the same fishbone pattern of black and white tiles as the rest of the floor. He walked on it carefully, grateful that his poor Lunnzian shoes were too soft to make a sound. As he moved towards the closed hardwood door he noticed with a shock that he was not alone. Sprawled in front of the dying embers of an open fire lay two bodies – a man and a woman, so still that at first he feared that they were dead. He could not see the woman's face, but a thick curtain of dark glossy hair flowed over the emaciated chest of the man beside her. The man's mouth and eyes were slightly open and his skin had a strange waxy cast, corpse-like, though he still breathed shallowly. Rej tiptoed past and was jolted half out of his skin when the woman groaned and moved. She raised one bare arm and brushed her abundant hair from her face, rolling slightly towards Rej himself to reveal her features, lost in the grip of heavy sleep. Her face was very pale and her lips unnaturally red, but there was no mistaking Donna's fine beauty. Rej felt sick, dizzy, shocked. He forgot the chicken and his danger and stumbled towards the door.

Why should she not lie with anyone she chose? She was of an age and her mother was, after all, a courtesan. Attitudes were different Above. She was not his – they had made no agreement, so why did the sight of her next to a man plunge him suddenly into a kind of inner darkness? She did not need rescuing – that, at least, was certain.

Rej tried not to stare at the man, tried to resist the urge to stab him where he lay. He forced himself not to falter, for to falter, to hesitate in this alien world of Above, would be disastrous – he had to keep going to do whatever the frakk he had agreed to do, for Light's sake. He could not quite understand what these two people were doing together, here, at the heart of what was supposed to be the torture chamber of Lunnzia. Where were guards, or had Barna made a mistake and was he somewhere else entirely? He wished he were somewhere else entirely, wished he'd never seen Donna. For the briefest of instants he thought of the poison pin and of the stories his mother had told him, romantic tales of men unmanned by love. That was not what happened in his world. In his world the hero squared his shoulders and did whatever had to be done – in this case a mercy killing.

He pressed his ear to the door, trying not to look at the couple, frightened that Donna might wake and that he would have to face her. He concentrated more completely on trying to hear through the door. He could make out nothing, but then the door was very solid, formed of thick planks of dense hardwood; it was possible that a substantial militia force could be waiting outside and he would not know. He did not care; he had to get out of the room and away from Donna.

He opened the door. An old man in the livery of the militia half dozed in his chair; another leaning against the wall for support rubbed tired eyes.

'Where d'you come from?' he said, reaching at once for his fauchard.

'I was bringing drink for the master,' Rej replied shakily, surmising that they defended the unknown male in the room rather than Donna.

'I didn't see you go in.'

'I'm not sure you were looking my way,' said Rej, wishing to suggest that his interrogator had been asleep without actually saying so.

'What's going on in there?' the guard asked, and Rej thought that he seemed afraid. 'What's the Inquisitor Capla up to now?'

Rej felt even sicker. The man beside Donna was the torturer – the man who would destroy Grimper, if he had not done so already. Worse than that, Rej had been blessed by Lady Luck herself, been given an opportunity to kill Capla as he lay, and he had not taken it. He didn't respond to the guardsman's next remark, indeed didn't hear it; he was still trying to grasp what Donna had done. Had she known what Capla was? He was surprised by the sudden proximity of the guardsman breathing the pungent smell of raw onion and ale into his face.

'I don't recognise you. I've not been napping and I know you didn't get past me. Who did you say was your boss? You're no slave – for all your bruises. Where's your mark?'

Rej couldn't think of any kind of answer. He knew nothing of the hierarchy of the place. He opened his mouth. 'I'm new here. I was cleaning when Capla and a lady came in and then I was afraid to make myself known.' He spoke rapidly, in a cowed, frightened voice. It did not take much acting on his part. He was shaking anyway with the shock of what he'd just seen.

The guardsman's eyes gleamed. 'It's not right. If Capla gets to hear of it he'll have your eyes out of your head. He'll have mine too for letting you in.' That thought seemed to give him pause. 'Get away with you back to your master.' He spoke tersely and Rej saw the flicker of fear in his eyes. 'Don't tell no one where you've been, or I'll kill you myself.'

Rej nodded gratefully and scuttled away down the corridor with his head bowed, like a broken man, a slave, or, worse, a man who has just discovered someone he loves in the arms of an enemy.

Chapter Twenty-six

Donna struggled to escape from the dream; it clung stickily to her thoughts like the foul-smelling glue she had used in her work tour with the cobbler. She had been with someone in her dreams, some dark basilisk figure. They had flown together, wrapped around one another like lovers, or like predator and prey. Her mouth was dry and tasted of something cloyingly sweet, and her whole body ached. Her limbs felt weighted down with lethargy, her eyelids were sealed with something worse than the aftermath of sleep. She tried to move and someone stirred beside her. Her hand touched the slickness of somebody else's sweated flesh, she sensed the rise and fall of another's breath. She opened one eye and saw – Capla.

It took moments for her to form some mental image of what had happened. Her skin crawled, as logic and reason reconstructed the fragments of remembered sensation into some coherent picture of events. She had not suspected the fragrant poison in her bath, absorbed through the skin, inhaled in a perfumed cloud: bergensalve – dulling the mind and increasing the susceptibility to ajeebamor. How could she have been so foolish? Her mother would die of shame that she should have allowed such a thing to happen. Donna could identify the fifty major poisons before she was ten; how could she not have noticed bergensalve?

She recoiled from the still sleeping Capla; he had touched her, they had shared a dragon dream. She tried to extricate herself from her too intimate proximity to the Inquisitor. He did not stir. Perhaps her mother's training had encouraged a quicker recovery time from the effects of poison, perhaps Capla had consumed more ajeebamor than she had, but he lay there in a position of complete vulnerability. She would have liked to have placed something over his face to suffocate him, a foot on his wind pipe to murder him – her mother would have done that. His smell was on her and his dream image still flew in recent memory. Self-disgust made her weak and it took some effort to stand. Ajeebamor had liquefied her bones; its after-effects froze them so she felt stiff and fragile as shards of ice. Perhaps she could kill Capla with a knife. Wincing with the pain in her brittle joints, she stepped carefully across the cold stone floor to the table and the knives that still lay there. She felt a sudden piercing pain in her back. Each step sent a jolt of fire through her spine. There must have been other substances in the ajeebamor to leave her quite this debilitated. It was hard to see; her peripheral vision blurred out of focus.

Someone was standing next to her in the livery of a soldier. She did not recognise him. He smiled at her and pulled a red-tipped dart from her back. She felt him rip it out and realised at the same moment that she was in serious trouble. Her extremities were rapidly becoming numb and she could expect to lose awareness very soon.

The militia man helped Capla to his feet. She heard Capla say, 'Put her with Immina – she has her gift.' Then everything stopped.

Donna woke later but how much later she did not know. She had no sense of the passage of time. She was nowhere she recognised. She regained awareness slowly. She was very cold. She could not feel her feet or her hands and cold air made her face parchment-stiff. She was lying down on something in darkness. She sensed the presence of someone but, as she could see nothing, she had to listen hard for breathing.

A long time later someone came with a candle and Donna saw that she was in some cave or dungeon of red rock and that Immina lay beside her. Perhaps she breathed still. It was hard to tell; she looked dead. The walls and roof of their cell glistened damply.

The someone with a candle spoke.

'Can you walk?'

Donna tried to get up but her body seemed paralysed, impervious to her will's commands. She tried to speak and, as nothing happened, for one terrible, heart-stopping instant she thought that her tongue might have gone as Immina's had. But, no, she could move her tongue, though it felt leaden and swollen and no words could form.

The man shone the candle in her eyes. She tried not to look desperate.

'Still frozen, eh?' He kicked her hard in the

abdomen and, though she felt the pain of the blow, which winded her, she could neither scream nor move. It seemed too long before she breathed again. Her eyes teared and she hoped he did not notice. The man laughed and might have done it again, but for the arrival of a second person with a green glass lantern.

'We could do anything we liked with them, you know,' the first man said.

'We could,' agreed the second, 'but how long do you reckon you'd last once he found out?'

'How'd he find out?'

'Bruises; and they'll talk, these girls – well, the one with a tongue will. He makes everybody talk.'

'No, these aren't talkers, these are the dreamers. These are for the Contrivance.'

Donna would have held her breath had she had enough control. She strained to listen.

'Are you sure? He's doing the talkers today. We've had to dump one corpse already – another little present for the combers.'

'No,' the first man said decisively, 'this one is for the device. I'm sure he'd never find out if we were to have some fun with her.' The smell of his breath in her nose was sickening and Donna wondered if she was meant to die of fear – to prove that Melagiar was right. But she did not die.

The first man spat into her face. 'I'll take this one – you bring Stumpy!' he said, indicating the prostrate Immina with a nod of his head. He hoisted Donna over his shoulders, carrying her like a sack of meal into another room.

The roof of the cave or dungeon was not high and

Donna felt the rough surface of the stone graze her back; she could not shout a complaint, then or when he scraped her arm against the side of the roughly hewn door and bashed her head as he dumped her inconsiderately in an awkward position against another equally hard wall in another dimly lit chamber. Feeling was beginning to return to her hands, her fingertips tingled minutely. She was able to move her neck a fraction and then she saw it: the thing that had to be the Basilisk Contrivance.

Its form made no sense to her. It was like nothing she had ever seen before – an object of polished wood, silver and Lunnzian glass. It was about the size of a drover's cart. There were several pallets with leather restraints arranged concentrically around a huge glass disc the diameter of the largest pan lid in the barracks kitchen. It may have been of silver – it reflected the flickering light from the oil lanterns with a moon-pure whiteness. There were also strangely shaped vessels of blown glass connected to one another by a brass-hinged wooden armature that linked the pallets to the disc. It was set at regular intervals by lumps of crystal cut in a rudimentary way so they all bore the same number of facets. It was not at all clear to her how this machine could bring any creature from anywhere. She did not know what she had expected, but it was not this peculiar construction.

Immina was dumped by her side. Donna did not like the loose way her head snapped back and hit the cave wall. She wanted to object, but her tongue still seemed too large for her mouth. There was a scuffle and the two guardsmen suddenly organised themselves into something approaching a military bearing as three men entered the room. Donna recognised two of them. One was the Arkel himself, the other Capla. The third was a man she had not seen before. It was this man who spoke first.

'With the unfortunate loss of the notes of the Doctor Esteemed Melagiar, it has been, of course, more difficult to gauge the settings.'

'What settings?' said Capla. 'Doctor Esteemed Garvell, I can see nothing worthy of adjustment but the tightness of the straps of the harness!' He chuckled but his levity was rewarded only with silence. After a significant pause, during which Donna observed Capla colour slightly, the Arkel spoke.

'Inquisitor, I have no doubt but that the power of the beasts of the region between sleep and waking can kill. I saw it myself many years ago. If you would be so good as to concentrate your not inconsiderable talents on persuading these young women to do as we wish and deliver the basilisk to our will, you will have done all that I require of you.' His voice was crisp and Capla, so lately this man's slave, seemed to cringe, retreating back into himself.

Garvell looked pleased. 'There are in fact a number of adjustments that can be made to the angle of the lens, the orientation of the crystals and the distance between them and the lens.' He demonstrated as he spoke. 'The crystals create a space in which the power of the dreamer is multiplied so that the phantasms of Between will be drawn here as if by the power of the lodestone. The direction in which they will be obliged to become manifest can be altered by the angle of the lens.'

It still made little sense to Donna. Her experience with Capla had clarified one thing at least. She became the dragon of her dreams. She *was* the dragon. There was nothing else to be brought from the place Between – just herself and the other dreamers. It was clear that she was supposed to be used in some way as an adjunct to the Contrivance to bring about the manifestation of the creatures from Between, but she could not see how that could be. She was afraid but too bemused to panic. She prayed to God behind Arché, the indescribable and all-knowing, that it would not hurt beyond bearing, that she would not be used to harm Rej, her mother, Grimper, or even the others on her work detail. Then someone else entered the room and, had Donna had the power of free movement she would have gasped, because the someone was an elderly militia man carrying her mother's poison chest.

Chapter Twenty-seven

There was nowhere to hide in the frakking mausoleum of a mansion. Rej realised that the moment he left the guards behind. The building was of vast proportions – its high mosaic ceilings and wide corridors opening on to a series of huge doors made him feel exposed and vulnerable. Light streamed in through a glass cupola above. It was a vista with few shadows and he feared the return of the space queasy. He did not know where to go, and though inside the building, seemed no nearer fulfilling his mission than had he stayed safe in the frakking tomb of a tunnel underground. Were there dungeons here? If so how would he find them? His problem was solved by his much-maligned Lady Luck, disguised as an ill-tempered bald-headed servant struggling under the weight of a large sack.

'You, lad, take this to the Holding Room.'

Rej did his best to look both obliging and moon-witted, an act he had largely perfected since he'd come Above. He slackened his jaw and tried to seem unfocused.

'Oh! Don't tell me you're the only man in the place who doesn't know the Holding Room. It's where His Inquisitorship softens them up first. You need to take these to the guard on that door over there.' He pointed down the endless corridor. 'I want nothing to do with this.' He indicated the sack with a strange expression of disgust and thrust his burden into Rej's hands.

It was heavy and smelled foully of decay, but Rej did not refuse it. He dared not believe that his Lady could favour him so generously after his failure to deal with Capla, when she'd brought him such an opportunity. An old comber expression came to mind: 'Never question Luck, she is fickle and follows no whim but her own.' He bowed his head meekly and walked off in the direction he had been sent.

The door the bald man had indicated was heavily guarded by armed militia. There were more armed men in this mansion than Rej had seen in the whole of Lunnzia. Those on duty were not particularly attentive, but he felt uncomfortable under their uninterested gaze. His height made him conspicuous and he unconsciously stooped to disguise it. There were four men at the door, not young men, but well-armed men. In the combes, where good balance and nerve often counted for more than strength in a fight, he might have stood a slender chance against such odds – here he was at their mercy.

He raised the sack for their inspection. It was stained at the bottom, like the meat bags they used in the combes.

'What's in the sack?'

Rej shrugged.

'I don't think he knows,' said another, mockingly incredulous, and Rej knew that they were going to make him find out. He steeled himself for something very unpleasant.

'Open it up, lad, and see what he's brought us today.'

The smell had warned him already, of course, but he still had to fight back nausea and reflexive disgust when his hand touched the severed head of one of Capla's victims.

He found the hair after a moment and tried not to think about what he was touching. He yanked it out of the bag, keeping his own face impassive.

He didn't say anything and the soldiers themselves were quieter than Rej had expected. Instead of the coarse humour at his expense that he'd anticipated, there was a kind of shocked stillness.

'Isn't that the apothecary from Lion Street in the old Blue Quarter?' said one.

'Word was he was accused of dealing dirty with Below,' another said quietly.

'Whoever he was, he gave in easy – he's still got his eyes and ears,' said the larger of them heavily, without irony. It did not seem that he found it any easier to accept than Rej. Rej did not want to meet his eye.

'He – that Capla – tries to bring someone in that the prisoner knows. It's usually a wife or something,' the man continued in a low, subdued voice. He glanced at his companions.

'I can't do it today. I've been on duty here six straight days and I'm done with it. Anyone else feel like rubbing this poor bastard's nose in it?'

Nobody answered. At last one of the men said, 'I think this one's the Devarra heir.'

'So anyone feel like some old aristo-baiting?'

The soldiers – middle-aged men all of them – looked away from the head still hanging by its greying hair in Rej's hand.

Rej glanced down at the men's leader. He was shorter than Rej by half a head, his eyes were bleak, harrowed.

'Put it back in the sack.'

Rej dropped the severed head back into the bag. It was not something he could do gently.

'You do the honours, lad – show the prisoner the head. There's a spike …' The soldier swallowed hard. 'There's a bastard spike you can stick it on. Make sure the prisoner sees it and then you can come back out. Don't worry, they don't usually attack – they're too shocked. If he gives you trouble, yell.'

The soldier opened the elegant double door that must once have led to some grand salon. Rej tensed himself against what he would find.

The room was huge. Cold sunshine from two large arched windows crudely protected by barbed bars flooded the room. In the stark light the repeated pattern of the black and white floor tiles and the pale cream plaster of the walls served to emphasise the frightening sense of space. It made Rej want to cower in the corner.

A solitary figure sat upright on the only chair in the room. By some extraordinary gift of Luck, his Lady, it was Grimper. His face was bloodied and his left eye swollen and bruised the colour of a dark plum, but he met him with a clear eye and nodded at Rej, familiarly.

'What have you brought me, boy?' he said softly. If

he was afraid, Grimper did not let it show; he seemed calm. Rej did not know whether Grimper recognised him or not; he felt awkward. It was one thing to agree to kill someone – it was another thing to do it. He did not know how long the soldiers would give him alone with the prisoner.

The spike the soldier spoke of already bore a trophy, a ruined face, unrecognisable as anything human. Grimper indicated it with a nod of his own head. 'I knew him once, never liked him. Now, who else have you got for me to contemplate?'

Under the powerful eye of Scrubber's brother Rej showed his trophy. It was no easier to plunge his hand into the sack a second time, knowing what his fingers would find. Grimper's expression did not change but something in his posture altered subtly, and Rej knew that he was relieved – it wasn't Scrubber or Donna and it wasn't the Low Lady Estelle.

'He was a friend, but he hadn't much to say to harm us,' Grimper said, as if that somehow made it all right. 'There is no flame here, my friend,' Grimper said conversationally to the severed head, and Rej briefly wondered if Grimper were as sane as he had at first appeared, 'but let my hot fury, my passionate desire for vengeance stand for the burning flame: *May the breath of Arché take you back through the breath of death to life in the place from which all breath comes.*' Rej had not known that the Abovers used the same ancient words for their own dead.

Time was passing; he expected the door to open at any moment. 'I have brought you another gift from the Low Lady,' Rej said urgently. He dropped the head irreverently back into the bag – he could not face removing the existing occupant from the spike – and, taking great care not to prick himself, took the pin from inside his tunic. Grimper was only a stride away. With fingers that shook far too much he removed the protective cap on the pin's end.

'It is her own pin,' Rej said. Grimper's smile was beatific. He raised his chin to better expose the vulnerable place at his neck which was the best site from which to administer the poison.

It was hard even so to plunge the pin into Grimper's neck. It hardly bled at all, though Rej felt Grimper wince involuntarily. He looked Grimper in the eye and held his own hand on Grimper's broad shoulder in what he hoped was a gesture of comfort for that long count of six. He waited for Grimper's next breath, hardly breathing himself, until Grimper's next breath did not come. The man slumped dead and Rej could not move for a moment. He had killed a man and yet he felt blessed by Grimper's silent gratitude.

'Light the flame of my vengeance,' he whispered. And then, because Grimper had cared enough to repeat the ancient words himself, he murmured: '*May the breath of Arché take you back through the breath of death, to life in the place from which all breath comes.*' He took the pin back and hid it at the bottom of the sack. The puncture mark it left in Grimper's neck was explanation enough for his timely death. Rej still could not bring himself to touch the decaying head on the spike and so left the bag on the floor where he had thrown it.

The guardsman let him out, without comment and

without checking the prisoner. Rej believed he'd told the truth: he'd had enough. He did not want to watch another man's pain any more. The rest was easy. He could not return the way he'd come – could not walk past Donna. He walked out past the Watch, claiming to be on an errand for the master.

'Need some air, do you, lad?' the duty Watchman said, perhaps noticing Rej's face. He felt as though he'd aged fifty years since he'd entered the Melagiar Mansion, and that surely must be visible to all – maybe it was. 'I was like you when I first started here – sick to my stomach most days. But it gets easier – you've got to think of it as a job, that's all – a duty and a job. Don't be long – they don't like us lot outside. They can smell it on us – all that pain.'

Rej nodded at him blindly and forced himself not to run. The sunshine seemed cleaner outside. As soon as the small inner door of the Mansion closed behind him he ran, careless of who saw him, reckless of pursuit, back to the dockside. He was relieved to have done his duty by Grimper, but he ran from the memory of Donna and from the death of a hope he'd not known he'd harboured.

Chapter Twenty-eight

In the unknown somewhere to which Donna had been brought, Capla looked at the Low Lady Estelle's poison chest and smiled.

'Yes, dear one, we have your mother – didn't I mention that? Perhaps not – we didn't talk much last night, did we?'

Under the Arkel's watchful eyes Capla touched Donna gently, stroking her face as tenderly as a mother might her child. Donna's skin crawled, but she was still held a paralysed captive by the freezing potion in her blood.

'You think this one is stronger than Immina?' The Arkel's precise voice seemed to resonate with suppressed excitement.

'Immina is strong, but her brother so abused her that she has found refuge in a most unhelpful intermittent madness. I believe that Melagiar thought he could encourage her cooperation through torture – I have a different theory and, moreover, my Lady, Oppidan Donna, is a much more accommodating person.' Capla leered at Donna and stroked her hair proprietarily. 'She will help us release the basilisk – won't you, my dragon queen?'

Donna, of course, could not speak, but she did not think the Arkel knew that. What had they done to her mother? Surely she would have used the last exit? Her mother would not have allowed herself to be taken alive. She must not think of her mother's suffering; her mother would not have allowed that suffering to happen. If the Low Lady Estelle had been captured she would be dead. Donna's eyes filled with tears. She blinked them back – she had that much control. The Low Lady Estelle would not expect her daughter to crumble; she would not expect her daughter to be accommodating. Donna had to believe that the Arkel could not harm her mother; she had to believe that they had no hold over her, beyond the administering of pain or pleasure. She did not quite remember now what had happened with Capla, only that her will had been subverted. She had been mistaken about him in the first place and foolish to trust him in the second; those were errors of judgement she would not make again. Inside the immovable shell of her frozen body she tried to stiffen her resolve, tried not to make herself feel humiliated and sullied by her misjudging of him, tried to make herself the heir to a Poison Lady instead of the weak, foolish girl who had allowed herself to be used as an Inquisitor's doxy. She did not know what they were going to do to her, but she had to keep fear at bay.

The Arkel looked at Donna curiously. Donna had not looked at him properly before. He was far from being the monster she had expected. Instead, he was conventionally handsome with the same piercing blue eyes as her mother. No, she could not bear to think about her mother if she were to survive this. Then, she finally understood. Perhaps she would not survive it. She was not meant to survive it. What she was facing was not some terrible ordeal but her own inevitable and imminent death. Something strange happened to her inner parts, the parts unaffected by the poison. She felt her stomach and heart churn, loosen. It is only the final exit, Donna, she repeated to herself with something resembling her mother's hard tone: a Poison Lady's final mark, a Low Lady's last call.

The Arkel was still staring at her with his intense, penetrating gaze. 'Who is she?'

Capla sounded smug – that was the worst of it, smug and self-satisfied. 'I believe she is the whelp of a courtesan – an old contact of mine from Lambrugio.'

'Which courtesan?' The Arkel's voice was sharp.

'In those days they called her the Low Lady Estelle; in these days I believe she is an outlaw, a smudge.'

The Arkel's face darkened and Donna wanted to die of shame. Capla had known her mother! Why that made things worse she did not know, but it did.

'I do not want her treated like Immina, Capla, is that clear? Do what you must to ensure her cooperation but do not harm her excessively. Judge it fine.' The Arkel moved towards Donna and lifted her chin, indicating for the guard to bring the lantern nearer. 'She is beautiful, isn't she?' he said, regretfully. 'But no doubt she is as evil as her mother. No true woman trespasses on the place Between, the preserve of Arché. It is right to use their vile gift to good purpose. Freedom from the combers and decisive victory over the High Verdans will be a good purpose.'

Strangely, Donna thought that this sounded more like a question than one of the Arkel's famous definitive statements of belief. She thought she glimpsed doubt in his eyes, then he turned away.

'What have you doped her with?'

'Bergensalve, freezeroot and ajeebamor will still be present in small quantities.'

The Arkel tapped his foot impatiently. 'These are not going to help, are they?'

'Anything that induces fear and confusion helps, my Lord.'

'I don't like it – I have never liked the indiscriminate use of such pollutants. They corrupt the soul, and she is a young woman.'

'A very strong young woman,' Capla replied.

'Be sure you don't overreach yourself, my friend. If this attempt fails you are on borrowed time, and I would remind you that fear and confusion have destroyed much of Immina's usefulness. You would be foolish to make the same mistake.' The Arkel signalled to his guards and left, leaving Capla and the Doctor Esteemed Garvell together.

'Interesting,' said Capla conversationally to the doctor. 'Why does the Arkel care about the delectable Donna?'

Garvell's expression was cold; he did not seem to care much for Capla. 'I'm surprised you haven't worked that one out for yourself – Master of Secrets.'

Garvell's tone was lightly mocking. He made some adjustments to the Contrivance, before adding with studied nonchalance, 'Pavenos – the Arkel – had a sister called Estelle. I do not know what became of her, but presumably *he* does. I believe she had a child, and even the Arkel might look less kindly on a man who abused his niece.'

Donna could not tell if Capla were surprised – she was too shocked herself. Surely the Doctor Esteemed must be wrong, or was thinking of some other Estelle. Surely her mother would have told her if she had been related to the Arkel? The answer, she knew, was nothing more definite than 'maybe': the Low Lady Estelle kept her own counsel, and she was especially close-mouthed with her daughter.

Donna did not have much time to consider this possible new revelation, because Capla was carefully extracting vials from her mother's chest. He concocted something in a plain glass beaker – she could recognise only a couple of its components. He opened her mouth. She could not resist; she could focus her eyes and she could blink but she could not clamp her jaw shut as she wished to.

'Don't make a fuss, beauty – better do what your uncle says. This should counteract the freezeroot – you'll be able to writhe again in moments.' His expression was closed, unreadable, though his voice was gloating.

'I will tell you what you are going to do. In a little while I'm going to give you something else. I call it the dream-maker; your mother probably gave it another name – it is made mainly of ajeebamor. It heightens dreaming but it leaves the body very susceptible to pleasure and to pain. It is a crude generalisation but, broadly, pleasure produces good dreams; pain – bad. I expect you can guess which one we want you to have.

Don't try to fight; there is nothing that can be done. I know my job – you will survive and with no major injuries. If this works we're going to need you again. The Arkel believes that you will enter the realm of Between in the right frame of mind to act as a channel for the beasts of that region. I have no such belief, but we will see. However it is achieved, you will briefly do the Arkel's work. This is to be a practice run in which we destroy the combes before we set out on our mission to destroy the army of High Verda. The Doctor Esteemed seems to think that this Contrivance will enhance the power of your dreaming. You will of course have Immina to help you – close contact in sleep for some reason encourages shared dreams.'

He smiled and Donna found herself squirming at the memory of their shared dream. She pushed the thought away. The cold liquid he had given her was, perversely, beginning to thaw her frozen limbs. She twitched her foot and was delighted to feel it respond. He knew his business then, Capla – she had never really seriously doubted that.

Immina made some strange noise in her throat as Capla administered the philtre to her too. Donna was able to twist her neck to see Immina's vague blue eyes seem suddenly focused again. She was back from wherever she had been.

Capla turned his attention back to the poison chest and another similar box she had not previously noticed, filled with further coloured bottles. Donna did not want to know the components of his dream-making potion; it would not help. Poison would take its course. She feared it of course, and she feared the pain. Her small hope of remaining strong, of being worthy of her mother, of Rej, was slowly beginning to evaporate. She reached for Immina's slender hand beside her and squeezed it. Immina responded with a gentle pressure of her own. Immina's eyes were no longer mad, but she looked terrified, and her hand shook. Donna too was trembling uncontrollably when the guards came to put her into the Contrivance. They tied their hands together – Donna's right to Immina's left. She could no longer see Immina's face, but the touch of her hand, though no part of Capla's plan, was a comfort. There was no way out – no way to fight. Capla took a long drink from whatever was in the cup and lifted her head to help her drink whatever vile poison he had made.

She had no hope when, spluttering, he made her swallow it. She fell at once into the dragon dream.

Chapter Twenty-Nine

No one pursued Rej. He did not know why not – running was unusual in Lunnzia. He ran through the Golden Quarter and on through to the Green and then through that on to the city wall and to the Liberty. Why did nobody think it worthwhile to chase him? He was expecting to be chased. It was only the physical effort of running, braving the space, making his lungs scream and his limbs ache that stopped him from crying out in anger, in fear, in rebellion. These powerful but unacknowledged emotions coursed through him, giving strength to his arm as he hauled open the entrance to the combes, Scrubber's entrance.

The darkness was a shock, the smell an assault. His home stank of sewerage and decay, of mould, dampness and the numerous and nameless poisons that the city dumped there daily. Rat-shit but it frakking stank. Rej almost retched but he made himself breathe deeply; it was, good or bad, the familiar scent of home. He lowered the heavy door above him and rested, panting, until he'd caught his breath, until he'd stopped trembling. He had done right by Grimper; he should find Scrubber and tell her. He did not want to see the Low Lady – didn't want to talk about Donna. He didn't even want to think about Donna. He put his head in his hands and just for a moment wept, for Grimper, for the victims of Capla, and for himself.

He did not indulge himself for long – frakking moon-witted, piss-blooded fool that he was to indulge himself at all – but set off to find Scrub. Scrub. How could he face a slack-jawed, stenk-juice-dribbling Scrub? He had a memory, long ago buried, of seeing her like that once when he was very young. It had frightened him then and it frightened him more now that he understood. Scrub. How much worse could things get? Maybe the knowledge that her brother had died a clean death might help, might keep her from the frakking stenk. Odds were it wouldn't. Giving it up had cost her too much – odds were she'd no credit left.

He was weary, not just in his tired legs but in himself. Above had been a frakking disaster. There was no freedom, no soaring dragons, only tyranny and what felt like betrayal. What in Arché's name had he done to save the combes? What for Light's sake had he done to avenge Harfoot? The malign threat of the Basilisk Contrivance still remained. He did not know where or even what the frakk it was. There was little with which to comfort himself, except, perhaps, the fact that Barna seemed to have lost the inclination to kill him for his debts – perhaps Barna'd thought Capla would have saved him the sweat. That was something Rej could hold on to. He had survived, Lady Luck's blessing and honour intact – one good chip in his hand of craven duds.

The ghost tunnels were worse than he remembered and his weariness and distraction strained all his combe-acquired directional sense to find his way back to Scrubber's hide. There was no welcoming light there – not an auspicious sign – and by now the treaty lights were dark too. Darkness bothered him more than it had before, now that he'd seen the sun. He climbed into Scrub's hide, fearful of what might greet him, steeling himself against the disappointment of finding her crumbled and stenk-eyed. He found her lantern – it was in its usual place along with the flint – so order still reigned. She was not there. He could not ignore his relief: a heavy weight shifted from his heart. At least he didn't have to face that frakking soul-rotting sight yet. Tomorrow he might be stronger, tomorrow he would find Scrub and maybe Barna and the Low Lady – they might know where to start to look for the Contrivance, and after that he might find a way to save his world. What the frakk – a man could dream.

Scrub's larder box was still in the votive niche. He rifled through it for something to eat and found bread. It was no more than two days old. Had she got it before she heard about Grimper, or after? His internal time sense was skewed. He tried to count the days since he'd left the combes. It didn't matter. He had food for now and some clean water in the canteen by the food box. He also found his own belt pouch, its weathered leather familiar as his own hand. Scrub must have brought it down from Above. He strapped it round his waist again. He touched the gaming dice and was reassured; he felt like a comber once more.

He had light too – Lady Luck still smiled on him. He was too frakking tired to think. He lay on Scrubber's corpse stone, looking at the shadows thrown by the light of the lantern; he'd done that when he was a child. He shut his eyes. Sleep came abruptly, velvet curtains closing out the light.

The dark basilisk waited in his dream, watching from the Melagiar Mansion as two great dragons soared and wheeled. Rej felt as if he flew with them, as if he himself was a third giant lizard of the sky, his wings gleaming as bright as the roofs of the Golden Quarter, scaled with living gold, swooping and rolling as the air currents cooled and caressed him. He was close enough to the other dragons to touch them, but they would not play; it was as though they were focused only on each other, as if they had no interest in him; they shunned him. The light must have faded gradually but he did not notice. It grew cold there, Between, as cold as the frozen air of Above, and as unwelcoming. Blue sky became grey and then darkened like a bruise to a deep purple-black tinged with sickly yellow light. There was going to be a storm. The sweet scented wind dropped and died away and in that sinister stillness the sudden clap of thunder sent a shock through his wings. He almost faltered, he lost the uplift, scrabbled against the air, wings beating wildly out of time; he almost fell. Lightning cracked the sky and briefly lit it, shattering the darkness into a thousand jagged-edged fragments, like broken Lunnzian glass.

In the sudden light Rej, with his limited peripheral

vision, noticed that the dark basilisk was gone from its perch. At the same instant he saw the two linked dragons twitch convulsively as though struck, though he was sure the lightning had not hit them. Their spines arched as if in a spasm of agony and their wings beat rapidly, thrashing the air with desperate energy. One beast produced a great keening cry, the other remained dumb but flame blossomed from its open mouth in his direction. Brilliant light flashed and almost blinded him as the sky was torn by another ragged fork of lightning. He saw the scales on the dragons dull and darken, turn from living gold to the dark green of deep water. As he watched, their necks twisted and lengthened so that where, moments before, the golden dragons had flown, two massive dark basilisks now flamed the sky. They turned on him baleful eyes, burning like coals from the fires of Arché. He looked away. Their talons extended like birds of prey, like the ominous figure in the library of Lunnzia, and they swooped towards him. The leathery sound of their bat-like wings flapping was loud in his ears. He saw their flame bloom like some malignant, misshapen flower in the suffocating darkness. It almost scorched his dragon scales, and Rej fled.

Rej woke in Scrubber's hide breathless and terrified. The light had gone out and he was momentarily disoriented. For a moment he couldn't breathe as the darkness choked and smothered him. It was the distinctive smell of Scrubber permeating the covers on the corpse stone that reminded him of where he was. Before he could feel relieved and before his heartbeat returned to normal he realised that he could still hear the basilisks' roar.

Rej stumbled to the hide's hearthstone, his body weak as though he had truly flown 'Between'. His heart still beat too fast and his hands shook. He peered out into what should have been darkness to see the Styx on fire, like oil from a spilled lamp or the lava flow from the fire mountains he'd seen in a book. People screamed their terror. It was more noise than he'd ever heard Below, echoing round the cavernous combes.

Rej did not hesitate. He swung out, finding handholes easily across the apparently sheer face of the combe wall, climbing towards the screams. The heat from the river burned his face and the left side of his body, and gave him more light than he needed to find his way. He followed the burning river towards the Light Hall. The rock was hot but he was unwilling to risk the spider ropes which were overcrowded with fleeing combers and likely to give at any moment. He recognised some of the combers swinging their way towards him. He thought he saw Moon and many of his gestation fleeing the Hall. A young girl passed him on the rock face, Nel, if he remembered her name right. Her face was panic-stricken and her whispered words came in frightened gasps.

'Wrong way, mate, frakking basilisk's loose in the Light Hall!'

He did not at first believe her, which was stupid whichever way he looked at it because, unlike the rest of the Lady's luckless, long-benighted combers, he'd known it could happen. Then, as his feet found their familiar rhythm and he climbed the unnaturally illuminated face of his dark home, he felt the burning heat of the Styx and he knew that everything had changed, that Below was invaded, that he'd failed in every way and that Luck, his Lady, had finally abandoned him; but when he came to the Light Hall it was still a shock and he still forgot to breathe.

The Light Hall was a large space, almost large enough to contain the domed library of the University of Lunnzia. The rock formed a natural high chamber lit by the largest treaty light in the combes. The natural circle was surrounded by two semicircles of rock, honeycombed with burial niches – the most desirable of the comber hides. The river flowed under it, making it the only large space below ground. It was always busy, even at night when it would be lit by braziers and full of knots of people gambling and gaming or coming for the food and other allowances. This night it was still full of people, all of them screaming because Nel was right – filling the vast space was the gargantuan figure of the dark basilisk.

It was the basilisk of his latest dreams, Rej was sure – grounded in the real world, graceless and squat. The wings that gave it elegance and a certain malevolent beauty were constricted, half-folded like a crumpled fan. The thick vanes that stretched the leathery membrane of the wings stood out like cords of vein on an old man's hand; they had that same blueish tinge. Rej was careful to avoid the basilisk's eyes – it was said that the coal-black eyes of a basilisk brought death in its stare. He had never believed it before, but then he had never believed that he might see a real, living basilisk in his home. This was no dream creature, but a thing of form and fire and substance. Its vast head almost scraped the treaty light. It half extended its wings, its great muscles bulging as it tried to unfurl them fully. He could see the creature strain against the rock which confined it. In the flamelight the beast's dark flesh seemed smooth as obsidian, smooth as the combe worms – the creatures of some nether world, neither snake nor eel, that lived in the damp ground of the Styx's banks. Somehow the basilisk elongated its slick, slug-dark tail and, using it for balance, partially fanned its wings so that the jet of flames that issued from its mouth burned hotter and more brilliantly. Rej watched in horror as five or six men fell from the cliffs on to the stone beneath. The flame licked at their hair and clothing, the blazing fire illumined their open-mouthed terror as they fell, and only the roaring and piss-freezing hissing of the creature drowned out their screams and the sound of the impact of their fall.

Rej found that he was screaming too. The image of the avenging basilisk was part of his childhood nightmare, the dark beast that symbolised the end of all things – the destructive power of Arché, the apotheosis of chaos. He was in a sweat-bathed panic. His body was petrified as if he had looked the creature in the eye but he frakking hadn't and this had to be fear; fear that made his thoughts scatter like a loser, a prime twazzock. His heart battered at his ribs arhythmically like it was trying to escape, though the rest of him refused. He believed for the first time that Melagiar was right – that it was possible to die of fright – and then, in the ever-shrinking, still-calm portion of his brain, he remembered the Basilisk Contrivance. Was this the triumphant consequence of the Arkel's weapon?

Chapter Thirty

Deep underground in the hidden part of the combes, bound together, strapped to the Contrivance, Donna gripped Immina's hand tight. At first she flew in a blue sky with the two golden dragons she knew of old, joyous and free, but the dark basilisk of nightmare looked on. It was good to fly, to feel the sweet wind, and then, abruptly, it wasn't good any more and the pain began.

The dragon dream was full of pain. Donna was full of pain. She ached with tension. Her arms were broken wings and every downbeat sent spasms of pain through her shoulders. She roared her agony, for to make a sound persuaded her that she still lived, still breathed, still fought against the forced perversion of the dream and the pain no dreaming masked. Immina was there, screaming silently in her tongueless agony. Flesh to flesh she felt Immina's horror, felt her withdraw to the inner places even Capla could not reach. Could Immina will herself away from the dream, move beyond the dream into private madness? Donna was afraid she could. Donna was afraid and did not want to be alone. She would not let Immina go. Donna set her will against Immina's fading, her retreat. In the dream Donna willed Immina to remain. Donna needed her, wanted her there; it was better not to be alone.

They flew together, Donna and Immina, deaf to all sounds but Capla's voice, his insistent murmuring that they could not fail to hear, even in the dream place Between. With his voice reinforced by pain he forced them to fly down, as if through the earth, down below the streets and troubled city of Lunnzia into the caves and secret tombs of the combes.

Donna wanted to fly away but knew that there was nowhere above the ground or below it, no high pinnacle or cave or secret place that would hold them safe from Capla. She believed utterly that his potions and his gift of excoriating pain would flush them out. Would Capla let them die? If she tried to dash herself across the rock of Below would he find a way to wake her to greater agony? Pain made her mindless, made her thrash and turn where Capla willed it, made nothing matter, made her speechless, powerless, without will of her own or hope. The world narrowed to one sole desire: Make it stop!

Donna did not know what was happening but her dragon wings seemed shrunken and dark. There was fire and burning everywhere. It hurt. The stench of burning and the sizzling of roasting flesh terrified Donna – was it her flesh or Immina's? Her vision was blurred and she felt unsteady. She was constrained in a place of darkness and burning and she had to get free.

Capla's voice was in her head, taunting her, shrieking at her, demanding something of her, but it *hurt too much for her to understand; she would do it, whatever it was that he wanted, if only he'd make it stop, if only he'd let her die. But the words she didn't understand went on and the pain didn't end and she fought harder and more desperately to get free. It hurt – all that fire and the burning and the pain was worse than fire, and it wouldn't end.*

Rej watched, fascinated, as one of the impossibly tiny figures in the Light Hall stood his ground and started waving something at the creature. It did not seem that the creature saw him, but then two or three others joined him with their belt knives raised and began screaming at the monster. No words carried against the terrible roaring, but the intent was clear enough. A couple of small combers with buckets began cautiously filling them with fiery liquid and threw the burning contents towards the basilisk's head. Their attempt was futile, but it gave the combers purpose; more seemed set to join them. Then the basilisk reared, maddened, banging its head against the stone ceiling of the cave, shaking the combes with the impact. It moved blindly, wildly, unreasoning, as if it too was frightened into madness. And it plunged into the Styx itself. Its hide seemed impervious to the flaming water. It extended its narrow viper-like head blindly, as though feeling its way forward, and began to wade towards Rej and the greater part of the combes, flaming everything in its path.

Rej's first instinct was to run but his frakking legs went weed-wet on him and he couldn't. It was as well because if he'd been able to move he wouldn't have seen the still stranger sight of a second basilisk emerging from shadows where no basilisk could have been. It was the smaller, frailer form of the second of his dream beasts. Its head jerked in spasm and flame dribbled from its mouth; it seemed uncertain, bemused even, wading through the Styx. Several figures fell before it and did not get back up, crushed by the lumbering, unsteady advance of its taloned feet. It seemed reluctant to follow the larger, more confident beast, until both were simultaneously wracked by a muscular tremor that sent the larger one roaring with what sounded like pain and fury.

Perhaps because he was afraid, perhaps because he could not even believe it himself, but it was only then that Rej began to make sense of what was going on. The two basilisks had to be the work of Donna and Immina, brought from Between with the help of the Basilisk Contrivance. The recognition scarcely helped him: by all the Light of God what could he do about it?

Chapter Thirty-one

Donna let go. She had been trying to let go for a long time. She had wanted to let go and die, but Capla would not let her. Now suddenly his control faltered, now at last she could sink into the dreamless comfort of unawareness. The fire and the pain disappeared; she thought that she might be dead, but it was a good thing, death. Nothing hurt any more and it was dark and cool and she could not hear Capla in her head or feel him doing things to make her hurt. She would be happy to stay dead for ever.

Rej finally managed to move, climbing swiftly back towards Scrub's cave. Reason told him the best way to fight these basilisks was to destroy the Contrivance that had brought them to the combes. He did not know how to do that, but he knew that the answer did not lie in confronting the great beasts in the combes. His fingers and toes sought footholds automatically; his long limbs moved effortlessly across the face of the combe cliffs. He needed to get away to think; there was no shame in that. Arché's arse, there was no frakking shame in that. He imagined that the hot breath of the basilisk would be at his neck any moment, and fear at last gave him the speed he needed.

Suddenly the flames of the Styx went out. Rej turned back to assess his danger and there was only darkness; the basilisks had gone. Incredulously, he made his way more slowly back to the Light Hall. The rock beneath his fingers was cool, the damp air cold against his face; he began to doubt himself. Had he experienced some powerful waking dream, a vision brought on by his disturbed state of mind? He did not now want to go back to the isolation of Scrub's niche; he needed company. He swallowed down his fear and headed back to the Hall of Light.

Pale, filtered dawn light spilled into the Distribution Chamber. In the dimness he could see figures gathered in small clusters; that was not so unusual, though it was early to be gaming. As he got closer he could see that the combers were gathered around the fallen bodies of his vision. He shivered when he recognised them: it had not been a vision and these men were truly dead.

Barna saw him approach and surprise registered briefly across his face. 'Rej! You're here. Did you get to Grimper?'

Rej nodded. 'He's dead. What –?' He did not finish the question – he did not need to.

'Did you not see the frakking basilisks – two of them came from nowhere. There's about twenty people dead.'

'I saw … at least … I wasn't sure if it was real.' Rej looked at the broken body of the nearest fallen man. 'Why is he not burned? I thought I saw him burn.'

Barna shook his head. 'None of them are burned,

there is not so much as a singe mark anywhere. I held a bucket of flaming liquid – it burned my hands, but ...' He spread his strong hands in front of him. They trembled slightly but they were not burnt.

'What happened?'

Barna shook his head. 'The Arkel has begun his war on us, that's all I know. False fire or real fire, these beasts were real enough to kill. We cannot let this happen. We will declare war on the Arkel and the Redmen Above.' He turned to two of his men. 'Send word out to the resistance of Above. We have no other choice. I will call a meeting of all combers at mainlight.'

Rej did not ask how Barna would achieve that. It was said that only the quasi-mythical Distributor knew the location of every hide. It was not his concern. Rej turned his attention to the sprawled figure on the floor before him. Blood formed a dark corona around the man's head; it was Dove Grey. Rej felt sick. He'd known him well – owed him plenty too. Worse still, Dove Grey was only one gestation older that Rej himself.

They burned the bodies according to custom in a massed pyre. After they'd chanted the words of committal, Rej spotted the Low Lady Estelle, in comber dress, at the back of the congregation. There was no way he could avoid her; it was better to get the conversation over with. He walked towards her. She bowed her head in Abover fashion in polite acknowledgement.

'Barna says Grimper is dead,' she said, without preamble.

'I gave him the death you asked for,' Rej said, uncomfortably. He had not liked doing it, even though he knew it was right. 'I don't think there was any pain, and he was grateful.'

The Low Lady nodded briskly. 'Did you find him before he was questioned?'

'He'd been beaten, but I don't think Capla had spent any time with him.' Rej paused, trying to find a reasonable way of describing his condition. 'He was bruised but he was lucid.'

She nodded again, a little less firmly. 'Thank you,' she said flatly, her voice drained of emotion, but she took Rej's hand in hers and held it tightly. 'He was my life partner, my friend since long before Donna was born. There is only Donna left now. Tell me – did you find out what Capla has done with her?' Her hand gripped his painfully; her eyes bored into his. It was impossible to lie.

'I found her with Capla.' He tried to find a polite way of putting it, though why he felt so constrained talking to a courtesan he could not say. 'I think that she had lain with him.' It was an old-fashioned euphemism; he did not know where it had come from.

Estelle's expression did not change, but her hand shook and she closed her eyes. 'He has her then. If you knew Donna better, you would know that he has poisoned and compelled her. He has used her like they used her mother.' She gripped Rej hard and he realised that she was struggling to stay on her feet. He helped her away from the crowd to one of the circles of rock where, on less tragic days, combers gamed.

'It was Donna who brought the basilisk here, wasn't

it?' She said it calmly and he was not sure whether she expected an answer. He gave her one anyway.

'I think Donna *was* the basilisk,' said Rej, surprising himself with the insight. 'There are no beasts Between, only our own dreaming selves. I do not know why I did not realise it before. When I dreamed I dreamed I was a dragon. I see it now. Immina and Donna were the other beasts. I saw them in my dream, flew with them as a dragon. I watched them change from dragon to basilisk, and when I woke they were here.'

'You do indeed have that gift too, then?'

Rej shrugged. 'Is it a gift if it can do this?' He indicated the still burning pyre. 'I don't know, but I think to kill the frakking basilisks we may have to kill Immina and Donna if they are one and the same.' There had to be another way, but he couldn't at that moment think what it might be.

'Perhaps it is a curse,' Estelle said, giving him a sharp look before continuing. 'But I know that Donna would not have done this willingly. If we must kill anyone it will be Capla.' She had recovered herself and spoke with authority. 'From what I've been able to learn, Melagiar started doping Immina with the dreaming philtre, with ajeebamor or some such potion, in midsummer – I mean in "Bright-light season".' She knew the comber terms, then. Rej tried to remember when the dragon dreams had started. It was hard to recall the time before his obsession with them. He shrugged. He couldn't see that it frakking mattered, anyway.

'It is important, Rej,' Estelle said sharply. 'I believe that Immina managed to pull you into "Between", or whatever we are to call it, in midsummer, when her own dreaming intensified. Maybe they began experimenting with the Basilisk Contrivance at the same time. You did not dream before?'

He shook his head. 'But there were no dragons appearing in the skies in frakking Bright-light season or surely you would have seen them? But now we have all seen the basilisks. How can that be?'

'Perhaps the Contrivance did not work properly then. Perhaps all that Immina did then was to draw in those with some dreaming talent of their own. Let us assume that it was so and that the Contrivance was built at around that time. It may help us to track down where and how it was built, and knowing that may help us to track down where it is now. Someone must have acquired materials to build it. Think! Is there anything else you know from your dreams that could be of use to us?'

'There were four of us,' Rej said carefully. 'Three dragons and the dark basilisk that had just started to watch us fly. One must have been Immina, the other Donna.'

'And the dark basilisk?'

'I don't know. Someone with the dreaming talent? Someone who did not know how to fly as a dragon and could not know the freedom and the pleasure of it?'

She shook her head. 'I don't know. Perhaps whatever has made Donna into a basilisk had already corrupted that person – perhaps ...' She stopped. 'I don't know – I don't know enough about it, but it might not matter. Can you go to Donna in "Between" –

tell her we're looking for her? See if she knows where she is?'

'It's not like that. I can't choose to go there. We don't talk there. I thought it was just a vivid dream.'

The Low Lady Estelle let go of his hand. 'We'll just have to find them the usual way, then.'

Rej looked at her questioningly.

'I have many contacts and so has the Lord Distributor,' she said, though without much hope.

'The Lord Distributor?'

'Barna, Barna – the Lord Distributor. Scrubber was right. You are an innocent.' She sighed. 'The time for secrets is over.'

It was growing brighter, but the improvement in the light did not make her expression any more readable. It did reveal the fine lines that creased the corners of her eyes and mouth, the slight slackness in her jawline that made her look less youthful than he'd supposed her. She would have been a good comber; her eyes gave nothing away. She looked at him very directly.

'Listen carefully! It is important that you understand the game you're in. This is the final hand, and if we don't win this we lose everything for ever. Barna is the Distributor, has been since the beginning. Grimper, with my help, led the resistance against the Council of Ten. We have always worked with Barna, though mainly through Scrub, who until recently did not know that Barna was with us. Between us we have a network of spies to match those of the Arkel himself. It has gone badly lately and many have been captured and tortured. In killing Grimper you have saved many lives and left us with a chance of finding

Donna, with their assistance. Even so, it would help things greatly if you could try to find her in your dreams.'

Rej found himself nodding.

'My poison chest was taken, but I can make you a sleeping draught that will help.'

He found himself nodding again – the Low Lady had that effect on him. Moreover, she did not think that Donna had been with Capla willingly; that made more difference than it should have done.

Rej followed the Low Lady to one of the burial niches overlooking the Light Hall. He did not want to know what was in the drink she gave him. It smelled slightly of attar of damask rose, of Immina and Melagiar's opulent rooms. That would have made him fearful but he had so little to lose. If they could not stop the basilisks they may well all die anyway.

He drank the slightly bitter liquid and arranged himself on the corpse shelf. He was tired and his eyes became heavier almost at once. The Low Lady seated herself stiffly on the floor beside him.

'I will wake you if you get into trouble.' Her voice seemed to come from the bottom of a deep pit and, though he would have liked to reply, nothing much seemed to happen when he tried to move his lips.

Suddenly he was in the place of his dreams they called 'Between'. There was nothing there. He flew in a dark sky without landmarks of any kind. He could see nothing, though he knew his wings beat strongly. He could feel the powerful downbeat, feel the air buoy and resist him. He was as he had always been when he'd flown with dragons. Now there were no dragons. It was terrifying to fly in the darkness, worse than the ghost tunnel – wide open spaces and total darkness, the worst features of the combes and of Above. He fought sleep, desperate to resurface into wakefulness, but the draught that the Low Lady had given him kept him where he did not want to be. He flew in great wide circles seeking the basilisks or, better still, other dragons, but there was no sign of life. The idea came to him eventually that without Immina and Donna to dream of it there was no 'Between'.

Chapter Thirty-two

Rej opened his eyes, disorientated. Scrub was standing above him, looking down. The lamplight exaggerated the hollows and planes of her face. She looked anxious.

'What have you frakking done to him, Estelle? He's ice-cold, and his eyes are open – like he's dead. Did you have to do this?' Her voice slurred slightly, but she sounded as aggressive as ever. Rej felt profound relief – she was not so far gone in stenk as he had feared.

'There is too much at stake here, Venetia, to treat a grown man with kid gloves. You already know what we've sacrificed.'

Rej saw tears form in Scrub's bloodshot eyes. He wanted to tell her that her brother had not suffered, but the words would not come; his mouth wouldn't move. It was a strange sensation. He would have panicked but his body was still relaxed and quiescent under the influence of the Low Lady's potion.

Scrub's voice was hard and cold when she spoke again more quietly. 'I'm sure that they're at the end of the stenk tunnels – that they've built their frakking Contrivance there. I know those passages as well as anyone. Someone's stomped all over the best yield rocks, and not one of my regular harvesters either. Even stenked-up they're not that moon-witted.'

'How could the Arkel's men have got there without being seen?'

'Don't be a twazzock, Stella. It's not such a great feat to open a new trap door – just because it's not legal doesn't mean it's not being done.'

Rej was intrigued, not least because he could not have imagined anyone calling the Low Lady Estelle a 'twazzock'.

His body was beginning to return to him and he managed to blink his eyes. Scrub, watching him like a combe-mother, noticed at once.

'He's coming round – he'd better be all right.' Her voice broke and Rej was surprised to hear the worry in it.

'I am all right, Scrub. What about you?' His voice was thick and muffled-sounding, his tongue felt too large for his mouth.

Scrub grinned and her teeth were only slightly blackened. 'Better,' she said. Her small, strong bird's claw of a hand clutched his shoulder painfully. 'Thanks for what you did. I couldn't bear the thought of Leo – Grimper – being tortured.' She spoke tightly, her face a mask of strain.

'I'm sorry he had to die, Scrub.' Rej's tears coursed down his still immobile face and he was powerless to stop them.

'There was no other way, Rej, no other hope.' She sounded wearier that usual, but sober. She helped him to a seating position and endured his hard look.

'Deve off, Rej. I know I've been a piss-hearted rat-turd. I was wrong. With you gone and then Leo, I despaired.' She shook her head. 'I'm old, Rej, and I just got too tired and desperate to fight it – but I won't fail again. You can bet on it.'

His face still felt stiff but he managed a smile. 'I was worried,' he said simply.

'Did you find Donna?' Estelle's patience was spent. She looked almost as dishevelled as Scrub. Her hair was coming down from its elegant knot; her greying mane was as thick and heavy as Donna's own.

'There was no one there. There was no "Between".'

'I don't understand.'

'I don't think Between exists without Immina and Donna. They don't discover it, they invent it.'

Estelle brushed hair from her eyes absently. 'I'm not a philosopher – I'm not interested in Between. All that matters is Donna. Where can she be, if not there?' The Low Lady had lost much of her calm and poise. She sounded raw, agitated. Rej wondered if she were perhaps as uncomfortable Below as he had been when first Above.

'Calm down, Stella – it's not his fault. Listen to what he's saying. If Between only exists when they dream of it then all that Rej has discovered is that they're not dreaming.' Scrubber was impatient, but the Low Lady was distraught.

'And what must that mean – that they're dead?'

'You're not dreaming and you're not dead! Get a hold of yourself, Stella – you're a frakking Poison Lady, not some rat-turd aristocrat!'

Rej was surprised that the Low Lady took the

insult, but perhaps she too listened to what Scrubber didn't say. Scrubber resonated with furious energy, and if she could tear the combes apart with her bare hands to find Donna, Rej suspected that she would. Instead she shared bread and water from her waist pack and tapped an irritated foot against the ground.

'Did you say you knew where they might be holding her?' Rej said after he'd drunk deeply of the water; it cleaned his throat of the residual effects of Estelle's potion, and made his thoughts less sluggish.

Scrubber nodded. 'The Distributor – Barna – has called for every able-bodied comber and resistance worker from Above to attack the Council of Ten, the Arkel and the Redmen, and anyone else turd-brained enough to stand with them Above. The Arkel is about to remember why he's kept us sweet all these years. Barna's sure the Contrivance is Above. He thinks I'm yearning for the stenk tunnels on my own account.' She looked momentarily angry. 'I suppose I've only got myself to blame. Anyway, I know what I know, and I know the difference between stenk dreams and truth. I'm going to go back to the stenk tunnels – when I've eaten. D'you want to come?'

Rej nodded, though his body did not feel up to much attacking. His many recent abrasions and injuries seemed to hurt the more now that life had returned to his numbed body. He had already sworn to himself to destroy the Contrivance but he did not understand the Arkel's tactics – he had taken too large a gamble in failing to wipe out the combers with his first attack. 'He took a huge risk in using the Contrivance. Do you think it was meant to kill us all?'

'Yes, I think it was,' said Estelle, thoughtfully, 'but, you know, Pavenos has made many such mistakes. He always did think he knew better than anyone else, and he's no tactician. Why else did you think we wanted to overthrow him?' She spoke so passionately that Rej was a little taken aback.

Scrub laid her hand on the Low Lady's shoulder. 'Our time has come, Stella. Now are you ready to storm the basilisk?'

It was ridiculous to think of two old women, even with Rej's help, storming anything, and yet Rej was not tempted to laugh. The Low Lady Estelle was a Poison Lady, while Scrub's reputation was formidable. Nonetheless he felt that something important was missing.

'I'm in,' he said, because he was. He'd never picked the right games, just the ones with the highest stakes. Then, remembering belatedly what was missing, he added, 'But we have no weapons.'

'Rej – what you don't know would fill the Library of Lunnzia twenty times over. We've had stocks of weapons for years. Apparently Barna is distributing them, though what kind of frakking state they're in after all this time Light alone knows!'

Scrub's tone was disparaging, but Rej's quick glance in her direction told him that she was struggling against her stenk craving. She was paler than usual, though he would once have thought that impossible. Her hands trembled and her eyes were feverishly bright.

Their conversation was interrupted by the arrival of perhaps one hundred Abovers, escorted by some of

Barna's less frightening henchmen. The Abovers looked shaken, scared, poorly dressed and undernourished. Most of them were oppidans but Rej noticed here and there the stained face of a slave. The combers looked at them suspiciously at first – they stared at each other, Abover and comber, shuffling and uncertain, and then Barna emptied a barrel of swords on to the ground, upturned the barrel and stood on it so that everyone in the now crowded Light Hall might see him.

'My friends and soon to be brothers and sisters in arms. We were always one people, separated by hard rock and habit, and united again against a common enemy – the Arkel and his men. We've both had it hard in our own way, but the rules that separated us are broken now and I speak for all of us combers when I say "Be welcome!"'

He jumped down from the barrel, to Rej's relief, as he was not sure how long wood kept underground could sustain the weight of Barna – but the coopers had done a good job and the barrel was sound. As Barna moved to welcome the Abovers, others followed in his wake. They offered food and water to the outsiders, awkwardly and hesitantly, but they offered, and were gratefully accepted.

Rej spotted the lame Belafor and Gayla of Donna's work detail and made his way towards them. He had nothing to give, having downed Scrubber's food supplies immediately. Another comber handed him a package of bread and salt meat.

'They've been starved up there by that turd-head Arkel,' the comber said by way of explanation. 'Barna says we share all we have and fight full!'

Rej took the package and stood before Belafor, feeling uncomfortably like the moon-witted twazzock he'd pretended to be.

'Belafor, Gayla, be welcome! I didn't know you were with the resistance.'

'We didn't know you were a comber and could speak,' rejoined Gayla. Fear made her sharp.

'You don't know where Donna is, do you?' Rej asked, not expecting a reply.

Belafor shook his head. 'She told me about the murders in the Barracks of the Wise and she said to go to the Liberty and ask for the Lady. We've only just joined the resistance – in time for the showdown.' He sounded nervous but Rej couldn't blame him. What did Belafor know of fighting? He seemed to guess what Rej was thinking, because under Rej's perhaps disparaging gaze he straightened his slightly twisted shoulders as best he could.

'Don't you worry about us. I want a go at those monsters who killed my mother, who've kept us starving and sent my brother to die against High Verda in some pointless, useless battle we can't win. Don't worry about us – any of us – we've all had to be tough to survive that Arkel's rules. We won't let you combers down, you can be sure of that.'

Rej felt moved by his honesty and his unexpected courage. 'Will you fight your friends?' He couldn't help but ask the question – it was too important to remain unsaid.

'Most of them will join us. Who will fight for the Arkel but those with too much to lose if he loses?

What have we oppidans to lose?'

Rej nodded. 'Sorry for asking,' he said. 'I've been distrusting Abovers for too long – my whole life. D'you want something to eat?' He offered Belafor the food, which he all but snatched from Rej's hand. The oppidans ate ravenously.

'No food at all yesterday,' said Gayla. 'It's getting worse, and one of the girls in my sister's detail died of the cold last night.'

Rej felt vaguely ashamed for underestimating their desperation and their courage – they were like combers really, though less pale and marginally worse dressed.

Scrubber was wrong about the weapons. When Rej and the oppidans joined the throng of people gathered around Barna inspecting his illegal stockpile of militia and army equipment, Rej was surprised to see that they were in good condition. Though some of the velvet decorative covering on the sallets, the steel helmets favoured by the militia and the army, had degraded badly, the metal itself was sound. None of the younger combers had ever fought in armour. Managing the fauchard, the long-bladed staff also regularly carried by the militia, was going to be awkward enough. Rej eyed the weapons dubiously.

'I can manage a short sword,' he whispered to Scrubber, 'but I'd make a right twazzock of myself with the rest of the stuff. I don't know how to use it.'

Barna and some of the other old men clearly did know how to use them, though why anyone would want to cover themselves in inflexible, weighty metal to climb their way through the combes was rather beyond Rej.

Scrubber seemed of the same opinion. She picked up three short, serviceable daggers from a bucket of knives on the ground. Most of the combers were more interested in the sword collection. A gaggle of them were trying them out while more inspected the edge of the fauchards. Only two others had, like them, gone for the daggers. Rej knew them both slightly – good gamblers both of them, and fair men. Most importantly he didn't owe them anything, though one was a cousin of Dove Grey.

Scrubber watched them carefully from a distance.

'Know how to use a short knife,' said one of them, aware of Scrubber's evaluating gaze. 'Wouldn't know how to fight with a frakking bucket on my skull.'

Rej nodded. 'Me neither. You don't want to be worrying about your kit in a fight,' he agreed. 'Scrub thinks she knows where the Arkel's weapon is,' he continued, casually, conversationally.

'The thing that let loose the basilisk?' the man asked, his interest kindled.

Rej nodded tersely.

'It killed Dove, my cousin.'

'I know. Would you be interested in coming along? There's just Scrub and me and Scrub's old mate, Estelle.'

'Why isn't Barna going there?'

Barna was at that moment describing his plans to attack the Council Chamber from his precarious position on top of the barrel. A large group of increasingly belligerent semi-armed combers were shouting their support. Rej strained to hear him above the throng but he had the combers with him, cheering his every phrase.

'He's after the Arkel, I think,' said Scrubber, moving in closer to better hear the conversation. 'He doesn't believe me, because I saw what I saw when I was stenked up,' she shrugged. 'Barna has wanted this chance for a long time. He's not going to give up his dream of attacking Above for an old woman's tale. Anyway, the more frakking militia he can tie up Above, the better it will be for us.'

The men were silent for a while, sharpening their knives on the whetstones Barna had left out for the purpose. When the taller had finished, he asked, 'Where do you think it is then, this basilisk-maker?

'The stenk tunnels.'

The man laughed aloud but then stopped suddenly at the look in Rej's eyes.

'I believe her,' said Rej. 'The Arkel didn't know for sure what the weapon could do. You put a siege gun near the wall you want to breach, not above it. If I were the Arkel I'd put the weapon as near my targets as I could get it unseen – that would be in the combes, not Above.'

'I think they've opened a trap over the stenk tunnels and are using one of a number of small caves there. There were signs that someone had been there, and sure as frakking Light it wasn't anybody I know. It's chest-rotting there. Even my harvesters wouldn't go that deep, the ground's slick as a water rat's arse. It's too damp for good stenk and it smells worse than a basilisk's fart. If I wanted to hide anything I'd do it there.'

Dove's cousin nodded firmly. 'You could be right. I'm in – for Dove.' He gave his companion a questioning look that turned to a smile when he too nodded.

Rej tried to hide his relief. Estelle and Scrub were indomitable women, but two more fighting men who knew what to do with a blade could only make things better. Belafor and Gayla remained silent through this exchange.

'D'you think Donna is with this basilisk-maker?' Gayla asked.

Rej had more or less forgotten about the Abovers – the followers of the Humble Way were too good at somehow becoming invisible, at deflecting attention from themselves.

'Yes, I do,' he said shortly.

'Then we want to come and help you find her. We don't know much about weapons. Would you pick us a suitable blade each?'

He was about to refuse and looked to Scrub and the Low Lady Estelle for support. Scrub shrugged. 'If they're honest and will not let us down they can come. Will you vouch for them?'

'Yes, I think they were mates of Donna's … but what about your leg, Belafor? The way will be hard.'

'My leg is always a problem, but it's my problem. Gayla will help me. I want to get the Arkel where it hurts most, and if we can help a friend too, all the better.'

Belafor's face was grim and Gayla looked equally determined. He could not refuse them.

Rej did not know at what point Scrubber and

Estelle had ceded him the leadership for their small group, but it was his, he knew. He picked up the two smallest, lightest daggers and belt sheaths for Belafor and for Gayla.

'You stab with the sharp end,' he said drily. They did not smile but strapped the belts on carefully. They looked clumsy and scared, but strangely heroic.

'Take us through the frakking stenk tunnels then, Scrub,' Rej said and fell in behind her as she led them by the simplest routes away.

Chapter Thirty-three

Someone was stroking Donna's hand. It didn't hurt. The touch was as gentle as the touch of a butterfly; it didn't hurt. Everything else did. Opening her eyes felt like lifting boulders with her little finger and when, against all the odds, she succeeded, she wanted to shut them tightly again and never reopen them. She was still strapped to the Basilisk Contrivance. Capla straddled her, shook her, hurt her. Only the gentle pressure on her hand reminded her that she was more than a subject of suffering, that she was still Donna.

Donna could not see Immina – she could not turn her head. The pallet on which she lay was damp with sweat and other things – blood, perhaps. She must have bled – where there was that much pain there must have been blood. Her head pounded. She had dreamed of darkness and fear; she remembered wild fury and a headlong, destructive recklessness that made her uncomfortable and guilty. She had been trapped and something fearful and bad had happened, but pain disconnected her thinking, destroyed time, made everything one long continuous present, an eternal moment of agony. She felt as though she had been trapped, somewhere dark and oppressive where walls of rough stone had closed in on her, trying to crush her in a vice more terrible even than Capla's, but she no longer knew what was real and what was part of the dark dreaming that Capla's vile potions engendered. The dreams offered no escape. Fantasy and reality merged seamlessly into a ceaseless, hopeless, pain-filled experience from which there was no escape and to which there could be no end.

Capla's eyes were bloodshot, his bleached face mottled with purple blotches and small spots. His dark hair had escaped from its binding and hung limply on either side of his narrow face. His expression was, fortunately, unreadable. Her hatred of him wore her out. She had moved beyond hate.

'The job's not done yet, Donna, my dear one.'

She was too soul-weary to wince at the endearment. He could say what he liked to her; her body would never be free of the pains he had imposed upon it. He carried on talking anyway, coaxing, as if he cared. She tried to escape inside herself as Immina had done, but even Immina could not retreat from his current onslaught.

'There's more to do. My beauty, eat something. You need your strength and we need your lovely voracious energy.'

Capla did something to her knee which sent a pure, thought-destroying spasm of pain through her entire body. Through a haze of agony, she saw him looking at her gravely.

'It gives me no pleasure to hurt you,' he lied, 'but know that if we are to serve the Arkel it is with the dark basilisk, not the bright dragon, and the basilisk is born of pain and fury.'

He left her then and something of what he said stuck with her, resonated with hidden meaning. Her faculties were frozen, beyond thought, beyond reason. She did not see where he went – it was out of her field of vision. His absence brought a kind of exhausted joy. The torment had stopped for the moment and, though it might be worse when he returned, for a few minutes she was pain-free and she had never known how precious that was.

She did not really understand what Capla had been talking about, but the daughter of a Poison Lady felt that she needed to understand it. *'Use everything you have.'* The memory of her mother's voice, her mother's tough-minded advice, caused her a new kind of pain – of loss and of guilt; she was still a failure. With a huge mental effort Donna focused on Capla's words: pain and fury, he was saying something about pain and fury. Immina carried on stroking Donna's hand; her touch spoke, as Immina could not, of something beyond pain and fury. Donna squeezed Immina's fingers gently, fighting the urge to crush their frailty as Capla was crushing her. Why did the abuse she had suffered make her want to pass such suffering on? The thought came with difficulty – she was handicapped by the aftermath of her suffering; weakness, confusion, as if her whole self had been exposed, picked over, broken, forcibly rearranged and then abandoned. She and Immina were being used as a weapon in some way and it was their pain and fury that Capla wanted.

'The basilisk is born of pain and fury.' Did he mean that she became the basilisk when angry and in pain? He wanted her to want to hurt him back. He wanted her hatred. She would not willingly give him anything he wanted. What if she could resist? If she could resist, would the basilisk cease to be? It was a ludicrous idea. She could not resist the pain – that was ridiculous; pain blotted out all thought, all feeling; pain reduced her to raw, screaming animal agony. But what if she could resist the fury? Was that what Immina was telling her though the gentle, loving, human contact of her touch?

Her fingers found Immina's palm and traced two words there, letter by letter.

No fury.

Her fingers ached with the effort and when she had finished she opened her own palm, resisting the urge to clench her fist, to draw in on herself. After what she had endured, even opening her palm, unclenching her hand seemed like an intimate exposure. Immina's finger weakly wrote: *dragon.* Donna curled her fingers around Immina's and held on. She held on when Capla returned. She held on while he made Immina writhe and scream her terrible inarticulate scream. She held on and she tried not to hate, tried not to feel the burgeoning fury.

Then, more things happened to Donna; bad things that made her forget that she was or ever had been Donna. Capla had given her some water to drink that wasn't water, and the dream or the reality of Between (she no longer either knew or cared which it was) began to take her. She heard Capla's voice say: 'Direct the Contrivance at the combes again.' And then everything became lost.

Donna struggled to feel the gentle pressure of Immina's fingers. She did not know what she felt any more, because even through the strangeness of being another kind of creature she could still feel the maddening pain. She saw with the eyes of her dream self something that looked like a rope of snake-like dragon flesh connecting her with the other flying creature, a dark basilisk: Immina. She was thrashing wildly, her skin smooth as an eel and the dark, deep-water green of the basilisk. Flame bloomed briefly from Immina's tossing head, like steam from the nostrils of a frightened horse in the winter streets of Lunnzia. Through the cord that joined them, she felt Immina's unreasoning fear, but Donna was still lucid, as Capla chose to minister to them one at a time. In the brief respite when he left her more or less alone, she remembered what she had to do.

She tried to think about Immina, not about herself; she tried to send waves of affection and concern through the dream cord that linked them. She knew instinctively that their linked fingers and the emotion they had shared had forged this physical bond between them in the world of Between, a strange, monstrous perversion of an umbilical cord. She knew that for all its strangeness it was the thing that she had waited for, the beginnings of hope. Capla had not intended for them to share this dream link; it was not part of his plan. In that at least they had surprised and subverted his intentions, and Donna knew that, like an umbilicus, this strange dream link was a means to nourish them and keep them alive.

It was hard to hold on to any thought for long. Capla's ministrations were relentless, pitched just below the level of pain at which the mind winked out. He was good at his job.

Donna struggled to picture Immina as she had first seen her in her dreams – as a figure of hope and beauty in a world made dull and hopeless. She remembered the magnificent golden-scaled dragon, basking in sunlight, and the pleasure of flight. She tried to hold on to that mental image in her mind, tried to envisage that image flowing through the cord between them. She willed herself to remember her admiration for Immina as a dragon, to send the memory of the dragon's strength and health-giving goodness. She tried to send Immina hope, tried to pump it like blood through their shared umbilicus, to wash away the anguish of Immina's pain and isolation. She did not know if she succeeded.

Chapter Thirty-four

Barna gathered his troops in good order and started to group the men into fighting units of twenty or so, each with a leader, one of his own old cronies from the combes. He seemed to know what he was doing and, alongside all his anger and his grief for Grimper and those others killed by the Contrivance, Rej could sense Barna's scarcely suppressed excitement. After all the years of planning this was his moment – his chance to defeat the Arkel.

Rej glanced quickly at the Low Lady Estelle, but her face was a mask in the dimmer light away from the main Hall. He did not think she felt much beside grief. The Low Lady had armed herself in her own way. As a Poison Lady she was expert in the tools of death. She'd taken a knife from Barna's hoard, but she also gave Rej, Belafor and Gayla a bag each of clay pots filled with some liquid. Rej recognised the bag he'd been given as Harfoot's satchel; it seemed like an artifact from another age, his age of innocence. The clay pots were heavy and, in spite of their questions, Estelle was non-committal as to their purpose.

Barna's army were leaving by all the many hidden exits that connected the combes with what lay Above, and they were leaving in a surprisingly orderly way for combers. Rej watched them climb like a regiment of spiders across the face of the combes. Watching them go he was briefly and achingly aware that with them went all that was familiar – the end to the way of life he'd always known. It was a frakking rat's turd of a life, it was true, but it was all he'd known. Whatever happened now there was no going back.

As he turned to follow Scrub, something, Rej could not say what, alerted him to danger. Before he could speak to the Lady Estelle, behind him something began to change and he felt a chill in the pit of his stomach. There was a sudden echoing roar, loud and discordant, which seemed almost to petrify everyone in the combes. Bodies clung more tightly to the handholds and spider ropes, tensed muscles, fought panic, and held on. A shadow darkened the huge chamber of the Light Hall and that shadow darkened and coalesced into the gargantuan form of the basilisk. For one frozen moment of shock and indecision no one did anything. Flames cast fiery shadows across the pale, terrified faces of the combers caught in the furnace of its breath, and then the combers fled, climbing away from the dark form and desolate, desperate roars of the beast.

'Do you really think that thing is Donna?' the Lady Estelle whispered, cowering away from the flame, though they were far enough away to be out of immediate danger.

'She sounds to be in pain.'

'I think it's Donna's dream form transformed by whatever they are doing to her in the Contrivance,' said Rej, with more certainty than he felt.

'Then she lives still?' There was hope in with the horror and the fear. 'Perhaps I should go to her – perhaps I could help?'

Rej shook his head. 'I think the only way to help is to find her real body and get her out of the Contrivance. This is like a shadow of her dream or of her nightmare; a shadow given substance.'

'But it's real, real enough to burn!'

'Real enough to kill because we think it's real – I don't understand it!' Rej didn't understand it, and yet it made a kind of sense to him – he couldn't explain it. 'Look, I think we should go, in case it becomes more maddened.'

The roaring was intensifying and once again Rej thought he could see a second beast somehow behind the first – Donna's weaker sister Immina, a shadow of a shadow, echoing her frenzy.

'Let's get the frakking Light out of here.'

Gayla was shaking too much to climb and it took all Rej's powers of persuasion and some straight-talking from Estelle to get her moving again. Only that kept him from going mad himself. When he listened to the bellowing, blood-curdling roaring of the beast, it seemed as if he could hear the true voice of Donna whom he loved, crying. They had to find her.

After a while the roaring stopped. Estelle touched his hand in the darkness. He answered her unspoken question.

'I don't know – Capla may be letting her rest or they may be flying Above. I never came here with them.' He pushed his fears away and concentrated on following Scrub's agile figure and keeping the Abovers from falling. It was enough to take his mind from Donna – almost.

Pain. It was there again, stronger than before. It made Donna gasp, blotted out the sun of her memory, but somewhere – she did not know where – she felt something else, something that was not pain – a pulse of gratitude, frail and slight like the butterfly touch of Immina's fingers. It was a tentative emotion, almost swamped by hatred for Capla, by terror and by suffering, but it was there. Donna was right. The dream cord that joined her and Immina seemed to act as a conduit for emotion, and maybe that could save them. She stretched her wings and willed herself away from the cavernous darkness that trapped her. With that thought the dark sky lightened perceptibly and a tiny shaft of pale sunlight shone on the strange physical link between them: it showed that the thickly scaled cord that joined them glowed with the gold of dragon scales. Something joyous blossomed momentarily within Donna. Perhaps it was hope. Pain wiped out all thought, all memory, but before the pain came, in the merest heartbeat between sensations, she sent that tiny spark of joy to Immina. Immina's gratitude flowed like life blood through the cord, and Immina's skin was no longer basilisk-green but glinted golden in the strengthening sunlight.

Somewhere else in whatever place he tortured them, Capla must have noticed that something had changed and moved to regain his total control. Donna did not *know it, but she guessed that at some point he must have drunk some more of his own poisoned chalice of the dreaming liquid that brought him to them. Suddenly he was there with them in the dream, as the dark basilisk. The pain only eased briefly, before some minion took over his tasks with no noticeable lack of alacrity, but in that moment the sun grew brighter and Immina beat her massive wings with sudden sensuous pleasure, sending herself and Donna soaring. Delight flowed between them, joyous delight and relief. It lasted only a minute, then everything hurt again, but that moment of freedom had showed them their power. For in that moment of freedom the sky had been bright with sunlight and the darkness had all but disappeared. When the darkness returned with the gut-wrenching, mind-twisting agony that wrung all joy from Donna, she still felt Immina's optimism, her unextinguished hope pulsing weakly through their shared cord, all the spirit they could muster between them. That was the moment of revelation. Her guess was right: they controlled this dream. Their joy made the sun shine, their fear made the clouds darken, and they could be what they chose to be: golden dragon or dark basilisk.*

Before Donna was able to think through the implications of that realisation, the basilisk that was Capla's dream form attacked; its cry chilled the blood. The darkness had again descended and it was difficult to see. Immina spouted fearful flames to fight it with and, in the hectic blaze of fire, Donna saw the look of triumph in the basilisk's eyes. She had been right. Capla wanted their hate and their fury – that was the point of the pain – that too was the point of his attack. She could not speak to Immina, could not reason, could not share this insight; their only contact was emotional. How could Donna tell her what they must do? Donna felt Immina's fear and hate, it flowed through the link between them, feeding her own. It would not help them, but she was powerless to stop it. Capla's every action had been wholly dedicated to driving them to such a state. She thought of the sunshine, Arché's Light and the soaring dragon of Lunnzia, the dragon dream that had first enchanted her. She thought of Rej flying with her, gliding above the city in a sky so blue it felt like she had been bathing in light itself. She thought of Immina's gentle touch, her fingers stroking and consoling her through Capla's pain. Donna sent her gratitude and something more: she sent her love to the pale, aloof woman who had asked for her help.

Only now did Donna begin to understand what Immina had suffered. She had suffered for so long and still found strength to offer comfort, to try to warn her. Donna thought of Rej, his slight stoop, his earnest look. She loved him too, and as she remembered all she loved, the sky brightened. Donna felt Immina's response instantly, her gratitude, her warmth, her tender concern. Some of the fury abated. Donna felt calmer, stronger, and Immina sent no more fire towards the dark basilisk. Immina's hide was growing more golden in the brightness and her great wings glinted in the only ray of sunlight in the sky. The basilisk that was Capla's dream form beat powerful wings so hard they felt the displacement of the air around him. In the light his flesh glistened damply, green as a toad with bat-dark wings, an image of malevolence. He dived towards them, flaming the air before him. He screeched with a sound of such venomous fury that Donna longed to stop her ears. Immina was afraid. Donna had gone beyond fear. Her basilisk mouth was unfit for speech but she spoke to herself nonetheless, striving for reason: 'Pretend he is a dragon, imagine he is the poor green-faced slave I pitied, hungry and cold. Remember him helping me – forget that he betrayed Grimper – remember that he saved me from the Watch that night. See him as a dragon, tawny-gold and lovely. This is my dream, mine and Immina's. If we are strong enough we may transform it.'

She could not let Immina know her plan, but something of her early pity for the man may have found its way into her curious mix of emotions. She tried hard not to hate and not to fear. She tried to feel any emotion but those that kept her bound to a basilisk's form. Donna did not know what emotion she passed to Immina – who knew what Immina thought? But the feeling she received from Immina, the feeling that surged through their shared link and made her almost burst with gratitude, was trust. Whether Immina understood or not, she trusted Donna. That helped. Donna redoubled her efforts to see Capla as a golden dragon, not a toad-green basilisk. She hung on to Immina's trust and would not let herself fear the poor half-starving, waif-thin man that Capla had been.

The sky grew less dark and Capla's fire went out.

Great bronze wings glinted in the growing sunlight. He seemed bemused, confused by the sudden shape change and quite unable to stall his headlong flight. He was bigger as a dragon – Donna did not know why. Basilisks were smaller, though more deadly, and the dive he had begun as a basilisk was one from which a very large dragon was too heavy to recover. Donna and Immina tried to elude his precipitous downward plunge, but the cord between them got in his way and, as he hurtled towards them, his weight severed the cord that connected them. There was a cannon-strike explosion of white light, and then blackness.

Chapter Thirty-five

The Lady Estelle did not speak much at all but followed silently behind Scrub and Rej as Scrub led them across the combes to the stenk tunnels. The Low Lady was not a natural climber and Rej's respect for her determination and courage grew. She did not complain and, although she fell and grazed herself badly more than once, she endured both the indignity of that and Scrub's nagging insistence on salving her with some lotion of Scrub's own concoction. She did not seem like a woman who feared the green death overmuch. Gayla pulled herself together under the older woman's silent courage. She was long-limbed and light, as all the Abovers were – but for her lack of upper body strength she would have been a natural climber. Belafor managed, though his lame leg was all but useless and would not support his weight. The combers helped him without comment and carried Belafor's clay pots, which were only hindering him further.

Scrub was right about the stench of that part of the stenk tunnels. The vile substance grew abundantly in the damp crannies of the rock – an innocuous-looking mould that stank like rotting meat. Rej watched Scrub in the flickering lantern light. She was slick with sweat and licked her lips constantly. The Low Lady stuck close behind her, holding her arm for support and whispering in her ear. Rej did not hear what she said but assumed they were words of encouragement.

'This where you send your stenk gatherers?' Dove's cousin asked Scrub, his disapproval clear in the tone of his voice.

She nodded tersely. Rej wanted to defend her for loyalty's sake, but it was difficult. The rocks were so coated with the slimy mould that it was difficult to gain any purchase.

'How many die?' the man asked severely.

'Some,' said Scrub calmly, 'but it is their frakking choice to hunt for me.' She did not sound defensive, only coldly matter of fact. 'It gets frakking worse in a minute, so you should save your breath for climbing.'

Rej had to stoop and soon even Estelle, who was as short as Scrub, was bent nearly double to duck under the outcrops of seeping rock. Rej did not know what liquid leaked through the sponge-like rocks, but it did not smell like water, and under the lamplight tiny rust-red flowers bloomed while they watched, like specks of blood.

Estelle looked at them gravely. 'So this is where you get them from?'

Scrub nodded. 'They only grow here, the darkest deadliest things, away where there is little light.' Her voice rasped painfully in her throat and the hands holding the lamp shook uncontrollably, sending the light dancing unhelpfully up the rock walls.

'Here, I'll take it.' The tall comber took the lamp

from her, courteously, and touched her shoulder. 'My brother took to the stenk. I know how it was for him.'

'No you frakking don't,' Scrub mumbled, but the lamp briefly illuminated a look in her eyes that spoke of gratitude.

They stumbled on, the only sounds their echoing breathing, their slithering feet and the musical drip of water.

At last Scrub spoke. 'I think the Contrivance may be behind this rock – I suggest we spread out and try to find a way in.'

'You do not know of one?' Belafor's voice, breathless and strained from his efforts, was accusing.

'I never frakking said I did. They will have got in from Above with the Contrivance, but I have never yet found a cave that did not have an entrance – besides, why disturb the stenk tunnels down here, if the only access was from above?'

Rej looked at the sheer cliff wall dubiously. It was slick with moisture and every toehold was green with stenk.

'Give me light,' he said flatly, and, dropping his burden of pots, began to climb along the wall, seeking some entrance to a tunnel, some fissure in the rock. The weak light from the lantern was of little use and he had to force himself to put his hand into stenk-filled ledges, which gave him little purchase. He climbed in the darkness until he found something, a narrow crack that might indicate the presence of a tunnel lower down. He had returned easily enough to comber ways and his tinder box was in his belt pouch along with some stubs of candle. He lit one with his left hand, while gripping the rock with his right; he conducted the difficult operation with the dexterity of long practice. He was sure he was right: the entrance to the cave lay a man's span below him. He waved his candle to signal to the others. He had no idea how the Low Lady would cope with so difficult a climb, but he would leave that problem to Scrub.

He had begun to recover a little from the memory of Donna in Capla's arms. Once the shock of it had worn off, he found himself inventing explanations for the scene which did not involve his Donna giving herself to the torturer. He did not know what had been done to her to make the dream world of Between turn dark, but he feared that it was not likely to be good. Fear for her began to kindle a reckless need to find her fast. He found that it had little to do with saving the combes.

He did not wait for the others. The gum candle had been made the traditional comber way, with a thin wire hook embedded in the gum, so that he could hang it on a small outcrop as a beacon. Rej dropped a small guide pebble from his pouch and marked how quickly he heard it land. It was dark below and he knew the dangers of jumping down into unknown blackness, but it was a risk that had to be taken. He would trust to Luck, his Lady, and Light.

He did not so much jump as allow himself to fall. He landed neatly on to the rocks below: a sound landing; no turned ankles, no treacherous outcrops. He lit the second stub of candle and fixed it near the flattest of the base rocks, a target for those following. The distance between it and the flickering flame above was great – surely too great for Estelle and Belafor, if not for Scrub. He dared not wait to help them. He felt the presence of the Basilisk Contrivance, knew that it was close. He cursed himself as a frakking moon-witted turd-head, but at some level he could not rid himself of that conviction. Donna was there, he knew it. He had only two candles with him and it would have been wise to wait for the others. He could hear their shouts above him, heard the Low Lady cursing and Scrubber telling her to jump. It was background noise; he could not wait for them. Besides, their frakking clumsiness might alert guards, militia men, Capla himself. He would like to kill Capla, the thought came to him unexpectedly. He might only have moments to find Donna. He would not waste any of them.

There was an entrance to the cave, tall as a man and narrow as Scrubber's ghost tunnel. He removed the bag of clay pots that Estelle had given him and pressed himself into the tunnel so that his nose all but brushed the cold, uneven rock, and the stench of rotted stenk made his stomach heave. He was afraid of the dark. It came to him suddenly, like the recognition that he wanted to kill Capla. His fear or the darkness itself pared him down to essentials. He was Rej, he loved Donna and light; he hated Capla and he hated the darkness, the claustrophobia of the combes, the dampness and the smell. He had always been afraid of the dark, but when you lived in it more or less constantly it made as much sense as to say you were afraid of frakking living. He closed his eyes. Remember the dragons – they had got him through the ghost tunnel when he had fled Barna – remember sunlight and the soaring dragons.

Closing his eyes was a mistake. Perhaps it was the pungency of stenk, the proximity of the Contrivance or his own desire, but he was plunged without warning into Between.

It was light there but colourless somehow. The sky was white as frost and bright so that it hurt his dragon eyes. Far below he saw a flash of gold and green, and cautiously, curiously, he flew down to investigate. Three creatures lay sprawled on rock so sun-bleached it too seemed white. A bronze dragon Rej had never seen before lay dead on the ground. Its neck was broken, one wing shattered, its brown eyes unseeing. Next to it lay two other golden beasts. He recognised one as Immina and she too lay dead. Next to her a golden snake-like cord curled around her wings, torn and shredded. Rej knew that the last creature, lying a little apart, was Donna. She had to be alive, or who else sustained Between – he knew that he could not; knew that without Donna there was darkness there. Her breathing was shallow and her body lay at an awkward angle. He lay beside her, his tail wrapped around hers, sheltering her with his wings, willing her to wake.

'What the frakk, Rej, wake up!' There was light in his face and Scrubber's foul breath and her dirty hands poking him, shaking him, her eyes wild.

'It's the stenk, Scrub – the scent in such a narrow space!' The Lady Estelle pulled him out gently and examined his eyes.

'Immina is dead,' he said. 'Donna is still alive – I don't think she has long to live.'

'Rej – is this a stenk dream?'

He shook his head. 'It's true – as true as Dove Grey is dead. I went Between, or wherever the dreams are.' His head thudded and he felt dizzy, but he was sure.

Estelle took one of the clay pots from the bag he had carried and smashed it into the narrow aperture. The pungent smell of some unspeakable solution filled the air.

'Douse the lantern – it burns like Arché's breath but it will kill the smell of stenk. Let's go.'

Rej followed his nose back to the aperture and pushed Scrub out of the way. 'Let me, Scrub. I'm all right now.'

He could not see her expression, but he imagined her disbelief and was surprised that she did not argue. She turned away, perhaps to help Belafor and Gayla, who must have been struggling.

'The bags won't fit,' Rej said.

'Take two of the pots each,' Estelle insisted. She had made them with rope handles long enough to strap across her body so that they hung at hip height. The pots did not hang so low on Rej but at least his hands were free for other weapons. The smell of the spilled liquid in the tunnel made his eyes smart.

'Is it poison?' one of the combers asked through a fit of coughing.

'No, though it is as good as for bringing death. Keep it away from heat. I don't think it harms you to breathe it – I have never noticed anyway,' Estelle answered calmly, and the comber fell in behind her. Rej presumed that he would not want to seem cowardly in front of her. He could hear Scrubber leading Gayla and the second comber following with Belafor.

The tunnel was not long and Rej soon saw the warm glow of lamplight that confirmed his conviction that this was the cave which housed the Contrivance. No one spoke. Rej got his knife ready.

Chapter Thirty-six

The tunnel opened into a small red-rock cave lit by two firebrands mounted on iron sockets in the wall. They were of ornate craftsmanship and had obviously been looted from some mansion of the Brandaccian period. A crude doorway had been carved into the rock and the heavy dark wood door of an old design had been roughly adapted to fit into the space. To add to the incongruity an elegantly proportioned spiral staircase had been installed at the end of the cave. Rej presumed that this led to the trap door above. He absorbed these impressions in an instant as, most significantly, both the stairs and the door were guarded by ageing militia men.

Without thinking Rej rushed the man at the door. The older man's reactions were slow, and, in spite of his superior weaponry, he was easily overpowered. The second man guarding the stairwell was on Rej in seconds but fell back with a knife in his back as a comber emerged from the tunnel. Rej suddenly remembered that as a combe brat Dove's cousin had been able to hit any target with a stone, and it seemed that as a man the comber was similarly skilled with a throwing knife. The militia man lay dead on the floor.

302

His sallet had slipped backwards as he fell, to reveal his white hair – and the gentle, lined face of an ageing man too old for this game.

They had made too much noise in the attack and the large rectangular door was pushed open and five armed men ran out towards them. They should have stayed where they were if their aim had been to prevent entry to the room beyond. Finding Donna was all that Rej cared about. He saw the men not as a threat but as a barrier between him and his target. He flung himself at the man closest to him, dodging the blade that was thrust too late in his direction. Rej's own knife found flesh that yielded to his blade. The man before him staggered and fell. Someone struck at Rej and he saw blood well through his tunic but felt nothing. The wound could not be serious. Someone was cursing, and from the corner of his eye he saw Scrubber smash her lantern into a man's face while she spat comber expletives at his companion. A comber had ripped the fauchard from the fallen soldier and was stabbing and slicing with it, protecting the Low Lady Estelle while Scrubber lashed out viciously with her short blade. Her movements were as violent and unpredictable as her language. Gayla and Belafor were struggling together to wrestle the fourth man to the ground.

Rej did not pause. He headbutted the next man, taking him by surprise and bloodying his nose. He knocked the fauchard from his hand and left him for the others to deal with. The soldiers had clearly not anticipated any attack and were bemused and slow to respond to the desperation of the small band of combers who came at them with such explosive force. Rej pushed his way clear of the door and into the main chamber.

The thing that had to be the Contrivance dominated the room. Its crystals glowed with eerie light and the whole looked like some extraordinary spider on a web of wire and crystal raindrops. It was strangely beautiful, unlike any weapon of war he had ever seen in pictures. Then he saw Donna lying semi-naked on a pallet, strapped to the machine and caked in blood. Next to Donna, her pale, bloodied wrist bound to Donna's wrist, lay Immina dead and already cold. He did not need to check her. He could see by her tongueless mouth, open as if frozen mid-scream, that she had not breathed for a long time. Donna was still alive, though her breathing was shallow and she seemed very deeply asleep. He kissed her cheek and her breath smelled of sweet decay, of stenk and attar of damask rose; she was still labouring under whatever potion Capla had given her to banish her to Between. Her breathing was even and there was little he could do for her until she woke. Her body was a mess of contusions and bruises; he could not look at what the former slave had done to her.

Rej held her gently, frightened to hurt her more than she had been hurt already. He looked for something to cover her with. Blood stained the front of his tunic, or he would have given it willingly. There was a cloak lying near her feet and he pulled it to wrap around her, then recoiled in horror from the corpse of Capla wrapped within it. He took the cloak anyway; it was a fine one of velvet and fur. Capla's face, denuded of his slave sign, looked raw and blotchy, even in death. Rej could see no obvious wounds upon him, only a look of shock on his face. He felt cheated; the torturer, the defiler, was already dead. He was tempted to kick the corpse, but it was a childish impulse and no revenge for what he had done to Donna.

It was a bleak scene. The chamber stank of fear and the poisons Capla had used upon the two women. Grimly, Rej took his knife and cut the bonds that bound Donna to her dead sister. He closed Immina's pale eyes, hoping that she had not died in fear and pain as he suspected. He could find nothing but her own shift with which to cover her face. There was blood everywhere. He turned to Donna. Her wrist was cut and bruised where the cord had bitten into it and her hand cool and white where the blood had almost failed to flow. He rubbed it gently to make it warm and, as carefully as he could, lifted her from the Contrivance. She was not heavy but she was deeply asleep. Rej staggered with her dead weight to the wall where he lay back and held her in his arms, as if she were a sleeping child, and then he passed out.

He was back in Donna's white world, his wings still sheltering her, his hot dragon breath still warming her. She stirred a little and opened wide blue eyes. Rej could not speak as a dragon, nor could he help her to her feet. Somehow she managed on her own. She was unsteady and awkward on land. One wing was lightly torn and she moved as though in pain. She staggered to the spot where Immina lay broken and cold, and then the sky darkened as storm clouds gathered, blotting out the bright bleaching sun. Driving rain fell in place of the tears that Donna as a dragon could not shed. Rej wanted to comfort her, but knew no other way than to wait with her, silently, by the twisted dragon corpse of Immina, as the wind lashed the wild rain into his eyes and all the light went out.

'What kind of a man is he anyway, forever passing out like a frakking pregnant aristo?'

Scrubber's harsh voice woke Rej again. Someone had taken Donna from his arms. He was instantly alert and looking for her. Rej's chest hurt and Scrubber pulled his tunic up to reveal a deep gash across his chest that oozed blood.

'You'll be fine – better than that frakking lot, anyway.' She indicated the bodies of the militia men lying where they had fallen. The Lady Estelle looked up. Rej was relieved to see that she was tending to Donna.

'She's in a bad way, but she'll heal.' Estelle was opening a wooden chest stowed at one end of the chamber and was examining the contents eagerly. 'I have everything I need – they brought my chest here! But I would rather get her somewhere warm and away from that thing.'

Scrubber nodded. 'I'll see where the stairs lead. Combe-mates, Belafor, Gayla – are you fit enough to come?'

All of them nodded, though none had escaped injury. Gayla's eyes kept flicking back towards the limp form of Donna. Gayla looked pale and shocked, but she gripped her knife so tightly that her knuckles were white. Belafor looked exhausted and leant heavily on her shoulder. The combers were in slightly better shape, though bloodied.

'I'll come.' Rej staggered to his feet but felt so dizzy he had to hold on to the wall for support.

'Rej, stay with Donna and Estelle. They may need you and I frakking don't – you can't even stand up!' Scrubber's tone was, as usual, softer than her words, and she flashed him a grin that sent fresh patterns of dirt-etched lines across her face. She was safe and stenk had not yet conquered her. Rej found himself grinning back at her despite the insult, like a puppy that did not know it had been kicked. She was limping slightly but Rej knew that she was proud of herself; proud that she'd fought the stenk as well as the militia and proved she was tougher than both.

The look on the Low Lady's face was enough to bring him down.

'What's wrong?'

'Donna's pulse is very weak. I don't know what I'll do if she dies.'

'She grieves for Immina.'

'Does she know she is dead?'

'She knows.'

'Go to her, Rej, find her for me. She has had too much of Capla's potion in her blood, her vital functions are suppressed almost to death. She has to fight – please help her.'

Rej felt sick at the thought of drinking more of the stenk-based potions, of flying again into darkness; how could he frakking help? In Between there were no words, no reason, and Donna controlled the brightness of the sky, even if she did not know it. But the Low Lady Estelle looked so desperate he could not refuse her – even though he knew it was hopeless.

'Let me hold her, then.'

He held her tightly, horribly aware of the narrowness of the chasm between life and death, one short stride in the combes. One of Donna's eyes was swollen and purplish blue, as if she had been punched. She was so still; he wanted to shake her, make her wake.

'Do I have to drink one of your potions?'

The Low lady shrugged. 'I don't know, Rej, do you? I have never been there – why should I know the way?'

She seemed tired, worn, old; no longer a Poison Lady, nor even a Low Lady, beautiful and deadly – just a woman, desperate and afraid.

Rej sniffed the goblet by Donna's side – Capla's goblet. Was that what had frakking killed him?

Rej did not take the goblet; instead, he shut his eyes and thought of the dragon of his dreams.

Chapter Thirty-seven

There was a Between, a grim and graceless place where the air smelled of nothing and the sky and the earth was all an undifferentiated greyness. Rej flew beside the ragged grey-winged dragon in the yellow light under the leaden sky and grieved. This was all that was left of the vision of beauty and hope and freedom that had brought him from the combes. This was all that was left of his dream of dragons. If this was it – he'd frakking had enough. He wanted the blue skies, the scented wind, the sunlight and the joy of flight. He had found Donna, they were fighting the threat to the combes. He was sad about Immina, Grimper, Dove Grey and the others who'd died because of Capla and the Arkel, but for Light's sake, they still lived! By all the many scents of shit, that was something he had not expected! Donna was still alive – he was still alive! The sky brightened perceptibly and a pale ray of sunlight caught the edge of Donna's wing and turned it from the putty grey of unfired clay to glowing gold. The wind blew warmer and the grey clouds parted. He did not know whether it was his will or Donna's that wrought the transformation, but something was going on, something good. Beside him

*the great golden dragon soared against a sky of a
clear, pellucid blue, and he felt his spirits soar.*

It was the Low Lady who woke him this time, shaking
him gently.

'Rej, we have to get out of here. The combers are
attacking Above, but the Arkel has rallied his forces.
We have to get out of here. We have to destroy the
Contrivance.'

The urgency of her tone stirred him before he
grasped the meaning of her words. He looked at
Donna – she was still sleeping but her colour looked
better. He struggled to his feet and stretched arms
which he half expected to be wings; it frakking hurt.
Estelle had dressed his wound but the pain remained.

'Where does the staircase go?' he asked, groggily.

'The Melagiar Mansion,' Estelle said tersely. 'It
always was a blighted place.'

Rej started to move Donna when there was a
sudden sound, a clash of swords, a shriek, and the
Arkel all but fell down the stairs. He was dishevelled
and bleeding from a cut on his cheek; he was clearly
fleeing and did not expect the scene that met his eyes.

'Estelle!' He looked with confusion towards the
Contrivance and the corpses of Immina and Capla.
'The girl!'

Estelle spoke firmly to Rej in an undertone. 'Take
Donna – I will deal with this.' She turned away from
him. Rej felt that she had entrusted her daughter
wholly to his care, and he was for a moment
overwhelmed.

'Your daughter still lives, Pavenos, though what she

has endured at Capla's hands I do not want to know. How could you do it?'

Rej almost forgot to breathe. The air between the Arkel and the Low Lady crackled with the force of their emotions, like the air before a storm. Estelle's eyes blazed, the Arkel flushed. Rej was trying to make sense of it. Estelle had clearly told him only half the frakking story. Donna was the child of the Lady Melagiar and Estelle's own brother. What she had not said was that Estelle's own brother was the Arkel, their enemy – the frakking Arkel was Donna's father. He felt duped somehow. He wished he'd known before. He picked Donna up in his arms and began to back away towards the open door that led to the stairs.

'I did not know she was mine.' The Arkel's voice was strained, defensive.

'I don't believe you.' Estelle was cold, her fury ice. She seemed more dangerous than the Arkel; she seemed to have the upper hand.

'She goes "Between" like her mother – spawn of the basilisk!' The Arkel screamed his response, like a curse – the persuasive silken-voiced Arkel was out of control.

'No! Your child, your baby, whom I have loved all her days. You are no servant of Arché, no brother of mine. You would have your own daughter tortured rather than face what you have done. You have destroyed this city – slaughtered our men in a war they cannot win, destroyed our trade, subjugated all of us – for what, Pavenos – for what?'

Tears rolled down Estelle's face as she spoke. Rej

could not tell if they were of grief, regret or fury, but the Arkel kept backing towards the door. Rej was conscious of Donna's weight and the tear in his chest which felt as if it grew wider with every step he took. He gritted his teeth, aware of the trembling in his limbs, the weakness that followed dreaming. He felt the sweat trickle down his tunic, the thunderous pounding of his heart. He had to get Donna to safety. The clay pot that Estelle gave him banged at his side, another hindrance. The Arkel shook his head at Estelle's words as if to shake her away, or to shake away the past. His head was bowed.

'It was Arché's will.' He shouted it defiantly back at his sister. Her verbal assault continued relentlessly. Rej did not know why the Arkel carried on listening to her, except that he supposed she spoke the truth.

'You killed all the witnesses to your days with the Basilisk's Breath – everyone who knew you in the Days of Decadence. You killed your Lady Melagiar – you killed all of them, and you would have killed your own daughter too.'

'I told Capla not to go beyond what was necessary!'

'Pavenos, I am ashamed of the blood I share with you.'

Estelle had her knife out, but the Arkel was ready, his dagger was in his hand. He towered over the tiny Low Lady whose eyes blazed with a ferocity Rej had never seen before. He felt he should intervene, but for a fraction of an instant her eyes met his and he knew with absolute certainty what she wanted him to do. He raced for the stairs as quickly as he could, Donna hanging still insensible over his shoulder. He had to use all the strength of his arms to haul himself up. Fortunately the trap door was open and Scrubber was there, ready for him – by the gift of Luck, his Lady or the intercession of the will of Arché – there and able to take Donna from him to allow him to do what had to be done.

'We've finished most of the militia in here – though there's still some holding out. Give her to me.'

'Estelle's fighting the Arkel down there,' Rej panted.

'Listen to me, Rej. Take the clay pots and throw them into the room – at the Contrivance – quickly. Estelle will use them if she has need.'

'I know.' Rej answered with what breath he had left. When he was certain Scrub had Donna safely, he leaped down the stairs and back into the chamber, only to realise that he was too late. The Arkel was pulling his dagger's blade from the prone body of his sister. His white gloves were stained with the terrible vivid redness of her spurting blood. The Arkel stepped back in horror at what he had done and began to sob wildly.

'Stella, I'm sorry – so sorry for all of us, but I did what I thought was right – say you forgive me, Stella, for Light's sake.'

It was clear that Estelle was dying. She slumped over her wound, scarcely breathing. She had trusted Rej to finish this, and he did not hesitate. He remembered what the Low Lady had said about the liquid in the pots. He grabbed one of the brands which still burned in its metal sheath on the wall. He threw the four pots he had with him into the room – heard the distinctive sound of breaking pottery, then threw in the burning torch and watched the room erupt into flames. He pulled the great door shut and ran for the stairs, closing the trap door behind him.

'It's ablaze! We have to get out of here.' He could feel the heat beneath his feet. *'At the beginning there was fire and at the end there is fire, may the breath of Arché take you back through the breath of death, to life in the place from which all breath comes.'* He yelled the words in defiance and grief, in memorial for Estelle's courage and in triumph at the destruction of the Arkel and the Contrivance.

He shouted the words with all his strength as with Scrub, the combers, Belafor, Gayla, and the still senseless Donna, he ran for his life as the Melagiar Mansion burned.

Chapter Thirty-eight

The streets of the Golden Quarter were littered with the bodies of Redmen and combers and the aged militia men. It was dusk and the cold air was black with smoke from burning buildings, the Melagiar Mansion chief among them. The smoke caught at their throats and made their eyes stream. Rej thought it was the smoke but it might have been tears. They had better hope for rain. Somewhere a woman sang the ancient tune that accompanied the words of the funeral commitment – it was years since Rej had heard a woman sing, and the rich timbre of her voice and the sorrow it conveyed sent shivers down his spine. He ached all over from his wound and he ached inside as if someone had punched his inner organs and twisted them out of shape.

It was all over, one way or another. He could never go back to the combes and to the life he'd once had. The battle for Lunnzia seemed to be over, and he did not know what came next. All the certainties were gone and he did not know if this burning, still beautiful city could ever be home. The Low Lady was dead and Donna still hadn't stirred.

They walked warily, expecting attack, but none

came. The combers walked with all the uncertainty that he recognised from his first hours above ground. They walked together, gazing at the stone buildings and the roofless space of Above with trepidation, veering towards the shelter of the looming walls. The streets were emptied of the living.

'Did we win?' Gayla asked, after a moment.

Scrub breathed deeply of the cinder-scented air. 'I don't know – we've lost Leo and Estelle and Light knows how many frakking others. We've finished off the Contrivance and the Arkel and my bet's on Barna having wiped out the Council. Does that mean we've won? I don't think this is that kind of a game. This is Seven-a-Jack for scrottle-heads – the winner simply loses less.'

Rej glanced across at her, marvelling at the coolness of her voice, and saw that her face was wet, her tears ploughing pink channels through the engrained grime of her face.

'Where do we go now?' Belafor said, his voice as low and lost as a man's voice could be. He was limping and in obvious pain, leaning heavily on Gayla.

'I think we will go to the Devarra Palace main entrance,' Scrub said firmly. 'If the Council are overthrown and Lunnzia returns to its previous form of government, you rat-turds will have to bow and scrape a bit because you're in the company of the last of the Devarras – the frakking heir to Lunnzia.'

'Are you serious?' Rej could not look on Scrub that way. He was astonished – he hadn't thought she'd be interested in such power.

'Of course I'm not frakking serious. Though I tell

you what – by Arché's arse, I wouldn't be the first frakking stenk-head to be in power – I'm not the one to sort this mess out, but someone's got to.'

They walked on in silence, taking it in turns to carry Donna. The city seemed deserted, abandoned.

'Will there be music again and dancing, d'you think, when this is all cleaned up?' Gayla spoke as if to herself, and Rej thought she might have lost her mind to think of such things while half the Golden Quarter burned and bodies lay unburied on the streets.

To his surprise Scrub answered. 'I hope there is music every day and dancing every night, and I hope I'll sing at your wedding, Gayla.' Gayla coloured as if she was afraid that Scrub was making fun of her.

'I'm serious. I used to love to dance when I was your age and wear fine clothes and sing – I was known as the songbird of the Devarras.'

Rej spluttered and was rewarded with a quelling look.

'Rej, Gayla, all of you – there's been too little joy here for far too long. The Lunnzia of your mother's memory, Rej, was a place worth fighting for, a place worth rebuilding.'

'With you aristos in charge?'

Scrub shook her head. 'No, I expect it will be Barna and his cronies who will rule for a time. He wants the power and is used to it, and his henchmen will enforce things for him, at least until the army returns – and then, who knows? Things will never be what they were.' She sounded regretful but then added, 'Anyway, you shouldn't listen to a sentimental moon-witted old stenk-head. If things had been that frakking good in the old days there'd never have been a revolution.'

'Why are you so sure we've won?' one of the combers asked, his voice frightened and too loud in the quiet street.

Scrub did not need to reply, because as they moved into earshot of the Devarra Palace they heard the cheering and rhythmic foot-stamping and the shouts.

'Barna! Barna! Barna!'

That first night of the liberation of Lunnzia was extraordinary. Barna ordered a huge bonfire lit of all the ledgers and records of the Council of Ten, the Book of Oppidans, all the prosecution documents against the combers, and the ownership documents of the slaves. In the light and heat of the bonfire the triumphant combers drank raided wine from the temple and ate bread and fish and salted meat from the Arkel's store and feasted and sang songs that only the old remembered, though the young were eager to learn. It was a strange gathering of the wary combers, the frightened oppidans, the slaves, the workers and the outcasts of the Liberty who had mustered to join the combers and fight the combined forces of the Redmen, the militia and the Watch. It was hard to say who was in the more wretched state. Of the seventy thousand who had once inhabited the proud city of Lunnzia, there were maybe no more than thirty thousand people who had survived the Arkel's rule. The merchants and many of the aristocracy were long gone and all the young men were still prosecuting the war against High Verda. The cold of the bitter winter and the near-starvation conditions had taken many more. There had been few children born in the last few seasons and the unproductive old had been dispatched by the Doctor Esteemed Garvell. A relatively small number had died in the fighting, but it was no wonder that the city seemed deserted – it was a shadow of its former glory.

Scrub drank too much and disappeared at some point during the revelry. She had lost her brother and her oldest friend in the conflict and was still fighting the stenk addict's endless craving. Rej knew that Scrub would need to be alone. He could not join the wild whirling crowd either. He stayed on the steps of the Devarra Palace watching his combe-mates celebrate, nursing the unfamiliar wine and waiting for Donna to wake.

He laughed and chatted with the others, of course. He found himself a hero of sorts and – Light be frakking worshipped and adored – everyone appeared to have forgotten about his debts.

It was not easy to work out exactly what had gone on. Rej heard a few drunken tales of three felled dragons lying in the square outside the Devarra Palace that were there, plain as a rat in the Light Hall, then gone like a stenk-dream a moment later. The tale of the defeat of the Council was more straightforward, though only marginally. 'We got 'em proper – like vermin they were – no courage like us combers,' Moon had enthused, though he was as usual out of his head, and beaming to show his blackened stenk-stained teeth. Rej felt a wave of unexpected pleasure to see him alive and triumphant.

Others were more circumspect. Rej gathered that

Barna and his men had stormed the Council Chamber from below as other groups surrounded the building. The Arkel's personal guard were no grey-haired militia force, but young fighting men kept back from the army to protect the Arkel.

'They were good men, brave for all that they were Abovers. Even some of the councillors fought, though a couple tried to escape and were captured as they fled for their lives. It was as well they were wearing red like the priests – it made them easier to see in the melee.' Towsler, a combe-mate to be trusted, was also far from sober by this point, but his understated delivery convinced Rej that his version was nearer to the truth; a comber victory then for Barna to be proud of – and not just a comber victory. Many of the oppidans, hearing the attack, had grabbed refectory knives, sticks of furniture, anything they could find, and had turned on the Redmen – few of *them* had survived.

It was late when the last reveller finally slept. Rej alone did not rest but kept watch over Donna, kept her dry with his cloak when the rain came, and fed the glorious heat of the fire from the heaped timber and ledgers on the Palace steps to keep her warm. Stray charred fragments of paper fell like black snow in the firelight and dissolved into damp dust in the puddles of rain. As the sun rose, Donna woke.

'Rej?'

He had kept some water for her and helped her to drink it. 'Donna, you're safe now – Capla and the Arkel are dead and the Contrivance is destroyed.'

'Mother and Grimper?'

'Both dead, but swiftly. Your mother saved us all. She saved you, Donna, and she knew you were safe and that was all that mattered to her. She died well.'

'She was not tortured? Capla did not get her?'

Rej shook his head. Donna cried a little then, but it seemed that it was partly with relief – she had obviously feared that Capla had done to Estelle what he had done to her or worse, for, after all, he had left Donna whole.

'I think we killed Capla, Immina and I. In Between you can make things whatever you want. We made him into a dragon and he fell and tore us apart and I think I was keeping Immina alive and she died.' Donna spoke hesitantly, with difficulty, and Rej did not know if it was still the after-effects of the poisons she had been fed, or grief or shock, or all of them together. She was going to be all right though, he was sure – she had her tongue still, and her wits and her life.

'You came for me. I remember. I was mad with grief and all that had been done to me and you came and made the sky brighten.'

Rej stroked her hair and tried to soothe her. 'I'll always come for you Donna, I –'

She put her finger on his lips. It was cold, and her touch felt like the kiss of paper, not of flesh, as if her experience with Capla had drained her of blood, of life itself.

'I know, Rej. Thank you. You saved me and I'm glad, I think, but – I've lost everyone, everything, and I can't think about anything else.' Then she broke down and sobbed uncontrollably, shaking as though afflicted with the ague, while he held her tightly, as if she were a very small child. He cried too, quietly and without fuss. He cried for all that he had lost, all the harm that had been done to her, and all the harm yet to come when he told her, as he surely must, about her true parentage. She would have to know that her beloved mother was in truth her aunt, that Immina whom she'd lost was her true sister, and that she herself was her enemy's child. He would help her all he could, but that was going to be another shock.

'You won, Donna,' he whispered through the tightness in his throat. 'Grimper and the Low Lady and Immina and Scrub – we won!'

She clung to him, then, hugging his neck as if he were the rock that overhung a chasm in the combes. She kissed him on the cheek with lips that were still raw and torn from Capla's work.

'Yes, we won,' she said softly. It was a strange, bleak kind of a triumph, but it was a triumph nonetheless and, as they held each other, a bright sun rose in the clear, blue sky of Lunnzia, more beautiful and more real than when he'd dreamed of dragons.